WAYS TO
HIDE
IN WINTER

WAYS TO
HIDE
IN WINTER

A NOVEL

SARAH ST. VINCENT

MELVILLE HOUSE
BROOKLYN · LONDON

Ways to Hide in Winter
Copyright © Sarah St.Vincent, 2018
All rights reserved

First Melville House Printing: November 2018

Melville House Publishing   Suite 2000
            46 John Street   and   16/18 Woodford Rd.
        Brooklyn, NY 11201   London E7 0HA

mhpbooks.com
@melvillehouse

ISBN: 978-1-61219-720-3
ISBN: 978-1-61219-721-0 (eBook)

Designed by Euan Monaghan

Library of Congress Cataloging-in-Publication Data

Names: St. Vincent, Sarah, author.
Title: Ways to hide in winter : a novel / Sarah St.Vincent.
Description: Brooklyn : Melville House, 2018.
Identifiers: LCCN 2018037662 (print) | LCCN 2018041697 (ebook) | ISBN
    9781612197210 (reflow able) | ISBN 9781612197203 (hardcover)
Subjects: | GSAFD: Suspense fiction.
Classification: LCC PS3619.T29 (ebook) | LCC PS3619.T29 W39 2018 (print) |
    DDC 813/.6--dc23
LC record available at https://lccn.loc.gov/2018037662

Printed in the United States of America

1 3 5 7 9 10 8 6 4 2

For Margaret Rome

PART ONE

1

The last of the deer hunters had come through for the day, and I was closing the store, counting the cash and watching the snow turn the gravel parking lot into a dappled expanse of white on gray. Someone had abandoned a car there a few weeks back, an ancient brown Subaru that was gradually succumbing to a shroud of whiteness, its tires deflating. A silence wound its way through the pines, slipping on the hidden, frozen creeks, drifting quickly on the wind. The hunters brought it in on their boots, brushed it from their hats, felt the remnants of it on their lips and fingers. When they ordered, the words were soft and gruff, as if this were no place for sound.

There was an old plastic broom on the porch, and I used it to knock the snow off the metal signboard before dragging it inside. *Sandwiches*, it announced. *Ice Cream. Hot Coffee.* Illustrated with silhouettes of a steaming mug, a man's hand giving a thumbs-up. The porch, with its picnic tables balanced carefully on eroding cement, was covered in a layer of dirt, a few spots of ash where the hunters sat if they didn't feel like leaving the cold. They would hunch there in their thick jackets, faces looking ageless behind their beards as they smoked. Sometimes for minutes, sometimes for hours, they would stay there, gazing at the old iron smelter that stood just down the hill, exposed to the elements, its proud limestone chimney slowly crumbling and falling.

There were still a few trail-hikers in the forest, too, the diehards, mostly retired men with time on their hands, even though it was dangerous to venture into the park at this time of year. The trails were overgrown, their markers obscured by snow, and the hunters—cautious as they were—had been known to mistake many things for deer.

I left the sign swinging in a corner and moved behind the counter. Outside, the snow was growing thicker, and I knew I should go—should have left hours earlier, in fact. I lifted the half-full coffeepot from the burner with my right arm—the good one—and tilted it over the sink, but then paused. On the other side of the window, the clouds seemed to trap the light against the earth, reflecting it from snow to cloud and back again, prolonging the dusk. The wind stirred the tops of the pines, making them ripple against the sky, bending and rising under the great invisible thing that moved them, as if they were underwater.

Watching them, the coffeepot heavy in my hand, I leaned against the edge of the sink. The wind grazed the edges of the building, humming. I chewed my lip.

Then, reaching for a styrofoam cup, I poured in a stream of the black liquid, dumped in a spoonful of sugar, and went out.

The store had once been a stable and was long and narrow, made from blocks of limestone probably hauled in from the quarries that had been just down the road. Standing under the low wooden roof of the porch, I leaned back against the wall, sipping the coffee and looking out over the mountains. Below me, the empty trail unfurled along the edge of a steep drop, past the fallen smelter and vacant campground, on its long, forbidding march from Maine to Georgia. Up the hill, the windows in the two-story brick hostel were all dark, giving the place a grim, haunted look; the manager, I knew, had left that morning to visit his mother in town, and there hadn't been a guest in weeks. The summer cabins up the road were similarly empty, surrounded by walls of stacked, frozen cordwood. Viewed from above, their roofs, like the store's and hostel's, would have looked like lost islands in a river of trees.

A cold tongue of wind touched my face, and I felt the familiar ache in my shoulder. Planting a hand in my pocket, I took another swallow of coffee. A car passed by on the state road just up the slope, sending vibrations through the hard, frozen air.

When it was gone, the park once again wrapped itself in stillness. Even now, in 2007, this was a corner of the world that had been left in peace, tucked away in the forgotten forests of Pennsylvania, high in the northernmost tendrils of the Blue Ridge Mountains. In my great-grandfather's time, the two quarries up here had crawled with the to-and-fro of laborers; now, they were just a pair of lakes where, if you were to stand on the bottom, you could look up and see the legs of swimmers and the bottoms of aimless canoes. Or at least, that's what you would see in the summer. At this time of year, you would be trapped under a foot of ice and—more often than not—the only other person for miles around would be me.

Finishing the dregs of the coffee, I crushed the cup and went in, plucking a dirty ashtray from one of the tables as I passed. The door banged shut behind me.

I slipped my library book into my purse and turned in a circle, making sure everything was turned off, the grill and the coffee machine and the deep-fryer that left my skin smelling like hot oil. My eyes swept over the small space, skimming past the blurred reflections of the young woman with the pointed elbows who turned with me.

Of course, everything was turned off. I had never forgotten.

Just as I was reaching into my pocket for the keys, the door hinges groaned behind me. Jumping in surprise, I spun to face the front of the store, realizing even as I did it that I was moving much too quickly, making a mistake. Pain sang through my hip and shot down my arm in a dart, hard and searing, the shock of it running through me like a blade.

Gasping and bending nearly double, I found myself standing with my back against the grill, staring at a wide-eyed stranger.

"Please don't scream! I'm so sorry. Please don't scream."

The stranger was tall and thin, wearing jeans and a padded brown jacket that was much too large for him, black hair protruding from under a dirty knit cap, a scarf wrapped over his nose and mouth. His hands were bare and half-raised, as if in surrender.

"What do you want?" I asked. My hip throbbed, and I gripped it with both hands, pressing down against the muscles that had seized over the bone. The pain sent a cloud across my vision, harsh and blue and electric, and for a moment I thought I would have to kneel on the floor.

The stranger's eyes were wide and black above the scarf. "I'm very sorry. Are you all right?"

With an effort, I nodded.

"I saw the light on," he continued, obviously alarmed. "I thought your store was open."

"It's not my store. And it's closed." Facing him, I caught my breath. "What were you coming in for?"

"Nothing, nothing—please don't worry about it." He lowered his palms and glanced around, seeming to take in the shelves of insect repellent and canned sausages, the ice cream case, the telephone that had been dead since the fire. "I was just looking for something hot to drink."

I gave him a long, doubtful look, keeping a grip on my side as I slowly straightened. "We're closed," I said again.

"I'm very sorry. I can see I've inconvenienced you." He stepped backward, reaching behind him and fumbling for the knob. His accent sounded foreign, the words rounded and stumbling, dropping like marbles. "I'll come in tomorrow."

"It's Saturday. We're not open tomorrow." I drew a breath. He was extraordinarily slim, a pale slice of a person, with a high voice and raised eyebrows. A musty smell seemed to emerge from his coat when he moved. "Is there something you need?"

"Oh, no, I don't want to trouble you. In fact, I'm really just looking for the man—the, ah . . . whoever runs this little hotel, up the hill. I thought you might know where he was. Or she." He tugged the scarf down, revealing thin lips and cheeks that were sunken, famished-looking, maybe feverish. He was young, I thought—or at least, a few years younger than I was. Maybe twenty-five.

"He's away. He won't be back until tomorrow."

The stranger fingered the buttons on his coat, considering this piece of information. "Is there somewhere else to stay?"

"No." I looked him up and down, beginning to grow curious in spite of myself. "It's a state park. There's nothing around here for miles. You'd have to go into town."

His eyebrows drew together, and he leaned back slightly. "Ah." A thoughtful pause. "You mean . . ."

"Carlisle. It's about ten miles north of here."

"Ten miles," he echoed. "I see."

Behind him, through the screen door, I could see the snow, even heavier now. A gust of cold reached me where I stood, still pressing a hand against my side, as if to silence a voice there.

The stranger looked over his shoulder, rubbing his bare fingers together as he took in the same sight. As I watched him, my conscience began to get the better of me; even so, I was surprised to hear myself speak.

"I have a key to the hostel," I said. "I could probably let you in."

He turned back to me. "Really? That would be most kind of you."

"Just until Martin gets back. Then you'll have to talk to him. I'm not sure if he'll want to keep the place open for just one person."

The key was on a hook behind the ice cream case, empty at this time of year except for a lone and inexplicable drum of strawberry, which I dipped into from time to time as I sat at the counter and read. Sometimes entire days went by without anyone coming in. The store's owner, a placid and forgetful man, long since retired to South Carolina, made most of his money during the summer; he kept me on during the colder months largely out of charity, I knew. I reached for the key without taking my eyes off the stranger.

"Is your car in the lot out here?"

He removed his hat and held it in his hands, knitting his long fingers into the fabric. His hair was limp and untrimmed. "No, I—I don't have a car, actually."

"You walked?" His shoes were odd, resembling dress shoes but cheap and rubbery, with heavy soles and fragile-looking laces. Not at all suited for hiking, and possibly not even suited for walking.

"No, I was given a ride. It would be a long way to walk, wouldn't it?"

I realized I was squinting at him, this man with the peculiar face and even more peculiar accent. "It would."

"My bag is on the porch," he said, still fingering his hat. "But of course, I can carry it."

"All right." I reached for my coat and pulled it on, fastening the buttons. It was long and gray, left over from my time in college, still warm despite the holes in the lining that I'd never bothered to fix. In a few more years it would grow visibly shabby, and then I would consider replacing it, but in the meantime there wouldn't be anyone to notice. My grandmother, with whom I lived, was increasingly blind.

He did have a suitcase, small and blue and wheeled. We stepped out from under the porch awning and walked side-by-side to the path that led up the hill. Above us, the hostel was still dark, a lonely mass of brick. Once a dormitory for the ironworkers who had journeyed across the sea from Ireland, Scotland, Germany, it was now a bare-bones refuge for the masses who came through on the trail—the Appalachian Trail, the one that put us on the map—in the summer. I unlocked the entrance, handed the stranger a set of sheets and towels, and showed him where to sign his name in the guest book. "You can pay Martin tomorrow. That's the manager. Pick any room with a cot in it."

"Thank you," he said, but I was already stomping outside in my heavy boots, going home.

The next morning's light was thin and gray, the clouds hanging over the sun. It was still snowing. I rolled over in the cold sheets, drawing the afghans around me. The pills sometimes made me forget where I was upon waking, giving me a long moment of confusion as I examined the stains on the ceiling. The feeling never lasted for long, though. Everything came back eventually, even if it didn't always come back all at once.

I did my best to stay wrapped in the blankets as I sat up and leaned against the wall, letting the world come into focus from my place on the mattress on the floor. Through the window, I could see the field with its mossy brown Herefords, the bleak gash of Route 233, the family plot with its row of gently leaning headstones. It was Sunday, and somewhere across the fields a bell sounded. A horse and cart appeared on the road and passed with the rhythmic, fading sound of hooves. Probably a Mennonite family heading to the church a few miles west in Walnut Bottom, I thought, gripping a blanket under my chin. Sometimes I wondered if they really felt as religious as they looked, the Mennonites, with their men in somber black hats and their women in those plain dresses and stiff-looking hairnets. Maybe they just got into the habit of doing things the way they did them, and that was why they bothered to rig up a horse and buggy every Sunday, even in the winter.

Aside from them, not a soul seemed to be stirring; even the cows were lounging on their sides, watching over their shoulders as the buggy receded out of sight. The railroad tracks that passed by the house were silent, stretching emptily to the east and west.

After a little while, there was a shuffling sound downstairs, a cough, a stream of water pouring from a tap. I could picture my grandmother standing in front of the kitchen sink in her robe, clutching a glass of water, returning to bed. Sure enough, the shuffling soon retreated in the direction from which it had come. Outside, a dog barked several times, as if it had spotted a stranger, and then stopped.

The stranger. Rubbing my eyes, I pushed myself to my feet and walked down the hall to the bathroom, turning the knob in the shower. If he was still on the mountain, I realized as the water struck my skin, then he was alone there, probably with no food. Martin's closet-sized kitchen rarely contained more than bread and milk, and the hunters would be crouched in silent, camouflaged lumps in the woods by now. Martin himself would be dealing rummy hands at the United Methodist nursing home in Carlisle until the evening.

I could have called him, told him he had a guest.

Instead I got into the Jeep and set off toward the winding roads that led upward.

Who was this stranger? Russian? Greek? I had never met a Russian, or any Greeks aside from the dark-haired, weary-looking family who ran the diner in Carlisle, but couldn't think of any other guesses. A married man, it seemed—I had glimpsed a gold band the previous day—but alone. Alone in rural Pennsylvania, in the woods. A state park built around some flooded quarries and an abandoned iron smelter. An empty hostel next to a store that sold little more than firewood and beans. A place that was miles away from anywhere, where even the telephone and electricity lines were unreliable thanks to the fire that had swept over the mountain a few months earlier. I couldn't understand it.

There was just no reason for a person to be there in December unless he was searching for a quiet place to shoot deer.

The radio signal faded as I made the steep climb, passing through the stands of live pines and, every few hundred yards, the stands of burned ones. Birches and maples. A few red oaks. The maples, when I noticed them, always made me think of the two trees in the yard behind my grandmother's house—the ones my father had planted when my brother and I had been born. It was my brother who had taught me to keep cars like this one running, or rather, had let me watch while he taught his friends; the rest I'd eventually figured out myself. I listened to the murmur of the engine as I steered around a bend, the whispering sound as snow and ice gave way under the tires.

The stranger was sitting on the porch in front of the store when I pulled into the lot, slamming the car door and approaching noisily in my boots. Same knit cap on his head, same tan scarf pulled over his nose and mouth. Looking out, it seemed, over the long, undulating slopes of the mountains draped in fog. He gave a jerk when the car first appeared, rising to his feet with a wary look, as if he might run. When he recognized me, however, he sat back down and even gave a small wave.

"Hey," I said neutrally, wiping my shoes on the cement and digging the key out of my pocket as I passed him.

"Hello!" His eyes were no longer feverish, but inquisitive, even merry. "Is something the matter? I thought your store was closed today."

"It's still not my store." The deadbolt turned back with a satisfying thump. "And it is closed, but I thought you might be hungry." I pushed my way in, dropping my coat and book on the floor. The lights came on with a flickering buzz. "What do you want?"

He followed me in, startled, looking like a courteous but starved wolf. "Oh, no. I don't need anything."

I crossed to the other side of the counter and folded my arms over my chest, trying to clear the last of the haze from my mind as I surveyed the terrain. "Egg sandwich? That's probably the best I can do."

He stood by the door, hesitant. "Well. If you really don't mind. All right."

"If I minded, I wouldn't offer," I told him bluntly, turning the knob on the grill. "Coffee? Tea?"

"Yes, tea would be delightful." The hat had come off; he was staring, forming his replies slowly. "Thank you."

"Sugar's over there by the door. I'll have to open some milk." I flipped the switch on the coffee maker, which doubled as the hot water machine, and pulled two styrofoam cups from the pile. The grill began to heat, and I scraped it carefully, even though it didn't need to be scraped. I could sense him behind me, watching, and suddenly became aware that my movements were a kind of methodical flurry, a hurried but well-practiced sequence of pushings and polishings and liftings and turnings, as if I had been programmed to do these things. Vaguely embarrassed, I slowed down.

"You're from Russia?" I asked, doing my best to sound indifferent.

"What? Oh—no." He cleared his throat. "That is to say, not really."

"Not really?"

"My family is Russian. But I'm from Uzbekistan." He paused. "It's in central Asia."

"I know where it is." The eggs cracked neatly. "Or at least, I have some idea."

"Really?"

I turned to look at him, raising an eyebrow. "Yes, really." There was, in fact, a map on the wall in my room at my grandmother's place, one I had tacked up years earlier so I could follow my brother's deployments. Over time, I'd found that I'd gradually begun to absorb its web of rivers, oceans, borders, all those remote places reduced to blots of blue and gray. "You can sit down, you know. There's a stool over there somewhere."

The egg whites crackled and hissed in the oil. I smeared slabs of butter onto English muffins with the spatula, dropping the upturned halves onto paper plates. Unwrapped the cheese, poured the tea, slid the eggs onto the muffins and moved everything over to the counter. "Here."

"Oh, I don't need that much."

"One's for me."

He drew the stool closer, pinching the hot sandwich between his fingertips and spreading a napkin on his lap, waiting for me to take a bite before he began. As we ate, our heads tilting toward one another, I tried not to stare at him—this stranger who was, indeed, so very strange.

"And you?" He swallowed a mouthful of the acidic tea, dabbing at his mouth politely. "Where are you from?"

I shifted, pressing the soles of my feet against the edge of a shelf beneath the register. "I'm from here."

"Here?"

I gestured behind me. "Down the mountain. Centerville. It's a small town—just a couple of houses, really. Well, and a fire station and a store and a library. That's about it."

The tea warmed my stomach. Through the steam, I could see him, the delicate-looking line of his scalp as he bent over his sandwich. The same slightly musty smell I had noticed the day before seemed to rise from his coat, and I found myself wondering if he'd slept in it. Then a troubling thought made me examine him more closely. "Was the heat on overnight?"

"You mean at the hotel?" He dabbed at his mouth again. "A little, maybe. Not really. But I had the blankets, of course."

"I'm sorry." I closed my eyes, frowning as I lifted the tea to my lips again. "I'll fix that."

"It's all right. I may be leaving before tonight, anyway." He was looking at me curiously. I was wearing a bulky hooded sweatshirt and men's jeans, my hair pulled back in a knot that was already coming undone and mouth probably set in that severe, distant line I had recently begun to observe when passing mirrors and shop windows. Where had it come from, that sad, wooden expression? I wasn't unhappy.

He wiped his fingers painstakingly on a paper towel. "May I ask what your name is?"

"My name? I'm Kathleen."

"Kathleen—that's a nice name. I'm Daniil." He extended his hand carefully and correctly over the paper plates, and we shook. "Thank you for the breakfast."

"It's no problem. I'll give you some soup you can heat up for dinner if you're still here. That's pretty much all we've got right now."

"Thank you." He nodded. "That would be nice."

"And then I have to go. After I turn on the heat."

"Yes, of course. Thank you."

After some searching, I managed to locate some cans of beef stew, which were so dusty I checked each one to make sure it hadn't expired. He handed me a pair of creased bills that looked as though they had passed through many hands and counted out another dollar in dimes and nickels. Then, almost timidly, he stood with the bag dangling at his side.

"Does it hurt?" he asked, touching his waist.

"What?"

"Your—your side. Yesterday it looked like it hurt you."

I stopped, standing behind the register, his money in my hand.

"No," I said after a pause. "It doesn't hurt."

"Oh. That's good. This morning you seemed to be . . ." He hesitated. "Well, walking a bit unevenly, I suppose. When you got out of the car."

Heat rose to my face; I could feel it. I pressed my lips together.

"No," I said again, quietly but firmly. "I'm fine."

"Yes, of course," he said hastily, nodding in embarrassment. "I'm sorry. At any rate, thank you once more. It was very kind of you." When I looked back at him without answering, he cleared his throat. "Well, have a good day, as they say."

My eyes narrowed, I watched him go, the bag of cans banging against the door as he closed it behind him. For a moment, I stood there, drumming my fingers against the Formica. Then I locked the store—after all, I had no reason to stick around—and walked to the car, pulling off in the direction of town. I never really relished going there, but I had things to do—groceries to buy, my grandmother's medications to pick up, all the little tasks that kept our lives moving like a second hand ticking around a clock.

I pressed my foot against the gas, letting the tires find the ruts in the snow that still hadn't been plowed. The road cut through the trees, white and smooth, like a path in a fairy tale. The woods seemed to wrap themselves around me as I turned on the headlights. It had an undeniable power, this place, a kind of majesty. I tried to disappear into the feeling of it as the forest passed by outside my window, dense and motionless, a wall of slender brown columns.

Then there was a gap, a long, empty stretch where a pair of ruts led down to one of the lakes. It appeared and was gone just as quickly, flickering by on my right. Slowing, I found myself looking back at it in my rearview mirror.

Before I knew it, I had pulled over.

There were two lakes in the park, Laurel and Fuller, both of which stood where the quarries had once been. When I was a child, bits of blue and green slag from the old iron smelter had still washed up on the sand that had been trucked in. My brother and I would walk along the shore and collect them, along with pebbles and snail shells and shining fragments of charcoal. Laurel was the shallower of the two and was always crowded in summer—small children with their mothers, Boy Scouts, softball teams, fishermen. Laurel had pavilions and grills, fire pits. When I'd gotten married, we'd had the reception there, outdoors, under the sun. Surrounded by hordes of happy, frolicking strangers.

Fuller was something different: smaller, deeper, darker, encircled by pines. Fuller was where, when I was sixteen, I would lie on the sand late at night, long after the park had closed, and look up at the stars in their endless, stoic expanse. Where I brought friends, the ones who could stand the silence. Sometimes, coyotes would bay, or a small nocturnal animal would crash through the brush, but otherwise nothing stirred. By day, it was just as still. Few people swam at Fuller. It was too isolated, too chilly, too overwhelming in its indifference, its unchanging beauty.

Grabbing my book, I tramped through the woods to Fuller, drawing my coat around me and following the slight downward slope until I could see a clearing through the trees. A few more steps and there it was: the great, pale expanse of the lake, ice streaked with snow that glittered under the empty sky. A ring of pines surrounded the void like sentries, stretching back over the mountain, dark and imposing, keeping watch.

A pair of picnic tables stood near the shore, and I walked over to them. With a gloved hand, I brushed the snow off one of the benches and sat, opening the novel I was carrying. The pines stretched overhead, seeming to bend and converge at their tips.

The wind stirred the pages, tugging them from my fingers. I put the book aside restlessly and rose, stepping closer to the lake that seemed to draw me toward it, its very blankness beckoning to me. How thick was the ice? I'd never seen anyone skating here, but that didn't necessarily mean anything. Most people, aside from the hunters, wouldn't care to risk the steep curves the road made as it wound its way up the side of the mountain. Not in December.

Edging up to the shoreline, I touched the ice with a foot, and something tightened in my chest.

It didn't matter what people thought they saw when they looked at me. I didn't limp.

I let out a breath. The cold air was sharp in my lungs, making me feel even more alert than usual to every movement around me, every sound.

Tentatively, I slid my foot all the way onto the ice, then took a step. The surface was firm beneath me, seeming to push back against my heels. The breeze reached through my clothes, and I shivered, feeling something inside me twist, like hard, dead vines being wrung tight.

I didn't limp. I didn't.

I took a second step, elbows pressed against my sides. There was a low sound as snow yielded under me, crushed into footprints. Otherwise, the world remained devoid of noise.

I looked out over the gray plain that stretched around me. Our wedding, mine and Amos's, had been held in a chapel on this mountain, St. Eleanor Regina—a falling-down clapboard place in a clearing, one with a handful of windows to let in the sunlight, a priest who came through once every couple of weeks.

It was what I had wanted.

I scuffed a foot against the surface. The twisting feeling grew tighter, as if something within me would rub together too hard and spark.

I stood still.

Then suddenly I was marching forward, half-running, feet pounding against the ice. My breath came quickly as I lifted my boots, one after the other, traces of snow scattering behind me. The hot, clenched feeling burned inside me, pressing against my heart and making me stumble. I banged my knee against the surface, hard, and gasped but pushed on. Slipping and scrambling, I went out fifty feet from shore, then a hundred, then two hundred, farther and farther.

Before I knew it, I had reached the center of the lake.

I came to a stop, panting. The ice stretched out around me, wide and smooth, a hundred yards or more to each point of the shore.

The cold had brought tears to my eyes, and I wiped them roughly with the back of my hand, legs trembling, pretending not to feel my hip burning and my shoulder throbbing where the pins had been put in. Steam rose from my mouth as I breathed.

When I shifted my foot, the ice creaked, sending a jolt through my nerves. I moved quickly to what felt like a thicker patch and crossed my arms over my chest, listening to the rush of my breath.

The space before me was deserted, as quiet and stark as the surface of the moon. Tipping my head back, I gazed up at the sky and the dark, ragged points of the treetops.

Sweat coated my temples and the back of my neck, and I could feel my pulse thudding. Feeling both sick and exhilarated, I let myself drop onto a thin layer of snow, sitting back and letting it soak through my jeans.

I would never know why I did these things, not really. Most of the time, for the past four years, I had felt as though I were enveloped in a haze of fear, a low sense of terror that hummed and crackled in the background, making me flinch when I lit the gas stove, when I drove in the rain, when I mounted the ladder to fix the gutter. And yet, every so often, I flung myself into danger as if it were the only thing I wanted, as if I could only be alive in moments as swift and violent as the one that had frightened me the most.

When the surface beneath me remained solid, I gradually began to relax, realizing I'd been holding my breath. After a few minutes, I unfolded backward, lying down to look up at the sky.

Okay, I thought, waiting for my racing heart to slow.

The mountain, I could guess, had never been a welcoming place to live, plagued as it was with blizzards in the winter, damp heat and clouds of mosquitoes in the summer. No doubt my great-grandfather had suffered here when he was mining, and the prisoners who had later been held in the camp down the road probably hadn't had an easy time of it, either. Although, I thought as I rested there, maybe it was just the same where they'd come from. They were long gone anyway, the prisoners, and nobody thought about them much anymore. Hidden in life and almost as hidden in death, remembered only by a few retirees who had time on their hands and saw fit to look into these things, driving up on sunny days to pester the park rangers with questions—uselessly, I thought, since the rangers didn't seem to know any more about it than anyone else did.

I picked up a handful of snow, squeezing it, letting it crumble in my fingers.

There were times when the days seemed to slip away so quickly, one after the other, like paper boats going over a waterfall, until one morning—this morning—I had found myself waking in the cold at my grandmother's, twenty-seven, alone, body curled tightly under the sheets like some hibernating thing. I didn't know how it had happened, how I had gotten to be this old, the years falling through my hands before I could catch them. Standing undressed in front of the mirror before I got into the shower, I almost hadn't known who I was, my face sharp with cares, my limbs shivering, wrapping my arms around myself to keep warm.

She never was able to light the woodstove properly, my grandmother.

I gazed up into the gray of the atmosphere. The longer I looked at it, the more it seemed to deepen, revealing itself to be finely graded, clouds blending into one another almost imperceptibly. I waited to see if a bird or an airplane would cross the sky, or something else would come along to break the stillness, but nothing did. I was alone, as alone as I could ever wish to be.

If I fell through, I thought, no one would see me. I would just disappear into the water. Maybe they'd find me in the spring, and maybe they wouldn't.

A strange feeling ran up my spine at the thought, but I stayed where I was. The sky above me remained empty, as if some previous sky had been erased.

I wasn't sure how much time had passed before I heard a sound in the woods; nothing much—a small shifting and crackling—but enough to make me come back to myself and peer around.

Rolling onto my side, I rocked forward and slowly pushed myself to my feet. Whatever it was I'd been trying to prove, I'd proven it. There was no reason to linger.

Carefully, I began picking my way back to the shore, passing my own footprints in the dusting of snow, trying not to notice that the left ones were slightly elongated. My breath quickened again with effort, and I leaned forward, appreciating for the first time just how far out I had gone. From here, the picnic tables looked like little more than children's toys.

At last I reached the sand and stepped onto it, exhaling with a startled sound. For a moment I bent in half, hands on my knees, stomach fluttering. My mind seemed to draw back together, rejoining itself from the places where it had scattered.

What a stupid thing to have done.

I stayed there, letting my head hang between my shoulders, feeling the weight of my boots in the snow. Finally I straightened, bracing myself against my knees and ignoring the ache that was spreading in my bones, the numbness of my exposed skin. I stumbled to the Jeep and turned the heat as high as it would go, gripping the wheel as I rested my head against it. Then I put the car into gear, continuing north through the forest that petered out into the foothills.

In town, I did what had to be done, taking care of my business the way I always did.

"Grandma," I said as I entered the house that night, pushing the door tightly against the jamb. She was in her orange overstuffed chair, facing away from me, her eyes on the television although she probably couldn't see much more than a blur of light. *The Price Is Right* was on, as it somehow always was. Someone, a brunette in her forties, had just correctly guessed the price of laundry detergent and was jumping up and down on the stage, her hands clasped over her mouth, ecstatic. A curl of cigarette smoke rose over my grandmother's head. "Where's the sewing box?"

"In the kitchen closet. On top of the old microwave." She didn't turn around. "What do you need it for?"

"My coat's torn." My joints were still aching, but I strode as evenly as I could back into the kitchen at the rear of the old farmhouse, opening the narrow closet. The sewing box—an old cookie tin that rattled with buttons—was there, a rusting dull green. I carried it up to my room and sat heavily on the mattress.

"Beth called," my grandmother bellowed from below.

"Okay," I said, drawing my knees to my chest and leaning back against the wall. It wasn't much warmer in the room than it was outside. I draped a blanket over my shoulders and glanced around at the bare space, the stacks of books and folded clothes in the corners, the map. *I need to remind her how to re-light the woodstove*, I thought, and opened the tin, searching for a needle.

When I found it, however, I leaned back against the wall and closed my eyes. It was amazing, I thought: the things we did that no one else knew about, that didn't leave a sign, that we ourselves almost couldn't believe.

When the night came, I turned off the light, curling up on my side and reaching under the mattress to feel for the paper bag I knew was there. Pinching two of the small ovals, I slipped them into my mouth and held them on my tongue for a moment before swallowing them without water. They were slightly bitter but otherwise tasted of nothing.

It was then that I realized I had never turned on the heat for the stranger. Even as the thought entered my mind, however, the deep red curtain fell over me, weighing on me, sending me into sleep.

2

The next morning was brighter, the sun slipping over the horizon as I stood in the bathroom, prodding my knee where I'd smacked it against the ice. There was an ugly bruise there, painful to the touch, but it was nothing. I pulled my clothes on, the fabric sliding up over the old scars, and turned my back on my reflection as I switched off the light.

Outside, I checked the mailbox, hoping for a postcard from my brother, as I always did. He'd left the valley years earlier, marrying a girl from Texas, someone he'd met in basic training, and moving from base to base before finally being sent overseas. I sometimes found a note from him among the bills and Publishers Clearing House envelopes, although not very often. When I did, the handwriting was always slanted and sparse, as if he were writing while running. Maybe he was.

The mailbox was empty.

The light was just breaking through the clouds as I drove the five miles to the gas station. At this hour, the only other people there were truckers, holding steaming cups of coffee as they chatted with one another, leaning against their rigs. One of them I thought I recognized from high school—elementary school, really. He was heavyset, with a pale, doughy face and hair in a crewcut. His father had been a trucker, too, I remembered, driving eighteen-wheelers for the potato chip company down in Hanover. John, the son, had always had a gravelly voice and almost dog-like friendliness, rasping good-naturedly to anyone who passed by. We'd been confirmed in the same church, long ago, two of the only Catholic children in the area, our families holding out somehow against the gulf of stern Scotch-Irish Presbyterianism and fiery Lutheranism that surrounded us. I still remembered kneeling next to him at our First Communion, envying his dirty knees and scuffed shoes as I sat there in my silly white dress.

I walked into the station as briskly as I could, staring straight ahead. The truckers' eyes followed me, then dropped down to their cups. Only John continued to watch, his gaze meeting mine accidentally. I nodded, not knowing what else to do, and he nodded back, giving me the shy, cautious half-smile people had been giving me since the accident. Some of them remembered the rumors and were uncomfortable, I could tell; others simply didn't know what to say. It didn't matter; I wasn't angry with them, not anymore. After all, I didn't know what to say, either. Maybe there was nothing to be said.

The sun shone through the trees as I wound my way back up the mountain, a rapid patter of light and shade playing against the windows. The bottoms of the trunks were still blackened in places, but the branches were uplifted, tall and defiant, as if there had never been a fire. Farther on, the blue-and-gold memorial to the three girls passed by, a dark blot backlit by the sun. I wondered, at times, who maintained it. It had been there for some seventy years, the signboard with its short, stark sentences, and yet it never leaned, never faded. The paint was always fresh. One of the more thoughtful retirees, I imagined, some aging farmer who snuck out early in the morning to touch up the gold lettering and returned home before anyone could discover this strange impulse of anonymous kindness, this sentimentality about someone else's long-ago tragedy.

The porch outside the store was empty, which gave me a small twinge of pleasure as I pulled into the lot. A few minutes later, I was sitting at one of the dusty tables, feet propped up on a chair, attempting to find my page. Martin, I noticed, had returned from Carlisle, a jumble of what looked like metal parts filling the back of his station wagon. I wondered if he had met the stranger yet—assuming, of course, that the stranger was still there.

The book was slow going. Even at the store, in the unbroken quiet, I sometimes found it difficult to follow the story, a fact that puzzled me. During my years in college, I had flown through books, consuming piles and piles of them, as if I were feeding them into a fire. Beth, my best friend, and I had shared a place for a while, two married women temporarily bunking away from our husbands, and together we'd devoured an almost unthinkable number of books. My husband, who was still living and working thirty miles away in Mechanicsburg, preferred that I didn't go out, while her husband was struggling to feed and house himself and Beth on a noncom's salary. And so we read, sometimes getting so lost in our conversations, our chance to try out ideas without anyone else there to say we were wrong, we forgot to eat the food in front of us. She was usually the one who was brave enough to say something first, and I remembered the sound of our laughter when we said something so bold we didn't know what else to do, looking around as if somebody would surely catch us.

Today, she was one of the few people I could speak to for a long period without losing my concentration, although as the months went by I felt less and less of a need to discuss anything with anyone at all. There was something to be said, I thought, for a quiet life, for self-sufficiency.

Around noon, Martin's wiry figure rounded the corner of the hostel, carrying an armful of branches. Waving with his free hand, he motioned for me to join him. I put the book down and mounted the hill.

"So!" he said, throwing the branches into a pile by the old stump he used for splitting wood. He was short, with a sharp, narrow face that should have been ugly but somehow wasn't—or if it was, I had long since stopped noticing. There was something oddly magnetic about the hopeful expression he always wore, a cheerful alertness that seemed to radiate from his very skin. "You'll never guess what I've got out in the trunk."

"You're right, I probably won't." I watched him pull a hatchet from his coat, testing the blade with his thumb. "What happened? Did your car eat some other car?"

"Very funny. I'm not going to tell you what it is, actually. I can tell you it's going to be awesome when I build it, though. And I mean totally awesome. Like, phenomenal." Bending down, he dragged a branch onto the stump and began quickly chopping it into kindling, pausing to smile up at me as he did so.

I watched him toss the handful of sticks into a pile. "But for some reason I'm not allowed to know what it is?"

"You'll see. I mean, you can try and guess if you want, but I don't think you'll get it." He picked up another branch and broke it into pieces with his hands.

I glanced up at the station wagon.

"Go ahead!" He laughed, his grin showing two gray teeth among the white ones. "Guess."

"Guess? I don't know. A medieval printing press."

"What? Come on—that's not a real guess. Try again."

"A Ferris wheel."

"All right, wiseacre, so you're not going to play along. That's okay—you'll see it soon enough. Man," he went on, the hatchet knocking against the stump, "I wish I'd invented this thing. I almost did! One of those blueprints I drew up last winter wasn't far off."

"Speaking of which," I said, "whatever happened to that grill thing you built? The one with the old oil drum?"

"That? That's ancient history. I raffled it off for the church last week."

"Raffled it off?" I looked up. "After all that work?"

"Sure! Don't worry, I'll build another one—maybe even better. Gotta keep busy up here somehow." He winked. "So how's your friend?"

I handed him a branch, smelling the deep reassuring smell of black walnut. "What friend?"

"The Russian guy. The odd one."

"Oh—good, you met him. I was worried he'd skip out without paying." I hadn't been worried, really; whoever he was, something about him seemed honest, although it had occurred to me that someone who had appeared so abruptly could probably disappear with just as little notice.

"No, he seems to have decided to hang out for a while. He's hitchhiking around or something and says he's enjoying the peace and quiet. I told him if that's what he's looking for, then believe me, he's found it." Martin straightened. "He's a lawyer, you know. That's what he told me."

"Really?" I pictured the tall, threadbare foreigner standing by the door, face half hidden behind his scarf, hat in his hands.

"I wouldn't lie to you." Martin gathered up the split kindling and tipped an imaginary hat. "Thanks for the help," he said, ambling back toward the hostel in his slightly bowlegged way.

"See you, Martin." Smiling to myself, I walked back down the hill. I liked Martin, I thought: he had never once asked me a personal question, and I returned the favor. It was one of the best kinds of friendship I could imagine.

In the store, I unwrapped the sandwich I'd bought at the gas station and ate it standing up. There was an old combination radio and cassette player on top of the ice cream case, and although the radio part was useless up here, the tape deck worked fine. Picking a cassette from the pile on the hidden shelf under the counter, I opened the cracked case and nudged the volume up. A woman's plaintive voice threaded its way through the room, accompanying me as I filled a plastic pail and reached for the mop, diligently erasing footprints and dust with swaths of water. Patsy Cline. I wrung the mop and pushed it methodically, back and forth, under the shelves, into the corners. It was warm in the store, at least, thanks to the grill and the rattling electric heater along the back wall. When I was finished, I made a fresh pot of coffee, leaning back against the counter and inhaling the sharp scent as Patsy warbled in her somehow luxuriant sadness, her melancholy pleasure. Then I refilled the pail and did the chore again, humming, letting myself drift off into the simple rhythm of it, my joints gradually loosening.

"Crazy," I sang with Patsy, letting my voice ripple through the empty aisles while the backup singers chimed in: *ah, ah, ahhhh.* "I'm crazy for feeling so lonely . . ." The wet strands of the mop kept time.

"Excuse me, is this your book?"

I turned sharply. The foreigner was standing in the doorway, wearing the same coat, the same scarf drawn over his mouth, holding a thick hardcover before him. His eyes were bright.

I switched off the tape and looked at him guardedly, taken aback by his seeming ability to materialize out of nowhere.

"Yeah, looks like it," I said shortly. "Did I leave it out on the porch?"

"That's where I found it, yes." He gazed at the cover thoughtfully, pulling his scarf down and running a thumb over the embossed letters of the title. "Is it really yours? You're reading it?"

I bent and lifted the pail of dirty water, trying not to show that this was difficult. "Yes, it's mine." Then, raising an eyebrow, "Why? Do I not look like someone who would read books?"

"Oh." He placed the volume on the counter and rubbed his glove-less hands together. "I'm sorry—that's not what I meant. It's just that it's a very good book. I didn't expect that that was what you would be reading." He winced. "Sorry, I mean that—well, you know, it's a Russian book, and—"

"Never mind. I knew what you meant." I emptied the water in a cascade of brown, then took my place behind the register, sliding the book onto the hidden shelf where he could no longer see it.

He stood with his hands folded in front of him, gazing hesitantly around the store. Something about him looked apologetic, I thought, although—as I remembered belatedly—I was the one who had left him to shiver through a second mountain night with no heat.

"You want something?" I asked, making an effort to sound, if not friendly, then at least slightly less hostile. "Coffee?"

"Oh—no, thank you. I left my wallet up there at the, ah—" He gestured uphill. "Not the hotel. What did you call it?"

"The hostel." I reached for the glass pot. "It doesn't matter—just take some. Whatever I don't drink by the end of the day just goes to waste anyway."

I put a cup on the counter and filled it. With a quick look at me, he took it and held it in both hands, as if to warm them.

When he didn't show any sign of leaving, I had the unfamiliar sensation of realizing I would have to think of something else to say.

"Um. Have you been out hiking?" I glanced around in search of a task with which I could busy myself.

"Hiking? Oh, no. I wish I could, but it's not good for me to be out in the cold air for very long, unfortunately. I've just been, you know, looking around a bit here and there." He took a sip of the black coffee and grimaced. I pushed the tall glass sugar jar toward him, and he tipped it carefully, watching the thread of sugar disappear into the liquid.

There was something about his face—the set of the eyes, maybe, or the fine-looking line of the jaw, like a bird's bones—that almost compelled me to look at it. Disconcerted, I turned away from him and settled on cleaning the coffee machine even though it was still hot.

"You're really in a very pretty place," he said behind me. "This park, I mean."

"I've always thought so," I replied, wetting a napkin. It was, in fact, a place so beautiful I sometimes felt as if my entire soul were bound up with it, although I wasn't about to explain that to a stranger.

"So are you the only one who works here?"

I pulled out the used filter and wiped down the dull metal inside the machine. "I certainly seem to be."

"I see." There was a slight pause; I could picture him sweeping his gaze over the small space again. "You've been here for a long time?"

I shrugged, keeping my back to him as I rubbed at a stain. "Depends what you mean by 'a long time,' I guess."

"A year or two?"

"Something like that."

"Oh. Longer?"

I scrubbed harder. "I don't know. Maybe."

"Since you finished university?"

I stopped and looked down at my reflection in the scratched surface of the machine.

"Martin says you're a lawyer," I said after a moment, turning and throwing the napkin away. "Is that true?"

He seemed to be studying me. "Martin is the man I met at the hostel?"

"Yes."

He smiled, although I didn't see what was funny. "Well, in a sense, yes, I'm a lawyer. I was a lawyer in Uzbekistan, although that isn't very useful here, I'm afraid."

"So what brings you here, then?" It was my turn to study him, looking over the rim of my coffee cup as I raised it to my face.

"You mean, to America?"

"Yeah, I guess." There were thin lines at the corners of his eyes, I noticed, and his brows seemed somehow weighted, as if he spent much of his time thinking about problems that could only be solved with great difficulty.

"I'm a student," he said simply.

"Oh. You're on your winter break or something?"

"Yes, something like that." He rolled the sugar jar between his palms. "So, you like Dostoyevsky?"

I narrowed my eyes—was he about to mock me?—but his face was sincere. I looked down, fingering the book under the counter.

"Yeah, I do," I said softly, surprising myself with the honesty of the words. Then, "Well. I don't know, exactly. I mean, I read *The Brothers Karamazov* in school, and it—I guess you could say it drew me in. This one, though . . ."

He waited, watching me expectantly. "You don't like it?" he said finally.

I bit the inside of my lip. "It's not that. It's . . ." I remembered the hours I'd spent hunched over the opening chapters on the very day he'd first walked in, how vividly the scenes had played out before me in the emptiness of the store. "Actually," I admitted, "I like it very much. It's just that it's so focused on the psychology of the main character, the murderer. And as strange as it probably sounds, I still can't really understand why he killed the old woman to begin with."

A light came into his eyes. He spoke softly. "Do you happen to have the other chair? May I sit down?"

After a moment of hesitation, I walked to the broom closet and dragged it out for him.

He sat and faced me across the counter, folding his hands. "Perhaps you could tell me why *you* think he killed the old woman?"

His pose was so earnest that I almost laughed in spite of myself. "I thought you were a student, not a professor."

"Oh, I'm not a professor at all. It just happens that *Crime and Punishment* was one of my father's favorite books. He and I used to talk about things like that sometimes—over tea, much like this." He waved a hand at our cups of coffee, smiling. "He wasn't well-educated, but somehow he always used to find the best books, even the ones the government didn't allow. I used to see him sitting in his chair for hours, just reading, and then he'd call me over. I was a boy with his head in the clouds—I always thought foreign books were better—but those were some of my favorite times."

I blinked at the openness of the words, the frank affection in them. Nobody I knew would have spoken that way. I reached under the counter and retrieved the book, thumbing through the pages.

"My grandfather was a bit like that," I said, almost to myself. "All right, Dan—Dahn—sorry, how did you say your name?"

"Daniil—like 'Daniel.' You can call me that if you like. Or 'Danya'— that's what friends call me in Russian."

"Russian? Is that what they speak in Uzbekistan?"

He chuckled. "That's what *I* speak in Uzbekistan. I'm from a Russian family, as I mentioned."

"Okay. Daniil. Right." I held a hand to my cheek, looking down at the open pages. A moment passed as the wall clock ticked. If this man really was a lawyer, I thought, then he probably had twice the education I did. It would be absurd to go on.

"Please," he urged.

I looked up, surprised.

"Well," I said slowly, "the first few chapters make you think he did it for the money, obviously. You can tell he's desperate, wandering around penniless and in rags. And yet . . ." I paused. "Somehow, that doesn't seem to be what bothers him the most. He spends all those hours dwelling on his sister and how she's thrown herself away—marrying that older man—for his sake. And that other girl, too, the one who becomes a—a prostitute so she can feed her family after her father dies." I looked up with embarrassment, expecting to find an expression of disappointment on his face, but he was leaning forward, paying attention to every word. "I don't know. I guess I don't quite understand it, really. Especially since, after the murder, he just buries the jewelry and the money he steals and never comes back."

"Yes, that's the mystery, isn't it? He goes to all the trouble of planning and carrying out the murder, and then he seems to care very little about the money." The stranger gripped his cup, the light glancing off his ring. His eyes held mine. "Do you think he kills the old woman, the moneylender, just because he can? That's what some people say."

I let out a small laugh and shook my head. "I'm not sure why you're so interested in what I think. I can promise you I know a lot more about hamburgers than I do about literature."

He leaned back and blew a puff of air through his lips. "Nonsense," he said, unwinding the scarf from his neck and placing it on the counter. It was tattered and stained, coming apart at the ends. "Of course I'd like to know. Otherwise I wouldn't ask."

I was still looking at the scarf, at his bright eyes and ragged hair.

"Okay," I said finally. "What I think, Daniil—"

"Danya," he interrupted with a quick smile. "No need to be formal."

"What I think, Danya, is that this Raskolnikov—the murderer—is driven insane by living in a world where people suffer so much, and for no reason, and where there's this kind of horrible, relentless cruelty everywhere you look. And the people who are cruel, or who even just exploit others, like the old woman he kills, are never punished. They rarely even seem to feel guilty about what they've done." The words sounded jumbled and confused, but I pressed on. "To him, killing her is like evening the score, or—I don't know how to explain it. Taking an eye for an eye, I guess. In some ways, I think it's that simple."

He remained silent for a moment after I'd finished, watching my face. With a flicker of irritation—what was it about the fact of my standing behind a counter that made people feel free to gawk at me as if I were an animal in the zoo?—I turned away to pour the last of my drink down the drain.

He stopped me by drawing a breath and reaching for the book. "May I?"

I made a vague gesture.

"I agree with you in some respects," he said. "But what I've always thought Raskolnikov can't bear is that so many people around him are . . ." He drew a breath, seeming to choose his words with care.

". . . Sacrificing themselves for others. All the best characters in the story, the most noble and honest and innocent ones, do that. And ultimately it causes them great pain without giving any real benefit to the people they intended to help." He closed his eyes, speaking almost as if to himself. "I think it angers him, knowing that so many of these sacrifices are useless. 'Futile,' perhaps, is the word I'm looking for. Yes, that's it—'futile.'" He opened his eyes again, giving me a self-conscious smile. "Sometimes these words just seem to escape from my memory, you know? I often regret that my English isn't better."

"What? Your English is perfect." I was relieved at the change in subject. "You must have been living here for a long time."

"Not at all, actually. In fact, I'm still a recent arrival, you might say." He continued to smile lopsidedly, rising to his feet and sliding the book back toward me. "But perhaps," he went on as he reached for his hat, "you could tell me what you think when you've finished? I'd be most interested to hear your views." He looked away, then back at me again. "Only if you'd like that, of course."

I watched him, reluctantly intrigued. "I don't know. I guess I don't see why not. You'll be long gone by then, though, I'm sure." I opened the cover to look at the due date, scratched there in pencil by a librarian with a shaky hand. Then, almost as an afterthought, I added, "You're lucky your winter break starts so early. I don't think most schools give the whole month of December off."

For the briefest of moments, he was flustered. I could see it in his face, an expression of unease that flew over his features, although it passed almost immediately. His hands twitched toward one another, a small involuntary movement. When he replied, however, his voice was as amiable as before. "Yes," he said. "It *is* very lucky. They want us to have a rest, you know—after our exams. And it's a good thing, I'd say. After all, this really is a beautiful place, isn't it? The perfect place to take a holiday." Then, with a wave, he was gone.

Through the window, I watched his dark, shambling figure step off the porch and climb the path to the hostel, his shoulders jerking awkwardly with each step, his head bent.

Sliding the back of the ice cream case open, I reached for a butter knife and began chipping away at the fuzzy layer of ice that had accumulated inside. My mind, however, kept drifting back to the conversation. It wasn't that anything he'd said was especially outlandish; if anything, his manners were almost painfully correct. But there was something odd behind the smiles, I thought, an uncertainty, as if he were afraid of something he might say.

On the other hand, who knew? Maybe he just wanted to be liked. It had been ages since I'd felt any impulses in that direction myself, but I could dimly remember what it felt like to care about that kind of thing. He was young and probably still did.

He would learn.

I swept the ice chips into my palm and stretched. It felt good to do physical work, even in such a small way. Before the accident, I had loved helping friends do farm work, stacking bales of hay, building sheds, mucking out stalls. There was something so pleasing about being able to see the results of all that effort, the stump that had been dug out, the crumbling wall that had been repaired, the door that had been re-hinged. There was something satisfying, too, about picking up a tool and knowing how to use it. *You want that old stall divider taken down? Sure.* Thinking of this, I looked down at the now-slightly-bent butter knife and smiled slightly. It was true that I couldn't do most of those things anymore, but I still did what I could. Maybe there was something in me of my grandfather's old stubbornness.

As afternoon slid into evening and I prepared to lock up, gathering my things into a pile, Jerry came in, bringing the smell of the woods with him. He was carrying a hunting rifle in one hand—an old one, I noticed, with a worn walnut stock. It must have been his father's or grandfather's, I thought as he propped it next to the door.

"Burger with onions," he grunted. He was a big man, with a thick beard and a bad back that had gotten him laid off from the Pepsi plant in town. A dusty black cap was settled on his head.

"Sure." I put the slab of frozen meat on the grill and covered it with a pot lid. It cooked more quickly that way, I had discovered. "You want the onions fried, too?"

"Naw, that's all right." He reached into his back pocket and fumbled for his wallet, his stomach bulging under his camouflage jacket. "How you been, Kathleen?"

"Been okay, I guess. You get anything out there?" I lifted my chin at the window, the woods outside.

"Nothing yet. Looks like it's gonna be a hard season."

"Yeah, that's what everybody's saying."

He waited quietly the way he always did, his cap pulled low over his eyes, like someone who could never quite get used to being indoors. I decided to throw an extra patty onto the burger and reached back into the freezer.

"Thanks," he said when it hit the grill with a hiss.

"No problem."

Then, reaching into his jacket pocket, he pulled out a brown packet—a paper lunch bag, as usual—and put it on the counter.

Without speaking, I moved the bag to the shelf next to the cassette tapes and extracted two twenty-dollar bills from my purse, giving them to him with his change for the burger. He was shifting from foot to foot, I noticed, as if trying to ease a pain that couldn't be eased. "How's your back?"

He shrugged. "Not so good. Nice of you to ask, though. I might need surgery one of these days, it sounds like, but I'm trying to put it off as long as I can." He began his slow stroll back to the door, holding the sandwich awkwardly in one hand and picking up the gun with the other.

"By the way." As he opened the door, he looked back over his shoulder without turning. I could see twigs clinging to the hood of his coat, a spatter of mud. "You oughta be careful, you know?"

I looked at him blankly.

"Out on the ice," he said. "I knowed a kid that drowned that way, back before you were born. It ain't safe."

I stared at him. By the time I opened my mouth to respond, he was shuffling out, the rifle gripped in his hand.

"Just because you're used to this place don't mean it ain't dangerous," he murmured, and then the door closed behind him, scraping against its sill.

"Okay," I said softly, watching through the window as he placed the gun on a rack on the back window of his pickup and climbed stiffly into the cab. A dog clambered to its feet in the backseat and put its paws on the window, panting, seeming to look at me as the truck drove away.

After he had gone, I opened the paper bag and looked into it, counting. They were all there, twenty of them, small and white and oval. I folded the bag again and held it in my hands for a moment, looking down at the floor, then stuffed it into my pocket and walked onto the porch, gathering the ashtrays and flipping the sign on the door so it read CLOSED.

3

The emergency room lights were harsh. My grandmother lay on her back on a stiff cot, shivering in her gown, looking angry. Her small eyes, focused on nothing in particular, were watering, and her mouth was set in a thin, contemptuous line. Her hand, when I tried to take it, was cold and papery, the skin wrinkled like a newborn dog's. She pulled it away and aimed her gaze grimly at the ceiling. Her breath came in short rasps, as if she were breathing through a straw.

It was a few days after the stranger had arrived. I had found her that morning, collapsed on her knees next to the couch, clinging to it with her yellowed nails as if she would drown.

"Mrs. McElwain," the doctor said, holding her file in a closed folder at his side, as if he already knew what it contained. I recognized him from my time with my husband. He was younger than most of the doctors I had met, in his forties, with two daughters who went to a private school the next county over. His curly hair made him look ridiculously, almost insultingly boyish, as if he'd discovered the secret to eternal youth and refused to share it.

My grandmother turned her eyes in his direction briefly before resuming her vague, sour examination of the ceiling tiles. The silence lengthened.

"What?" she rasped finally, gathering that a response was expected of her.

"Your chart shows you were diagnosed with emphysema two years ago." He spoke in a gentle, reassuring doctor–tone I knew she would hate.

"Yeah?" she said, nearly spitting the word.

"Mrs. McElwain, you need to stop smoking. Immediately. To be honest, I'm amazed you're not on oxygen already. Because what you're doing—" he sat on the end of the cot, crossing one leg over the other "—is weakening your lung tissue, which is going to impede your airflow more and more. So, when you get sick, like you did this morning, you're going to have a very difficult time breathing and could face some serious problems. In fact—"

Her eyebrows contracted and she looked away, raising a hand dismissively.

"Mrs. McElwain, I'm serious. I'm concerned about you." His eyes were a wide, deep blue. "I know it's hard, but please consider—"

She muttered something and coughed, still facing the wall.

"I beg your pardon?"

"I said, 'I don't know why everybody keeps calling me 'Mrs.,'" she snapped. "He's been dead for years." Although she was a small woman, the gown left her arms and legs bare, exposed in their motionless, lumpen whiteness under the lights. Her breasts hung slack under the fabric.

The doctor stood up, her folder under his arm. "All right, Mrs.— Lydia," he said curtly. "Just remember what I said, please." He went out, white coat flapping behind him as if he were some kind of over-grown dove.

"I hate him," my grandmother said when I helped her into the Jeep afterward. She glared out the window at the parking lot, the bleak exterior of Carlisle Hospital. "Dr. Blue Eyes. Always talks to me as if I were stupid."

"He's trying to help you." I put her seatbelt on and tightened it over her shoulder. "Are you going to do what he said?"

"Bah."

"Well, are you?"

She scowled at me. "Have you ever tried quitting smoking? After fifty years?"

I paused, my hands on the steering wheel.

"What?" she said after a moment. Something must have shown itself in my expression.

I slipped the key into the ignition.

"Nothing." I shook my head. "And no, I've never tried quitting smoking, but there must be—"

"Take me to that restaurant by the War College. I want dinner. They didn't feed me at all in that place."

I closed my eyes briefly, then put my hand on the gear shift. "Okay."

"Is he the doctor that patched you up?" She turned suddenly and regarded me intently, squinting.

"What?" I looked at her, startled.

"After the accident. You know, when—"

My stomach lurched, but I kept my voice even. "No, Grandma. They took me to Hershey."

"They did?"

"Yes. In the helicopter. You visited me there." I remembered the day clearly, my grandmother sitting starchily at a table in the cafeteria until the attendant had locked the brakes on my wheelchair and left. Bending toward me with her gruff expression, she had opened a cup of applesauce and fed me patiently, spoonful by spoonful, as if I were a baby, holding a bottle of water with a straw up to my lips and wiping my mouth carefully with a napkin. It had been my second trip out of my hospital room and the first time I had been able to sit up in the wheelchair for more than two minutes.

"Oh." She was quiet for a moment, touching her tight gray curls. "Well, that's a good thing, then. These Carlisle doctors ain't worth nothing."

I glanced at her; she didn't usually use words like "ain't." "Dr. Padovese is Catholic, you know."

She looked over with sharp surprise. "Where'd you hear that?"

"His daughters go to high school at Bishop McDevitt."

"Is that so?" Considering this, she smoothed her shirt, as if she were still wearing the gown. "I don't care," she finally pronounced. "He still ain't worth nothing to me. When's the last time he tried to quit smoking after fifty years, that's what I'd like to know."

We went to the diner near the Army War College and ate our grilled cheese sandwiches in silence, surrounded by stiff-looking men in civilian clothes. As I watched them, I thought of the stranger with his enthusiastic gestures, the way he leaned forward against the counter as he quizzed me about the park, Centerville, my progress through the book. He had kept coming in, buying a cup of tea with small change and wrapping his long fingers around it as he spoke, sitting tentatively as if afraid of overstaying his welcome but staying anyway. It was hard to imagine a greater contrast with the men who now sat chewing in the booths behind my grandmother, their backs straight and their eyes fixed on something invisible that seemed to hang in midair just beyond their plates.

When we finally arrived home in the darkness, the light on the answering machine was blinking.

"Beth again, I'll bet," my grandmother gasped wetly, picking her way toward the overstuffed chair and coughing. "You better call her back this time."

I picked up the receiver and carried it into the kitchen, dialing Beth's cell number, the mustard-yellow cord trailing behind me.

"Kathy!" Beth chirped, over the noise of an engine. I could picture her in her dented blue Jetta, steering with one hand. "How's my baby girl?"

"I'm good. Sorry I didn't manage to call you back before." I glanced at the clock on the oven. "Where are you?"

"Driving home from Target—I had to pick up some diapers for Dylan. You want to go out tonight? I can leave him with my parents for a while."

I looked through the doorway at the back of my grandmother's head; she was motionless, probably already dozing off. "I don't know. I mean, I'd like to, but Grandma's been sick."

"Oh, that's too bad. Well, whatever you want—I was thinking we'd just pop over to the Joyride, maybe shoot a round of pool, and come home. But it's up to you." Her voice had the bright, upbeat tone of the barista she was by day, although I knew her husband's latest deployment weighed heavily on her.

"All right, sure." I gave in. "You want me to meet you there?"

"No, I'll come pick you up. I think you need to have at least two drinks while we're out. Wait, I take that back—three drinks. At *least*."

"Here you are, a good Christian girl—"

"Yeah—" she laughed.

"A Sunday school teacher even, and yet you're always trying to corrupt me," I said, making an effort to smile even though she couldn't see me. "I can only imagine what you do to those children."

"Oh, whatever. There's nothing wrong with me living vicariously through you. Besides, you deserve to have a little fun, in my opinion." I heard her downshift. "Speaking of which, when I get there, you'd better not be wearing a sweatshirt."

"Do you have any idea how cold—"

"I don't care how cold. You're way too pretty to be dressing like a fourteen-year-old boy all the time."

By the time she arrived, it was snowing again. When I climbed into the car, she gave me a hug, rocking me back and forth slightly before letting me go.

"There," she said. "I feel better already."

"What's wrong?"

"Oh, nothing—same old. It's just still tough when Mark's gone. Of course, it's also tough when he's here, but that's another story." She pointed at the glove compartment, her short black hair brushing her cheek as she turned her head. "There's a cookie in there for you. We didn't sell them all today."

I pulled it out; it was gingerbread, smelling of cinnamon and cloves. "Not a lot of business?"

"Actually, I lied. I kept that one aside for you." The wipers beat rhythmically as she looked over her shoulder and swung into another lane. "Did I tell you the kid started running the other day?"

"He's old enough to do that?"

"Barely. You should see him—he gets all fired up about something and just starts pumping those little legs." She laughed. "He's still so tiny—but then, he was pretty much doomed to be short, I guess, given how Mark and I both turned out. He's gonna be an only child, too, so we've probably created a monster." She swung into the parking lot of the Joyride and stopped under a blinking Rolling Rock sign, its neon-green lights flashing into the night.

The bar was nearly deserted—it was a Wednesday, after all. Beth sauntered over to the jukebox and pushed the buttons for a new country song, something fast and jangly I didn't recognize. "What're you having, gorgeous?"

"I don't know—Jack and Coke?"

"I should've known. Would it kill you to try a girly drink?"

"It might."

"Ha." She spoke to the bartender, a stout woman in a Rusty Wallace T-shirt, returning with the mixed drink for me and a cherry Pepsi for herself. Even in her heels, she barely reached my shoulder. "Drink up. You want to break, or should I?"

"I can, if you want." I racked the balls with swift movements and hung the triangle back under the table, breaking with a fierce *crack*. Behind me, an array of smoke-stained posters hung on the wall— Corvettes and Mustangs and Roadsters. Their edges were curling, but the sunsets behind the cars, the palm trees and bright strips of beach, shone eternal.

"Damn," she said. "It's so hot when you do that."

I laughed. "Oh, please. I didn't even sink anything."

"That's not the point." She peered under the table, searching for the chalk. "You know, Mark took me to Good-Time Joe's when he was here on leave—God knows why; I think he just wanted to get out of my parents' house—and let me tell you, it's a little alarming how much the army has improved his pool skills. Also poker. I pretended not to notice." She shot at a striped ball and missed. Straightening, she caught sight of her reflection in a long mirror on the wall. Her face briefly took on a hard, scrutinizing expression as she sucked in her stomach and smoothed her shirt, twisting sideways to look at her hips.

I took aim at the six ball but watched it rebound sharply off the corner of a pocket.

"Boy, we're great at this game, aren't we?" she said.

I smiled again and sipped my drink, surprised by how strong it was. The bar, with its reassuringly bar-like smells, was beginning to feel smaller and warmer than before.

"So did you sign up for that master's program?" I picked up the chalk.

She sighed. "Actually, we just decided to push that off 'til next year. I still want to do it, and Mark wants me to, but I don't know who'd watch Dylan. I'm sure my parents would, but I hate to put that on them—they're already doing me a huge favor by watching him so I can go out and work. I think they know I'd go crazy if I didn't, but still." She bent to slip a finger into a shoe where it must have been chafing her. "You need a master's to be a CPA, so I do want to do it someday. It'd be nice to have a life of my own once the kid's old enough for school. I love him to bits, but right now I feel like my brain's rotting."

I missed my next shot, and she took aim again, looking at me surreptitiously. "Do you think you'll ever go back and finish?" she asked.

"What? My bachelor's degree?" I leaned against my stick. We'd circled around this question before, but she'd never asked it so directly. I shook my head. "No, not a chance. I mean, I wish I could. But I'm not earning nearly enough. I'm barely saving anything at all, working up there."

"You know, Mark and I were talking about that," she said, striking the white ball and sending both a striped and a solid into the pocket. "Shoot—that wasn't supposed to happen. Anyway, if I go back full-time, I could take Dylan and move into one of those student apartments, at least until Mark's back from Iraq. If you don't mind watching him sometimes—the kid, I mean—maybe we could live together and both take classes. You know, like before." A hesitant but earnest expression came over her face, and I looked away. "Mark and I would take care of the rent. It'd be worth it to us, to have someone besides my parents who can keep an eye on Dylan sometimes. I thought . . . well, I thought it could be good for both of us. If it's what you want."

I bit my lip, gazing behind her at the jukebox. "Oh." The bartender strolled over to the machine and picked a different song, an older one. "I mean, that's—that's an incredible offer, but . . ." I tried to imagine myself folded into a chair at the back of a classroom, surrounded by chattering nineteen-year-olds. Bending over a textbook at night. Standing up in front of a crowd of strangers to give a presentation, exposing myself to their stares. Inwardly, I shrank away.

Aloud, I said, "I just don't think I could. My grandmother needs somebody to keep an eye on her. And the tuition is just so much—it wouldn't really be within reach."

"Well," she replied brightly, "you were almost finished when you left, right? You'd probably only have to do it for a few semesters."

I avoided her eyes. It hadn't really been my choice to drop out in the first place, something I'd never seen fit to tell her, but which she probably suspected. At any rate, it didn't matter now. "I don't know," I said, looking for a way to change the subject.

"Okay, but promise me you'll think about it?"

Without answering, I pretended to concentrate on my next shot, finally sitting on the edge of the table and swinging the cue behind my back in defiance of my protesting joints. The five ball rolled into the pocket, and the bartender applauded. I smiled and shook my head.

"Show-off." Beth touched my shoulder gently as she walked toward the jukebox. "Well, whatever you decide, you know I love you. Although I still think you should give it some thought." Pinching her wallet from her purse, she flipped through the song list. "By the way, you heard from your brother lately?"

"No, not for a while. He's still near a place called Kandahar. That's all I know." I studied the balls that were left on the table, then glanced up at the car posters. There were women in many of them, of course, with long hair and tanned legs, sitting on the hood or leaning over to polish a strip of chrome, backs arched and breasts perfect. Somehow, I thought, they were never in the driver's seat.

"His wife doesn't call?"

"Not that I know of."

"Ugh, what a witch." She chose another song, poking at the buttons with a long, polished fingernail.

I laughed. "I don't really blame her. What would we talk about if she called, besides him? She doesn't know us, and it's not like there's ever any news up here."

"Truer words were never spoken. You could die waiting for something to happen here that's actually, you know, an event." She looked at me from the corner of her eye. "Not that that's an excuse, in my opinion."

For a moment, I thought about telling her about the stranger who had so mysteriously appeared on the mountain, but, looking down at the billiard balls that were scattered across the table, I decided against it. There was no reason to mention him. He was no one and he would soon be gone.

With a sharp, hard shot, I sent the thirteen ball down the edge of the table, but my aim was off and it ricocheted dumbly back toward me. I picked up my drink and finished it off, letting it reach my feet, making me hover above the ground as the room softened and grew. A group of men walked in, their boot heels striking hard against the linoleum, descending on the bartender in a blur of striped shirts and black cowboy hats. Beth wandered off to the bathroom, leaving an invisible trail of perfume behind her. The music changed to the deep, thudding chords of classic rock.

One of the men in the crowd glanced over his shoulder and, seeing me, kept looking, his round face shadowed by his hat but still familiar. It was John, I suddenly realized—the trucker I knew from childhood. He kept watching even as the bartender began to slide drinks across the counter, her chest shaking as she laughed a laugh I couldn't hear, the lines in her cheeks deepening as she smiled.

My back stiffened, but I turned on my heel, pretending not to see. I didn't care, I thought. Let him watch; let any of them watch. I wasn't even there anymore, anyway: I was miles away, in a world created by the single green-shaded bulb that hung over the pool table, a place none of them could ever reach. I was no longer myself, I was someone else—just a woman in a bar, anonymous, leaning on her cue stick, her hair falling onto her shoulders, no scars, no mended bones, no rumors that followed her. A woman who was whole and complete and mysterious, someone no one had ever tried to look through with their prying eyes or their X-ray machines. A woman with no name, or rather, any name she wanted. Who decided who could see her and who couldn't, who was able to vanish with a snap of her fingers. Here before you and then gone.

I knew it was the liquor that was giving me this illusion. I didn't care.

"Your turn," I told Beth when she returned, floating over to the bar on my suddenly weightless legs, cutting through the cloud of men with their wide backs and shining belt buckles as if they didn't exist, putting down my money, ordering another drink.

The next morning, before work, I called my parents. It was early, and I knew they would still be asleep. Fighting a sense of reluctance as I dialed the number, I rubbed my palms against my sweatshirt, shifting my weight in my shoes. My head ached and my eyes felt dry.

My mother picked up; I could see her rolling over in bed to grab the phone, her black hair disheveled and streaked with gray. "Yeah? What?"

"Hi, Mom. It's Kathleen." I waited, knotting the cord around my fingers.

"Oh." There was a pause. "Yeah? Listen, honey, could I call you back later? We were up—"

"No, sorry. The phone still isn't working at the store. This'll just take a minute, though. Listen, yesterday—"

She made a muffled sound, and I heard her mumbling something to my father in the background.

"Mom," I said patiently.

"Yeah?"

"I had to take Grandma to the E.R. yesterday for her breathing. I thought you and Dad would want to know."

"Oh." She seemed to be waiting for me to go on. When I didn't say anything, she asked, "Is that all?"

"Well, yes, that's all, but—"

"Yeah, yeah, okay. Let me talk to your dad about it. She's his mother. He might be able to swing by after work, but I don't know. The shop's been giving him later and later hours. And honey?"

"Yeah?"

"Don't call so early."

"All right, Mom." I hung up, rubbing my face with both hands. There were some Aunt Jemima pancakes in the freezer, and I pried two off the stack, heating them in the microwave. I didn't particularly want to go to work. I didn't particularly want to do anything.

I took my coat from its hook and grabbed my book from the dining-room table, poking my head into the living room to look at my grandmother. She was asleep on the couch under a blanket, her mouth slack.

The keys jingled as I pocketed them. I opened the door, wincing as the cold air struck my skin.

"Kathleen," my grandmother said.

Surprised, I stuck my head back into the living room. She was lying in the same position as before, but her eyes were open. "Yes?" I said, in case she couldn't see me. It was sometimes hard to tell just how bad her vision was these days. "How are you feeling, Grandma?"

She ignored the question. "I want to have dinner tonight."

"You mean with me?" We had dinner together nearly every night, or if not together, then at least in the same household, her staring at her TV shows, me perched on the edge of the mattress in my room.

Something in my expression seemed to pain her. She turned her face away. "Bring a ham from the grocery store. And some potatoes."

I did some mental calculations, remembering the pile of bills I had pulled from the mailbox the day before. "Okay."

"And green beans. Or peas. Canned." Speaking seemed to tire her. She shifted under the blanket, settling further into the cushions.

"All right. I can do that."

Grimacing, she closed her eyes. I left, forgetting to tell her that my father might stop in, although I doubted he would. Generally, they left it to me to take care of things. And I did.

"They're finally putting up the sign!" Martin enthused over lunch in the store. "I was starting to think they weren't going to do it, but when I walked out this morning, there they were, digging a hole for the post."

He had cropped his hair even closer than usual, giving him a fuzzy look. "What sign?" I asked, looking at the gray meat of my hamburger. I had overcooked it, and it was dry. I opened a Pepsi that tasted much too sweet.

"The Underground Railroad one. The historical marker. I heard a rumor way back when I first took over up there, but I never really thought it was true. I can't even believe it. Runaway slaves! In that very building!" He was rapturous, even more so than he'd been about the mystery project—which remained ongoing, if the parts currently stacked on the hostel's porch were any indication. "In some ways, it makes me feel a closer connection to God, you know? Like Moses and the Israelites—how they fled slavery in Egypt. Like the building was part of a deliverance."

I walked to the sink and poured myself a cup of tap water, peering into the bottom to make sure there were no bits of rust or dirt. "You're right, that's really something," I answered absently.

"Sure is. I'm going to look into it as soon as I get a chance. Maybe the county historical society has something on it."

I looked at him, his bright eyes and radiant smile, and for a brief, troubling moment was puzzled. What had we been talking about? My grandmother's face, her grim expression and narrowed eyes, appeared before me. I should have put more wood in the stove before I'd left. She'd be cold.

"So how are you?" Martin asked, taking a swig of his Dr. Pepper.

"Me? I'm fine." I returned to the present. "How's our friend?"

"The foreign guy? Busy. I put him to work."

"What? Why?"

"Because he can't pay," Martin replied nonchalantly. "He somehow got down to his last few dollars, it seems. So I told him I'd let him stay for free and eat whatever he can find in the kitchen if he helps me out. He's up there sweeping out the game room right now."

I rubbed a fingertip along the edge of the counter, frowning as I envisioned the stranger with his thin limbs, the padded coat in which he looked so slight. "What's he doing here, do you think?"

"I don't know—not my business to ask. I invited him to our Bible study tonight, but he didn't seem very interested. Hey, do you want to come?" His face brightened.

"I can't—I'm having dinner with my grandma. Thanks, though."

"No problem. It's a standing invitation. We always meet on Thursdays."

"Yeah, I know." Although if the older ones found out I had been brought up Catholic, I thought, they would probably chase me out of the building. Many of the churches in the area taught that Catholics weren't Christian, pointing to what they called idol-worship and who knew what else. I'd lost more than one childhood friend over it, although these days people seemed more inclined to focus their ire on Middle Easterners they'd never have to meet.

"All right, Kathleen," he beamed, slapping his money on the counter the way he always did. "I'll see you later."

The sky darkened during the afternoon, and in the evening a lashing rain came, pelting the windows and battering the ceiling. At six, I dragged the metal signboard in, locked the store, and walked as quickly as I could to the Jeep, holding a plastic bag over my head to shield my face. The drive to the grocery store in Carlisle—all Centerville had was Miller's, a combination convenience and hunting store much better known for its crossbows than its food—was a long one, the rain coating the roads in slick, half-frozen sheets. I steered the car carefully around the curves, watching for deer. They didn't usually come out during storms, but you never knew. I had once counted thirteen of them as I drove up the mountain on a foggy night, my headlights shining into their wide, frightened eyes as they stood by the side of the road, vigilant and vulnerable, watching. That had been years earlier, but I still remembered it, the wonder of it, thirteen adult deer stunned into stillness, one after another, poised to run but frozen in their beautiful, fatal uncertainty.

The parking lot at the grocery store was jammed, probably with people from Centerville and other rural dwellers leaving their jobs in Carlisle. It was a cheap, crowded place, and none too clean, but we all continued to go there out of habit. My grandmother had been a cashier there for a while, after my grandfather had decided working wasn't worth the bother. I parked at the edge of the lot and made my way toward the faded awning, feeling my hip begin to ache with the cold. Ignoring it, I yanked a shopping cart from the interlocking line of them and pushed it through the sliding doors, wiping the rain from my eyes.

I entered the bleak, brightly lit produce aisle and dropped two dirt-streaked potatoes into a bag. The hams were at the back of the store, and I was edging my way there past displays of holiday candy when I saw Amos's mother.

She was standing with her back to me in front of a row of Christmas cookies, wearing a stylish black jacket with a belt around the waist. I caught a glimpse of her in profile as I passed, her dark eyes, pert nose, and tanned skin, and felt my throat contract. I did not want to see her. Most of all, I did not want her to see me.

"How come you never talk to her?" my mother had asked once.

I had shrugged, or tried to.

"It makes it look like you don't like her," she had persisted. "Or like you feel guilty or something."

I had turned and fixed her with a long look.

"I do not want," I'd told her firmly, "to talk about this ever again."

This was shortly after I had left the hospital, when I was still as thin as a starved animal, with long red scars not entirely hidden under my clothing and an expression that struck even me as angry and raw-looking. She had stared at me, startled, and quickly turned away to do something else.

Amos and I had met when I was fifteen and he was nineteen, and gotten married on the mountain as soon as I'd finished high school. The marriage had lasted for four years, almost five, and then he had died. There didn't seem to be anything to say about him aside from that. When the lights come up, the show is over, and there really isn't much of a point in hanging around the theater.

The truth was that the whole thing—everything that had happened—still made me sick inside, although what I felt was more anger than sadness. More than once, I had opened my mouth to talk to Beth about it, but was always stopped by a sense of unsteadiness, almost nausea. Early on, when I had just come out of one of the surgeries, she had stroked my hair and said, "We can talk about it when you're ready, hon." But I was never ready: never ready to tell her, or anyone, that I wasn't feeling what I was supposed to feel, that instead of sorrow I felt a fury so corrosive it seemed to be eating away at me on the inside, hollowing me out like a snakeskin, making me grind my teeth at night. Women weren't supposed to be this angry; no one was, especially not someone who, according to everyone else, was grieving. Angry is what I was, though, and it was an absolute anger, the kind that comes from the cold, hard knowledge that something unfair has happened, something you will never be able to forgive.

In any case, I had no desire to come face-to-face with Amos's mother. The very thought gave me a sense of dizziness, causing me to wander, disoriented, into an altogether different section of the store. I stood for several minutes under the pale lights of the frozen-food aisle, staring stupidly into the frost-covered glass, before coming to my senses, grabbing the ham, and fleeing to the car.

At the house, my grandmother was waiting for me, her hands on her hips. Her housedress, I noticed, was stained, as if she had spilled something on herself that day. A cigarette was pinched between her lips. "You didn't tell me your father was coming."

"I'm sorry," I said, putting the grocery bags on the counter. She rifled through them, ash dropping onto the floor.

"Where are the beans?"

"What?"

"I told you to get beans." Her brows were so deeply furrowed that they seemed to meet above her nose. "And I don't know why you didn't tell me he was coming. Just because I'm old doesn't mean I don't care about my privacy anymore. Just because I'm old—"

"Yes. You're right. I'm sorry." I hung up my coat and moved toward the stairs.

"Where are you going?"

"Just—upstairs. I'll be back in a minute." I bolted upstairs with as much dignity as I could and stood in my room for a moment, facing the faded map on the wall, forcing myself to keep still. Uzbekistan, I verified, composing myself, was between Kazakhstan and Turkmenistan, west of a place called Tajikistan. It even shared a border with Afghanistan, where my brother was probably at that moment sleeping in a tent behind some nameless hill.

After a few minutes, I went into the bathroom, where I rubbed cold water on my face and made myself practice a smile in the mirror. Everything was fine, I reminded myself. Nothing had changed.

When I opened the door, I noticed, for the first time, a foreign aroma in the house, which usually smelled of smoke and dust and the cheap soap my grandmother always bought at the Dollar Store. The scent was heavy and sweet.

"I made a cake," my grandmother announced when I returned to the kitchen and began searching for the potato peeler, bending and digging through drawers filled with rusting keys and teaspoons and can openers.

"You what?" I looked up at her.

"I said I made a cake. Pineapple upside-down. It's on the table." When not perturbed, she bore a marked resemblance to the Queen of England, albeit in somewhat heavier form. She had the same gray curls the queen had in tabloid photos, the same round, powdery-looking face and soft jowls. Nodding pointedly, she disappeared into the dining room and returned bearing a gooey-looking casserole dish that was much too heavy for her, the cigarette still clamped in her mouth. I took the dish from her hands and placed it on the stove, mystified.

"It smells delicious. What made you decide to do that?"

"I don't know," she said carelessly. "It seemed like if you were going to go to the trouble of making a ham and all . . ." Her voice trailed off, and she turned to peer into the now-empty bags again. "And anyway," she added in a darker tone, "I needed something to do while your father was in here poking around and asking a bunch of stupid questions."

"Oh." I began covering the ham with sheets of foil. "What did he ask?"

"Just stupid things about my smoking and my lungs. I don't see how he has any room to talk—he smokes like a chimney himself. Menthols, too. Now *those* things," she said with conviction, "*those* things are disgusting. Full of nasty chemicals. You'd never catch me touching that kind of"—she searched for a word—"*garbage*. No, sir."

Turning on the oven, I stifled a smile.

"And he had a bunch of questions about how we went to the hospital yesterday, but I don't let him bully me. Just like you shouldn't let anyone bully you." Taking two plates from the cupboard, she fished some silverware from a drawer and walked creakily back to the dining room.

"Wait. What?" I looked after her, blinking.

"I said—"

"No, I mean, I heard you. I just wasn't sure what you meant." I stood facing her, holding the potatoes.

"Exactly," she grumbled, continuing to set the table and then settling into her overstuffed chair, from which she turned on the TV and sank into silence.

After a time, I heard her turn the TV off again and shuffle across the room to the record player she'd bought at a yard sale a few years earlier. Peggy Lee began belting triumphantly, her voice sailing over the dusty furniture and into the kitchen. Peggy, my father had once told me, had been my grandmother's brother's favorite. He would come home in his handsome army uniform and swing my twelve-year-old grandmother around the living room while the singer celebrated in her brassy tones. Then he'd gone to the Pacific theater and come back a changed man, sitting wordless and grim and staring obsessively at his hands until, eventually, he'd been put away somewhere. At my grandmother's wedding, he'd slumped on a pew at the back, attended by a nurse, crying inconsolably. Maybe he knew that my grandmother had married a hard man.

I put a pot of water on to boil and stooped over the trash can, working briskly with the potato peeler. The scent of roasting ham filled the kitchen, and for a moment, I wondered just how much of my day I spent standing over food, waiting for it to be ready. More of it than I cared to admit, I thought, at least when there were actually customers. It was a good thing I had the library to keep my brain from turning into paste.

Maybe Beth was right, I allowed myself to think tentatively, rubbing my forehead with the side of my hand. Maybe it was time to find a way to go back to school.

But no: even if I had the money, which I didn't, and even if the woman currently standing over the record player didn't need me, which she did, something about the idea made me uneasy. I wasn't ready, I thought. That person wasn't who I was anymore.

And anyway, I had a settled life, one I had more or less arranged to my satisfaction. Maybe it wasn't all I had hoped, but it wasn't bad.

An hour later, we sat at the table. Peggy had been replaced by Dean Martin. "This is good," my grandmother said, chewing a mouthful of potatoes and meat and wiping her mouth roughly.

For the first time that day, I felt a sense of calm. "Thank you."

She sniffed her glass of milk suspiciously before drinking. "Will you take me to Christmas Eve mass next week?"

"Sure. It's not next week, though. It's two weeks from now."

She shrugged and shook a generous amount of pepper onto her potatoes, sending the black grains flying all over the table. "It doesn't matter. Just tell me when the day comes. It's all the same to me."

"Okay." We finished the meal in silence, and I cleared the plates and sliced the cake. It was like caramel on the bottom, leaving sticky droplets all over the counter.

"It's good," I said, returning to the table and taking a bite. Then, taking another, "Really good."

"Well, I should hope so. It was my mother's recipe. They made that kind of thing back then."

"I can see why."

"Canned pineapple," she said. "We thought it was the greatest thing God had ever invented. That and the atom bomb. Shows you what we knew."

"Hmm." Absorbed in my own thoughts, I finished the slice of cake, then cut myself another, bending over it as I ate. My grandmother watched me.

"I'm not going to live very much longer, you know," she said.

"What?" I looked at her, a forkful of cake half-raised to my mouth.

"'What?' 'What?' Is that all you know how to say?" She raised her eyes to the ceiling. "I said I'm not going to be here much longer. That's what I told your father, but he can't accept it."

I stared at her, lowering my fork, unnerved. It suddenly occurred to me that there might be a reason for this dinner.

"I don't think that's true," I said.

"What, that it's going to happen or that your father can't accept it?"

"That it's going to happen. Not anytime soon." A shadow of hesitation flickered across my mind, an uneasy twinge that told me I did, in fact, think it might be true. I shook my head as if to wipe the thought away. "The doctor didn't say anything like that. Not when I was there."

"Puh! The doctor. What does he know?" She took a bite of cake and chewed, closing her eyes. "All I know is that it's coming. Which is why I'm telling you. So you know."

"Grandma," I said. "Don't talk like that."

She opened her eyes and lifted her chin regally. "I'm telling you," she repeated, "because I want you to be ready."

I glared back at her, a knot of anger and dread growing in my stomach.

"There's no way to be ready for things like that," I said, barely managing to refrain from adding the obvious: *and I should know.*

"Yes, there is."

I looked down at my plate with its slab of cake oozing caramel. Her breath was still ragged; I could hear it. The record player had at last spun itself into silence, and a car could be heard passing by outside the house. There was an old mansion on the mountain, to the east of the park, from whose enormous stone porch it was possible to look out over the entire valley. For a moment, I imagined how we must appear from that great distance: just a point of light, far away, surrounded by shadowed stretches of field and clusters of trees like inkblots. To anyone sitting up there, we would be invisible, she and I, as we sat here at the table under our single bulb, facing each other without speaking. Like prisoners.

"All right, Grandma." I reached for her empty milk glass and stood, taking my own plate in my hands. My head had begun to ache again, just as it had that morning.

She looked up at me, trying to read my expression with her clouded eyes. I ignored her and continued clearing the table, wrapping up the remainder of the cake and sliding it into the refrigerator. When I had finished washing the dishes, I wiped the floor with hot water and rearranged the utensils and knickknacks on the counter, leaving everything spotless the way I always did.

Mounting the stairs in the dark, I entered my room and closed the door without turning the light on, stripping quickly and pulling on sweatpants and an old T-shirt before sliding under the blankets on the mattress on the floor. The blinds were raised, and a mist of light rain coated the window. I rubbed my eyes and lay quietly in the darkness for a while before reaching under the mattress and pulling out the brown packet, the one Jerry had given me. Shaking two of the pills into my hand, I swallowed them quickly. It seemed as though I watched the moon pass across the sky for a long time, thinking about lonely, silent tents in the mountains of Afghanistan, before falling asleep.

4

The days passed, much like most other days save for the continuing presence of the stranger. Sitting across the counter, he would fold his hands almost primly as he chatted about the weather, stories in the newspaper, Raskolnikov the killer and his unthinkable deed. I would offer him something to eat, but he always refused—out of pride, I suspected; maybe he sensed that I knew about his dwindling funds. As he spoke, sometimes he would forget himself and begin to gesture, his hands swanning through the air, not seeming to mind that my responses were largely limited to nods and neutral murmurs. He always kept his dignity, somehow, and yet I had never in my life seen anyone who looked so singularly out of place. Perhaps he knew this; there was something in his words, a wistfulness, a hint of irony behind the smiles, that made me think he did.

When he wasn't at the store, he seemed to spend most of his time in his room, although a few times I spotted him outside, leaning against the hostel with his hands in his pockets, apparently gazing at nothing in particular. He didn't look bored, but neither did he look as if he were actively contemplating the principles of modern forestry.

"What are you looking at when you stand around like that?" I asked one day when he came in.

"What do you mean?"

"When you just lounge around up there. I can't tell if you're half asleep or if you just find empty space particularly captivating."

He laughed. "Well, at first I was waiting to see if there was a bus that came through here. Then I realized there was no bus. Now I just sort of think about things."

"A bus?" I looked at him in disbelief. "Do you understand where you are?"

"I certainly understand it now. I don't mind—I was just curious."

"Well, let me satisfy your curiosity. You are, certifiably, in the middle of nowhere. Nothing comes in and nothing goes out."

"Yes," he said. "I can see that. I suppose in some ways it's good—it helps to maintain the peace and quiet."

He rubbed his fingers together and blew on them. I looked him up and down.

"Do you need a ride somewhere?" I asked finally.

He paused. "No," he said at last, with his usual courtesy. "I couldn't ask you to do that. Besides, it would cut my holiday short. I've really only just settled in."

I peered at him, tempted to ask why someone who was supposedly waiting for a bus would want to settle in, but held my tongue.

It was a few days later that I arrived at work early and was horrified to find him attempting to chop wood.

The rain had eroded the snow, leaving only small, ice-encrusted patches scattered around the grass. He had propped a log on the old stump Martin used for such purposes and was standing with his back to me, holding a heavy axe in his hand. After a moment of scrutinizing the log, he raised the axe above his head, his back bending, and swung it down sharply. I cringed and watched the blade bounce off the wood, sending reverberations shuddering through his arms. The scarf was drawn tightly across his face, and he rubbed his forehead, examining the head of the axe. A minute later, he began to lift it again, his shoes sinking into the mud.

"No!" I called sharply, beginning to mount the hill behind him. "Don't."

He turned, surprised. Sweat shone on his brow, and his cheeks were flushed. "Oh! Hello." His voice was muffled by the tattered fabric.

"You're going to hurt yourself." I reached the place where he was standing and looked around, seeing a large pile of logs but no tools aside from the axe. "Where's the maul?"

"The what?" Even when he was short of breath, his words were carefully shaped, like the small carvings of birds my grandfather had once made.

"The maul, city boy. It's like a big mallet."

I was using words he didn't know. He squinted slightly, looking to the side. "I'm afraid I'm not sure."

"Martin should have given it to you. I'm assuming he's the one who told you to do this." I began marching toward the hostel, the puzzled stranger following behind me.

"Well, he didn't order me, if that's what you mean. I asked if there was anything I could do, and he said I could do this."

"I don't care what he said—you can't use the axe."

I strode toward a closet in the reception area, rummaging through the rakes and shovels inside. The maul was at the back, its wooden handle streaked with tar from some unknown source. I pulled it out and found a wedge on a high shelf.

The stranger took the tools from me, looking as if he were trying not to seem confused. I closed the door.

"You're right, you know," he said as we returned to the stump. "About my being a city person. I'm from Tashkent, the capital. We have electric heat. Electric everything. I've never done this in my life." He pulled the scarf down. "I have to admit, it seems very primitive. I never knew people in America still heated buildings this way."

"Well, Martin doesn't really need this. It's just for the fireplace. But yeah, there are some houses around here that still use woodstoves for their heat. Not so many anymore, although my grandmother's place still does." We stood facing the stump, and I took the wedge from his hands. "Here's what you do. You work this thing into a crack, like this one you've already made"—I pointed—"and then you hit it with the maul. That'll start to split the log, like you're driving a chisel into it, and then you can use the axe to finish the job. Or you can just keep using the wedge." I pushed the tip of the wedge into the crack and reached for the maul, gripping it and raising it above my head, swinging it down as hard as I could. The motion was difficult, but it worked. I had learned to make it work.

The maul hit the wedge with an echoing clang. I gripped the handle and struck again.

"Oh!" He stepped closer and took the handle from me. "I see. Thank you."

"No problem. That should at least make things easier."

"Yes, I'm sure." He paused, looking down at the maul's heavy, blunt head. I waited.

"May I ask," he said finally, "if you would like to accompany me for a walk later?"

I looked at him. His eyes were still on the maul.

"It's nothing . . . inappropriate," he added hesitantly, raising his head. "It's simply that I thought I could stand to stretch my legs a bit. And, you know . . ." He stopped, glancing away almost shyly. "Life passes by rather quickly, doesn't it? It seems that while I'm here, I shouldn't always stay within four walls."

"Well," I said, putting my hands in my pockets and shifting my gaze to the stump. The tree must have been two hundred years old by the time it had been cut down; the stump was enormous, sprawling out irregularly, more than a yard wide, a humbled but still imposing reminder of something great that had once been. It occurred to me to wonder if he were afraid of the woods. I didn't know why the idea hadn't crossed my mind before; people who weren't used to places like this always imagined the trail would dwindle and they would find themselves at the mercy of black bears and bobcats and whatever else was lurking in the unknown. Which, of course, was always possible; but then, a lot of things were possible. Many of us experienced the worst disasters of our lives while doing something perfectly ordinary that everyone did.

"May I ask you a question?" I said at last, looking up into his face.

"Of course." He laughed, sounding faintly relieved. "I believe you just have."

I studied him, unsure how to find the words that would do what I had long since learned not to do, that would ask something as direct as, *Who are you?* It seemed too much like an opening, a crack that could allow someone else's all-too-curious arm to reach into my own thoughts later.

"The scarf," I said instead. "I was just wondering. You always keep it around your face—you look like you're about to rob a bank."

"Oh," he said. "No, no. Is that why you were so frightened when I first came into the store?"

"Frightened? I wasn't frightened."

He raised his eyebrows. "You looked frightened."

"It takes a bit more than that to scare me, I think."

"There's nothing to be ashamed of in being frightened. In my view." Before I could reply, he continued, "I wear the scarf like that because my lungs are rather weak. It's no big secret."

"Weak? Have you been sick?" That would explain the almost other-worldly paleness, I thought.

"No. Well, not recently. It was a long time ago. I was taken in for questioning, in my country, and they made me sleep on the floor with other people. It was cold, and I got sick. After I got out, the doctor told me I should protect my lungs when I'm outside, so I use the scarf. There's some scarring or something in there, apparently." He gestured at his chest.

I looked down, prodding the muddy ground with my toe. "'They'?"

"Pardon me?"

"You said 'they' took you in for questioning, or something."

"Oh. Yes."

"You mean the police?"

"Something like that. Not the ordinary police, but a kind of special police. The police who do these things. It's difficult to explain."

"Special police? You mean, like, secret police?"

"In a sense. I forget exactly what it is in English." He pulled off his hat and scratched his head. "'Intelligence,' maybe?"

A vision of this fragile-looking foreigner shivering on the floor of a cell swam into my mind, and I winced. "I'm sorry. I shouldn't have asked."

"Don't be sorry! It's all right. As I said, it's no secret." He gave the maul a short, experimental swing, as if it were a golf club.

I looked at him.

"You know, it's odd," I said after a moment.

"What's odd?"

"That you would tell the truth about that, but lie about being a student."

His face tensed, but his response came in a light tone. "Why would I lie about that?"

"That's what I've been wondering, I guess. But it's all right. You don't need to answer." I scuffed at the ground again, then looked up at him. "I asked you if I could ask one question, not two."

He smiled wanly.

"I'm sorry," I said. "But listen. Remember what I said about using the maul first. If you just use the axe, it's going to take forever and you'll wind up splitting your foot instead. I have to go open the store now."

"Okay," he said, but cleared his throat as I turned to go. "Although you never answered my own question, I think. About the walk."

"Oh."

As I looked at him, I realized for the first time that a deep sadness seemed to suffuse his entire figure, making him look smaller

and frailer than he really was. Even when he stood straight, he looked
stooped.

"Sure," I replied, suddenly embarrassed. "I guess I don't see why
not. Maybe Sunday, if you're still here then."

"Okay." He shifted his weight, gripping the maul awkwardly.
"Thank you. You're—you're a good girl."

I must have looked at him strangely, because he turned back to the
stump, eyeing the log with the wedge embedded in it as if he had suddenly been put in charge of a military strategy, tasked with figuring
out how to crack enemy lines.

He labored most of the morning, until, I thought, blisters must
surely have left his hands bloody and sore, in spite of the gloves he had
found somewhere. Watching him through the window, I thought of
the prisoners of war, their vanished camp with its vanished guards, an
entire village that had left behind only rotting rectangles of timber and
cement, deep in the woods. Unlucky German and Japanese officers
who, I thought, had probably split wood and carried water from dawn
until dark, sweat soaking the shirts on their backs. Laboring alone
and unseen, trapped in the forest in a strange land. No one knew for
certain what had become of them, afterward. There was no list of their
names. Ghostlike they had come, and ghostlike they had disappeared
into the strange, winding tunnels of the past.

They must, I reflected as I watched the stranger, have been very
homesick when they were here. Even if they were soldiers.

Although of course, it wouldn't be right to pity them. They had
been on the side that was responsible for murdering all those people,
after all. And if they had toiled and sweated and maybe even died
hidden away somewhere in the woods of Pennsylvania, well, there
were worse fates.

By noon, the stranger was clearly tired. Nevertheless, his thin
arms in the padded, musty coat continued to move, up and down, up
and down, like a human piston driven by some invisible and pitiless
machine.

5

Sunday came, and I pulled up in front of the hostel, watching the stranger's slender figure peel itself from the wall like a shadow.

When I stayed in the car, he walked toward me, glancing around, hands stuffed into his pockets and scarf tied firmly around his face. It was a bright day, the nicest we'd had in weeks, sharp sunlight glinting on the ice that coated the trees. I rolled the window down. "Go ahead and get in. I'll take us to Tumbling Run."

He looked at the car nervously, twisting a foot into the gravel. "I really shouldn't go very far, I think. Maybe we could just stay close to here?"

I paused with my hands on the wheel. "I don't know. It's up to you, I guess. I thought a change of scenery could do us both good."

"Yes, I suppose," he replied uncertainly.

I watched him as he looked down at his feet.

"It's kind of a secret trail," I told him, somehow guessing the cause of his reluctance. "No one's going to see us. I can't remember the last time I saw anyone else up there."

He peered behind the car at the state road and the steep rise of the mountain beyond. "Are you sure?"

"Well." I shifted into park and cracked my knuckles, looking down at a cut on my palm. "I can't make any promises, I guess. But if anyone does see us, it'll be some guy out walking his dog who'll forget us as soon as we're gone. Nobody really goes there. It's just too hard to find."

It wasn't hard to find, of course, if you knew to look for it. But nobody did. An unmarked trail on private land, it didn't appear on any maps, not even old ones. Amos had shown it to me, long ago, maybe six months after we'd met. It had been spring then, the mountain laurels and rhododendrons blooming and the stream running. I had been stunned by it, thought it was the most beautiful place I'd ever seen, although at the time I hadn't made note of where it was. I was with Amos, my first serious boyfriend, the man with the quiet eyes and work-lined hands who said he loved me. It was hard to pay attention to anything else.

The truth was that much later I'd had to call Amos's mother to figure out where it was. Amos was dead. I had just left the hospital with a shattered hip and arm that had each been bolted back together through a month of surgery, two fractured ribs, and a disorienting double vision I hadn't mentioned to anyone, since it seemed impolite to have something else go wrong when I was the center of so much effort already. The morphine floated me along like a great white balloon. Everyone was very nice. They didn't talk about Amos, although they knew I knew, and gradually it came to seem as if he had been washed away by this month of stillness, of a small, hushed television in a corner, nurses making notes, pills in cups, meals on trays. When Beth visited, I cried, but I didn't know why. The rest of the time, I wasn't really sad. Just floating along, anchored only by the persistent pain of bones held together by metal.

I had called Cindy when I was home, even though I was still months away from being able to walk properly, let alone drive. "Cindy," I had said into the phone, sitting in my grandmother's dining room, and had instantly forgotten why I'd called.

"Kathleen," she had breathed on the other end. Then, with difficulty, "How are you? I was glad to hear you were out of the hospital."

"I'm fine," I'd replied dreamily. The two white pills I took every four hours were powerful stuff, making me feel as if I were miles away from my own body. Every so often, they made me giggle unreasonably, which always seemed to unnerve whoever was within earshot. I had no idea, at the time, that they would stay with me for so long. "How are you?"

"We're all right," she said, although she meant, of course, that her world was chaos, a whirlwind of sadness and despair, and that she would never know a moment of happiness ever again.

"I'm so sorry," I told her.

"It's not your fault," she replied, as if she had rehearsed saying this. Although she didn't know it, and never would, she was right. It wasn't.

"I was just wondering," I began, and then paused, struggling to remember what I had intended to ask her.

"Kathleen?" she'd said after a long moment had passed.

"Yes. I'm sorry. I was wondering," I'd said slowly, the thought gradually coming back to me, "if you know where Tumbling Run is. I'd like to go there, when I'm better. But I can't seem to remember."

"Tumbling Run?" she had echoed, surprised and perhaps beginning to grow angry, a combination of confusion and grief.

"We used to go there," I'd said, suddenly feeling very tired, as if I were climbing a long spiral staircase whose top I couldn't see. "A long time ago. Before we were married."

"Oh." She had reflected on this for a moment. I could picture her standing in her neat living room, looking stricken. She was a psychologist, one of the only professionals I had ever known, and everything in her house seemed somehow consoling but impersonal: dried bouquets on the mantel, needlepoint pillows on the couch. Amos, with his drawl and his dusty hands and boots, had always seemed out of place there. I probably had, too; maybe that was one of the reasons she hadn't wanted him to marry me.

"It's on South Mountain," she had said finally. "Right before the county line. There's a row of rocks. A semicircle. That's the entrance." She drew a deep breath. "We used to take the boys there when they were little."

"Yes. Thank you. I'm very sorry," I had said, and carefully returned the receiver to its cradle. A few minutes later, it had become difficult to remember who I'd been talking to.

The following day, I'd been surprised to find a card from her in the mailbox, small and white with violets on the front. "Please don't call again," it said on the inside in her rounded cursive, although it said other things as well that were meant to sound nicer. I had looked at it and then, for some reason, put it in a drawer. It was probably still hidden in my grandmother's house somewhere, gathering dust.

Six months later, when I could drive, I had gone up to the trail in all its solitary beauty, passing the state park and the general store on the way. While driving back, I had stopped at the store and spoken to the owner, my mother's second cousin's husband, an older man named Herman. The next day, I had found myself with a job that didn't require me to talk or move much, and that allowed me to rest for long periods on the porch when my pelvis began to ache, as it often did. The hikers were friendly but had little interest in prying into the life of the woman who was cooking their hamburgers. After a time, I was happy, especially when I had grown strong enough to walk down to one of the lakes in the evening, watching people wade and swim in the last of the fall light.

I had found a place where I could be at peace.

The stranger walked around the front of the car and opened the passenger door, bringing me back to the present. His expression was doubtful.

"Come on," I said. "It'll be fine. I think you'll like it."

He climbed in, his limbs bending stiffly, as if he were made of wire. I pulled away from the hostel and drove us west through the long corridor of trees. Sitting there, I had an unsettling sense of his nearness, but shook the feeling off.

"Where does this road go?" he asked, as I steered us around the bends. Small brooks of melted snow were running across the asphalt, shining in the light.

"Go?"

"I mean, if you were to keep driving for a long time."

I gave him a sidelong look. So much for the idea that he was some kind of hitchhiker, I thought. "Well, it runs along the mountain for quite a while. Eventually you'd wind up close to Gettysburg."

"Gettysburg?" He looked at me quizzically. "I've heard of that. There's something there."

"Yeah, that's where the battlefields are. From the Civil War. Aside from that, it's really just a tourist town. It's pretty small."

"Oh." Watching the trees and empty summer cabins pass by outside the window, he was quiet, knitting his hands together in his lap. A squirrel darted across the road, its tail a gray plume, and I swerved to miss it. Light and shade played on the windshield, passing over our faces.

"Do you ever think about it? The war?" he asked.

I looked at him. "My brother's in it. Of course I think about it."

"No, I'm sorry. I mean the Civil War, although of course—" He broke off. "I'm sorry, I didn't realize—"

"That's okay. It doesn't really come up." The road unspooled before us, through a stand of birches that had been charred in the fire.

He seemed to be pondering something. Eventually, he said, "What do you think of it?"

I glanced at him. "Of what?"

"Well, of—of the war. The one happening now."

"There are two of them, technically. Or the same one, but in two different places. So they say, anyway." I swerved around some black ice. "I'm not sure what there is to think, really. They're happening, and I follow what's going on as best I can. But . . ."

Hearing and disliking the edge of helplessness in my own voice, I tried to think of something else to discuss. But he persisted.

"Do you ever ask yourself if your country's done the right thing?"

"What do you mean?"

"I mean . . . going to war in those places."

I was silent for a long moment, considering being offended. But, I realized, that wouldn't be honest, and I didn't feel like inventing a feeling I didn't have. I looked at him, remembering the pauses that had sometimes formed in the gap between my twin bed and Beth's, between a question and an answer, late at night, when we knew there was something we shouldn't say but were turning over in our minds anyway.

He watched the forest pass by. The gray rocks that marked the bottom of the trail came into view, and I pressed the brake.

"All the time," I said.

The smells of damp earth and cold water greeted us as we stepped out of the car, closing the doors with a sound that echoed and made the stranger wince. There was a short path leading down to the gully where the trail actually began, and we trod along it, weaving around the jagged outcroppings of quartz and granite that protruded from the soil. Within moments, we could hear the low, mumbling chorus of the stream. The clearing revealed itself abruptly, the way it always did, hidden behind a sharp curve in the path and a dark, dense patch of holly.

"It's wonderful," he murmured, standing before the stream with its fragile bridge of lashed-together branches, the water trickling down through the tree roots before forming the ice-edged pool at our feet.

"Yeah," I said quietly as I looked around. "It is."

We crossed the bridge, holding our arms out like winter scarecrows. The mud bank on the other side was steep, and I led the way, prodding roots and stones with my foot to make sure they would hold. The stranger clambered after me, grasping boulders and branches. The sound of water filled our ears, and we walked single file as the trail narrowed, ducking under fallen trees, the light shining down into our faces. The stream was partly frozen, the sunlight making the rolling arcs of ice look even whiter.

"Are you okay?" I asked, glancing over my shoulder. "You can do this?"

"Yes," he said, breathing heavily. His shoes sank into the mixture of snow and mud. "Of course, it's fine."

Following the water, we made our way over patches of slippery dead leaves, loose rocks, thickets whose dried blackberry vines grabbed at our sleeves. I rubbed my hip to quiet the persistent note of pain that had begun to sound there, raising my feet to break branches and flatten undergrowth that stood in our way. It was something that made me feel more than a hint of pride, this knowledge of how to get through the difficult places. How to help us both make it to where we were going.

After what felt like an hour but was probably far less, we came to the waterfall that was halfway up, where a glacial cascade of boulders lay tumbled steeply, the tree roots growing around them and binding them in place. A cedar tree had fallen across the waterfall long ago, and there was a smooth spot where people would clamber across to sit on it, their legs dangling over the steep descending stretch of forest.

I pointed at it. "Do you need a rest?"

"Well, I—only if you—" He wiped sweat from his face. "I mean, yes, please."

We laughed.

"Be careful not to slip," I said, and sat down on the log, edging out over the empty space.

I made my way toward the middle and looked down at the water—melted snow from higher up—that glimmered back at me. The pang in my hip was becoming more insistent, and I shifted in place, trying to settle into a position that was more comfortable.

The stranger sat next to me, grasping the bark, seeming afraid to let go.

"I've never done anything like this," he said, still trying to catch his breath. "To be honest, I never knew I could."

"You don't hike?"

"No, I've literally never done this. I'm an indoor guy."

It was certainly much easier, I thought, to picture him hunched over a dozen books than slogging his way up a peak, even a modest one like this.

A thread of water trickled musically behind us.

"So," I said, turning to him, "I've been wondering. Are you happy here?"

"Here?" He jumped slightly and rubbed at a splinter that must have pricked his finger. "You mean right here? Now?"

"No, I mean staying up here on the mountain." I swung my feet, watching their reflections below. "You know, for someone like me, it's no big deal—I grew up here, I'm used to it—but I thought for you it might be . . . " I didn't want to use the word "lonely," maybe because it felt like some kind of accusation whenever anyone applied it to me. "I guess I thought you might miss home."

He looked surprised. "Well, yes, I do miss home. Unfortunately, home is a place I can't go at the moment."

"Oh." I pulled my ankle up to rest on my thigh. "I'm sorry. I didn't know."

"It's all right. There's no reason for you to have guessed."

We sat, listening to the quiet, glass-like sound of the stream.

"May I ask you a question?" he said finally.

"I believe you just did."

He threw his head back and laughed appreciatively. "I've been meaning to ask about that sign, down on the road. Not the road we took today, but the one that crosses by your store. What is it?"

"You mean the Underground Railroad one?"

"I'm not sure. It's blue, with flowers tied to it. I saw it when I first came here, but I never got a chance to read it."

"Oh," I said. "That."

"You know it?"

"Yeah, I know it." I leaned forward slightly, feeling the tug of gravity.

"What's it about?"

I looked out over the tangled roots, the branches heavy with softening snow. Although the stranger kept glancing cautiously around us, he seemed to be in good spirits, and I found myself reluctant to bring him to earth. "Nothing, really."

"I thought—since it had the flowers—"

"I mean nothing very cheerful."

"Well," he said after a moment, raising an eyebrow, "I'm rather used to hearing about things that aren't very cheerful, I'm afraid. Uzbekistan, as you may know, isn't an especially cheerful place. But of course there's no need for you to tell me—I can see you don't want to talk about it."

I realized I still didn't know a thing about Uzbekistan, although

I silently resolved to find out. A hawk that had been circling above us settled into a tree, shifting its feet and folding its wings, turning its head to watch us. I looked back at it; like so many things in the woods, it was unsettlingly large when seen close up, its ferocity giving it the grandeur only dangerous things have.

"It's okay," I said slowly. "I understand why you'd be curious."

I peeled a dead leaf from my shoe and dropped it into the water, watching it fall.

"The story is that there was a man who was passing through here," I began. "This was back during the Depression, nineteen thirty-one or thirty-two, I think. The man had lost his job somewhere else and came here looking for work, but he couldn't find any.

"He had three daughters with him, young ones. I think the oldest was maybe twelve or thirteen. Their mother was dead, although they had a stepmother of some kind, their father's girlfriend or fiancée or something like that. So, this man and the fiancée and the three girls, they were driving through Pennsylvania looking for work—he had a Model T or something—but there wasn't any to be found, even on the farms. They ran out of money, and then eventually they ran out of food."

The stranger was listening intently, gazing down at the toes of his shoes.

"We think the man tried, for a while, to find something to feed them, but there were three of them, plus the woman. It was hard, even when he went through town and begged. No one had anything to give.

"As the winter came, he realized there was no hope, at least not here. He decided to go out to California and look for work in the fields there. A lot of people were doing that, thousands of them, driving or walking across the plains out west.

"The girls, of course, weren't very strong, especially not having had anything to eat aside from what they could scrounge. He loved them, or so people say. But he didn't know what to do. And he couldn't bear to see them suffer."

I looked down at the pool of water that reflected our dangling feet, our hands poised next to each other, gripping the log. "So he drove them up here," I said, and fell silent.

"And he left them?"

"Well, yes." I replied. "In a manner of speaking."

The stranger's expression grew puzzled. Then he suddenly looked at me. "Wait. You mean he *killed* them?"

"Yeah."

"Oh." He grimaced. His gaze moved to the middle distance, as if the scene were being played out somewhere in the tree limbs. "You're right. That is terrible. Especially for a beautiful place such as this."

I flicked a hand dismissively. "Beautiful places are just like anywhere else. People still suffer."

He sat wordlessly, his face troubled. One of his hands moved over the bark, then came to rest.

"That's terrible indeed," he said after some time, as if he hadn't heard my words. "I can see why there would be a sign there. I suppose that kind of thing leaves a mark on people here."

"For a long time, we all heard something completely different, actually," I told him. "The father laid them all next to each other, just like they were going to sleep. And that's what everyone used to say—that he left them in the woods to fend for themselves, and eventually they got tired and curled up together, the younger ones around the oldest one. But then a couple of years ago one of the newspapers ran a piece on it, and we all found out the old story wasn't true."

There was a sound in the brush, and I looked up, but it was nothing, probably just some small animal whose winter rest we had disturbed. Or, I thought, the hawk had finally gotten its prey.

"'On this spot were found three babes in the woods,'" I said. "That's what it says on the sign."

"Do you wish they hadn't told you the truth?" he asked.

I thought about this for a moment. "No. No point in being sentimental about it, I guess. Nobody benefits from that, in the end." I turned slightly, and one of my joints cracked. "People do horrible things to the ones they say they love sometimes. Hurt them, abandon them. No reason to pretend they don't."

He reflected on this, putting his hands on his knees. For some reason, he looked less odd in profile, more like the thoughtful, if slightly shabby, student he'd claimed to be.

"Well," he said after a long moment, "I think sometimes we do things like that when we don't mean to. Sometimes we think we're doing the right thing, and it's not until later that we realize it was a mistake."

"That's not an excuse," I replied, more sharply than I had intended. As I spoke, I pictured my parents, Amos, the priest on his darkened porch. The stranger, of course, couldn't know this, and gave me a surprised look.

"I don't know," he said slowly. "We all do things we regret. For example, I . . . I know I've put my wife through some unpleasant things. Being a lawyer in Uzbekistan has its risks, you could say. And I knew that from the start, but . . ." He rubbed his thumb over a knot in the wood. "Sometimes things happen, and we do what we think is best. It's only later that we understand the consequences."

Neither of us spoke for a time. I busied myself scratching a series of shapes into the log with a twig.

"So your wife is . . . still there?" I asked.

He looked away and nodded. "Yes. She's still there."

"I noticed your ring, that first time you came into the store," I told him, for lack of a better idea of what to say. "It's nice."

"This?" He held up his hand, his expression lightening. "Yes, isn't it? I got it—and hers, too, of course—when I took a trip to Paris once for work. The authorities let me have an exit visa that time."

"Paris?" I couldn't hide my envy. "When were you there?"

"Oh, about fifteen years ago, I suppose."

I studied his face, his eyes. "That can't be right. You're not that old."

"I'm thirty-nine."

"What!" I gaped at him. "No, you're not."

"Oh, really?" He laughed. "I had thought I was. Have I been wrong all this time?"

"I had no idea. I thought you were ten years younger than that."

"No—I'm an old man, I'm afraid."

"I'll say. Twelve years older than me, and I'm already ancient." Stretching, I flicked a piece of bark at him. "Should we keep going?"

"Of course." He worked his way gingerly back across the log, holding out a hand to me when he reached the land. I could see the tiredness in his face, but he seemed determined to offer help, even though I didn't need it. His grip was warm and surprisingly firm.

Now that I knew, I could see his age, especially in the fine lines around his eyes. I had thought they came purely from worry.

"You have children, back at home?" I asked as we returned to the trail.

He was panting, attempting to scramble up a pile of boulders after me. "No, unfortunately. We couldn't have any, it seems. Can't," he corrected himself. "Can't have any."

"Does she get to visit you here?" I pulled myself over the rocks, their edges rough against my hands.

"No, it's . . . not that easy, I'm afraid. I wish it were." His foot slipped on a vein of ice, and he caught himself awkwardly on a branch. "I do hear news of her from time to time, when another exile from Tashkent comes over. We knew a lot of people there. But sometimes I don't hear anything for months, and sometimes what I hear isn't so good."

I gave him a questioning look, and he hastened to add, with seeming embarrassment, "Not that there are any other men, I mean. But that she's . . ." Climbing the last few paces to the foot of the slab of rock at the top, he searched for words. "Not safe."

"Oh."

When he remained quiet, I stopped and pointed. "We're just going up that short path and then over that ravine you can see. And then we'll be at the top."

Our shoes scraping against the stone, we made our way to the summit, standing together on the immense slab of rock and looking out over miles of evergreens and glimmering, ice-coated ashes and cedars. The gap where the park was fell away below us, the lakes and road hidden by the endless web of branches. On the other side, the mountain rose again, its rounded peaks undulating into the distance.

We sat down, and I reached into my coat pocket, pulling out two oranges. "Want one?"

"Oh—yes. Thank you." He took the fruit from my hands and held it, looking perplexed. "So the place where I've been staying, it isn't at the top of the mountain? I'd thought it was."

"Yeah, mountains are deceptive like that. You think you're at the top, and then you realize you're nowhere near it."

He settled back onto the rock and began peeling his orange. "Apparently so." There was some graffiti on a boulder near us, and he looked over at it curiously. "What's it called, this mountain?"

"This one?" I looked around us. "I don't think it has a particular name. We call this whole chain South Mountain. And the chain on the other side of the valley is North Mountain. That's all I've ever heard anyone call them."

"Oh." He considered this for a moment. "But what if you go south of South Mountain? Or north of North Mountain?"

I arranged my face in a serious expression. "You can't."

"What? Why not?"

"That's where the world drops off."

He smiled.

Sitting next to one another, we ate in silence for a while, juice dripping from our fingers onto the stone.

"You never seem to mention your husband," he said after a time.

I gave a start, but did my best to keep my expression blank. "No, I suppose I don't. There isn't much to say."

He smiled almost indulgently. "That can't be true. After all, you're married to him. I assume he's an interesting person. Does he work in the park as well?"

"Nope." I brushed dirt from my jeans with my palm. "He's dead."

The stranger flinched. "Oh. Oh, dear. I'm sorry."

"It's all right. It was four years ago. We were in a car accident." A cold breeze picked up, and I hunched my shoulders. "Although I do think it's odd that Martin would have told you I was married, but not that my husband was—" I paused, reflecting that "dead" sounded unfeeling. "—Gone. I'm assuming it was Martin who mentioned it."

"Yes," he replied thoughtfully. "I suppose I find it odd, too. In any case, I'm sorry I brought it up."

"It's all right," I repeated. Then, to my own surprise, I told him the thing I had never acknowledged, never said out loud. "People here think I killed him. It's very strange."

"What?" He looked at me, shocked.

"It's all right. I don't mind."

"But how could they think that?" he asked, still looking stunned.

"People think all sorts of things." I shrugged. "It's just how they are. There isn't really much point in trying to figure out why."

"But—but you're so kind."

The words were so unforced, so full of genuine distress, that for a moment I didn't know how to respond. "I'm just ordinary," I told him finally. "And anyway, it doesn't matter. They can think whatever they like."

"Well," he said, still sounding unsettled, but he didn't seem to know what else to say.

We perched beside each other, the only humans, it seemed, for miles in any direction. Our faces turned up, we watched the sun as it slowly traced the arc of one of the shortest days of the year.

When it touched the tips of the trees, I looked at him. A pink tinge was beginning to appear on his nose and cheekbones, probably from the sunlight. At last, I broke the silence. "Are you glad we came here?"

"What? Oh, yes, very. You were right—it's good to have the chance to do these things." There was something vaguely wistful in his tone, almost melancholy, but he laughed as he went on. "Although it does make me realize I should perhaps get more exercise."

"Well, this is a hard climb for anyone." I glanced back down the rocky path behind us. "But I'm glad you like it. It's one of my favorite places."

We resumed our silence for a while, watching the colors of the forest change as the sun began to set. When the cold became too much to bear, I stood up, shaking leaves and twigs from my clothes. The stranger did the same.

"Could I ask," I said as we stood next to each other, taking a last look at the valley before turning to go, "what you're doing here? I mean, what you're really doing?"

He exhaled and looked down at his hands. A short silence followed. "Yes, I suppose you would wonder."

"I do, sometimes. Although you don't need to answer."

He fingered the fraying end of his scarf and was quiet. Beneath our feet, the rock glittered with fragments of quartz, all but invisible except at this time of day.

"I did a bad thing," he said finally. "In Uzbekistan."

"A bad thing?" I looked up at him.

"Yes. That's why I can't go back."

For a moment, neither of us spoke. He scuffed at the rock with his shoe. "I would rather not talk about it just now, if that's all right with you."

"Of course. I'm sorry I brought it up."

"It's okay." He glanced at me and attempted a lighter tone. "Now we've both accidentally mentioned things. I suppose we're even."

"I suppose we are." I was still trying to read his face, but he smiled and I gave it up, tucking his words away in my mind where I could ponder them later. "All right, let's get down from here."

I hopped off the rock, landing heavily on the trail, the nerves in my leg burning all the way to my toes. The stranger lowered himself carefully after me, and we made our way down the mountain, leaning back and grasping at branches to keep our balance. Together, we raced against the diminishing light, arriving at the car just as the last of it drew back into a deepening blue.

When I dropped him off at the hostel, he turned to wave. I nodded and, belatedly, when he had already turned away, waved back.

6

On Christmas Eve, my grandmother and I drove to the church in Orrtanna for the candlelight mass. My grandmother was bundled into the stiff wool coat she seldom wore, her hands in the fur muff she had bought during some long-ago trip to Pittsburgh to visit my aunt, before I was born. Resembling a misshapen package, she hunched forward in her seat, seeming to stare watchfully through the windshield as we drove up over the mountains, passing the old apple orchards and the canning factories. What she thought she was watching for, I couldn't have said.

We arrived and squeezed into the last parking spot beside the church, a fading pile of red brick with a modest bell tower. Inside, the pews were garlanded with pine boughs, topped with rings of tall white candles at the ends. The altar, too, was festooned with dark green pine, the branches hung with shining white and gold ornaments. I didn't really believe in any of it—the actual Christmas stuff—but something in me always responded to the music and candlelight. I'd done my best to give a nod to the occasion, pulling on a red silk blouse that had once belonged to my mother and that I'd found at the back of a closet. At least I'd match the clusters of fake berries.

The priest, who was very old and braced himself against the altar as he spoke, delivered the mass in a quavering tone, facing out over the rows of flickering candles. As he recited the words, I helped my grandmother stand and kneel. For a long time—after the things that happened—it had been hard to look at him without anger, but those days had passed. I didn't know what he saw when he looked at me, but when I looked at him, I saw nothing in particular. He was just a man, an old man, like any other.

Afterward, before we all surged back into the cold, there was a reception in the vestibule, plates of gingersnaps and sugar cookies arranged on folding tables. I was piling some of the cookies onto a napkin—two for me, two for my grandmother, who was chatting with a former neighbor—when I heard a voice behind me.

"Kathleen?"

I turned to find John, the trucker who'd shown up at the Joyride a few weeks earlier.

"Oh," I said uncertainly. "Hi."

"Merry Christmas," he said, extending his hand. A smile creased his face. "Nice to see you. Been a while, eh?"

Not knowing what else to do, I took his hand. "Uh, Merry Christmas," I replied.

"How you been lately?" he asked, standing in front of me as the other churchgoers—mostly older people—flowed around us.

Did "lately" mean the past few weeks or the past ten years? I thought of my plain room at home, the long days at the store, the stranger as we sat together on the mountaintop. "I'm fine," I replied. But he didn't go anywhere, and I soon realized I had no choice but to offer the normal response. "You?"

"Oh, I'm all right—can't complain." Despite his bulk, he looked at ease with himself, hands planted in his pockets as he tilted his head back slightly. I had forgotten that he was an inch or two shorter than I was—one of those solid, compact valley men whose impression of strength and immovability doesn't depend on height. His face had a relaxed, open expression that was somehow startling, perhaps because I almost never saw it on anyone.

"I'm actually back in town for the first time in a while," he continued casually. "I was living down in North Carolina with my wife, but she—we—got a divorce, and I decided to come back home. Bought a farm out on Route 11, down near Quarry Hill. Beautiful piece of land, about thirty acres. Real nice spread." He rubbed the stubble on his cheeks. "Don't tell the priest, though. About the divorce, I mean." He winked.

"No," I mumbled vaguely, looking around. "Of course not." My grandmother was still engrossed in her conversation with the neighbor, which was unusual; there must have been some especially intriguing gossip about somebody she didn't like.

"I gotta say, it's good to be back," John was saying. "I missed this place. You know, we always made fun of it when we were kids, but when you get down to it, there ain't nowhere like it."

I stared at him in bafflement. If there was a purpose to his starting a conversation with me, other than some kind of morbid curiosity, I couldn't see it.

"I think I'll wind up leasing out most of the land," he went on, "but I'm definitely keeping the house, even though I don't really know what I'm going to do with all of it. Not used to having a whole place to myself." He chuckled.

"Anyway," he said, "I was wondering if you might like to come over for dinner sometime. Can't say I really cook much, but I figured I could pull something together. I remember you were always real interesting to talk to, and I thought it might, you know, make the place feel less big. At least for an hour or two."

Blinking, I stood stupidly with the napkin full of cookies in my hand, at a loss for words.

"Well, I . . ." I began. My hand opened and closed around the napkin. "Uh, sure," I stuttered, hoping he understood that I meant "absolutely not."

"All right, then, I'll look you up sometime. You take care, now." Shaking my hand again, he nodded and ambled off.

I looked after him mutely.

"Was that Johnny McCullough? What did he want?"

I turned around to find my grandmother standing behind me, grinning one of her rare grins.

"Nothing," I said, wondering how she'd managed to sneak around me when I wasn't looking. "We were just talking. Come on, let's go."

With her gripping my arm, we descended the cement steps to the parking lot, the sky a cold, starry vault above us.

We'd barely walked in the door when Beth called. "I'm giving my son a very important lesson in how to decorate a Christmas tree. You want to come over?"

"Yeah, sure," I replied, still disoriented by what had happened at the church. "I'll be right there."

The small ranch house where her parents had lived for as long as I could remember was draped in blinking white Christmas lights. In the driveway, two figures bent with their heads under the open hood of a Mustang, one trim and one with a wide back. When my headlights struck them, they turned around, and Beth's father—still in the jacket he wore as a maintenance man at the War College—waved welcomingly. "Hey there, Kathy!" he called. "Merry Christmas."

The larger figure didn't say anything, but nodded at me from behind his beard, meeting my eyes as I gave a small start. Of course, I thought, he would be here. I knew his relation to the family; I just managed to keep the world of the store so separate from the rest of my life that I sometimes forgot.

"Hey, Mr. Calaman," I said. "And . . . Mr. Calaman."

Beth opened the door, Dylan on her hip. "Are my dad and Jerry still messing around out there?"

"Yeah." Inside, the house smelled of butter cookies, the Irish recipe that had been passed down from Beth's great-grandmother.

"Well, boys will be boys, I guess. Not that I believe in any of that claptrap." She gave me a peck on the cheek. "You look beautiful, lady! Merry Christmas."

"Thanks—you, too." She must have just gotten home from work, I thought; she was still in her coffee-stained jeans and full makeup. Her lipstick—the same brilliant scarlet as the poinsettias on the table— left a smudge on my cheek, which she wiped away briskly and automatically with her hand, as if it were a smudge on her child's face. "Where's this tree I've been hearing about?"

Dylan pointed into the living room, his other hand in his mouth. A real spruce tree stood in the corner, surrounded by open boxes of ornaments. Beth and I set to work while the boy sat solemnly on the sofa, his legs extended, shaking a snow globe.

"We had Mark watching us on the webcam a while ago," Beth said, "but it's the middle of the night in Ramadi, so he had to go. There's something surreal about all that, but at least he was able to be here, sort of. It's already hard to believe he was actually here just a month ago." She stood on her toes to hang an ornament shaped like a rocking horse, probably left over from her own childhood.

"Webcam?" I said. "You can do video over the internet?"

She threw her head back and laughed. "Oh, darlin', you're in your own world. It's one of the things I love most about you."

The ornament fell, and I picked it up for her, hanging it myself. She looked up at me as I reached for the top of the tree.

"So," she said in a sly tone, "I don't suppose you have anything to tell me."

"Like what?"

She bent to rummage through a box with exaggerated nonchalance. "Oh, you know . . . like something about a new man in your life."

"What?" Flustered, I fumbled for a reply. "Where did you hear that?"

"Ah-ha! So there is someone." She pulled out a glass ball. "Uncle Jerry told me."

I blinked at her in incomprehension. "Jerry?"

"Yep. Apparently he was out hunting and saw you walking in the woods with some tall, skinny guy. That's what he said, anyway."

A tremor of surprise ran through me.

"Oh," I heard myself reply.

"Yeah. I don't know how he can sit out there in the cold, given the amount of pain he's in, but evidently he does. My dad keeps trying to get him to stop, but he's been kind of funny since Joanne left him." She sat back and put her hands on her hips. "Anyway, dish. Give me details."

"There aren't any to give."

"Oh, come on. I can't believe you're holding out on me. Who is he, some hiker?"

I was about to respond, but a timer rang in the kitchen, and she hurried away, Dylan looking after her. There was the sound of an oven door opening, the clattering of a baking sheet.

Looking down, I fiddled with the bent wire hook affixed to a ceramic snowman, still absorbing what she had said. *All right*, I told myself. So Jerry had seen us. It didn't matter; he probably wouldn't think anything of it. I'd just be more careful in the future. And there was no reason to tell the stranger, who would only be needlessly worried.

Beth stuck her head back into the room. "You want to come here and tell me if these look done to you?"

I followed her and examined the tray of cookies, pressing one gently with a fingertip. "Yeah, they're done."

"You're so freakin' *competent* at everything. Seriously, it kills me." Standing on her toes, she switched on the fan. "You go back in there with Dylan, and I'll be right out. We'll just let these cool down for a couple minutes."

Moments later, she returned, slipping off an oven mitt and tossing it onto the sofa, where Dylan regarded it with surprise.

"So, you're not gonna spill the beans, huh?"

"Honestly, there aren't any to spill."

"All right, suit yourself, but I'm going to drag it out of you sooner or later." She extracted a long strand of red tinsel from a box with a rustling sound. "Anyway, have you thought about the thing we talked about last time?"

"What did we talk about last time?"

"Going back to school."

Catching the loose end of the tinsel, I helped her string it onto the tree, each of us following the other in circles. "Yeah, I've been think-ing about it," I admitted. "But I just can't. My grandmother . . . well, and the tuition, and everything." I breathed in the smell of evergreen. "Maybe someday, when things are different."

"Is that a dodge?"

I sucked in my upper lip, going quiet for a moment. "No."

"Oh, really?" She raised an eyebrow. "How much is the tuition?"

"How much? I'm not sure."

"That's what I thought. You should call them and see what they can do."

"Maybe," I said, which was the word I always used when I meant "no." She knew this, and rolled her eyes, although she didn't fight me.

"So what did Mark have to say when he called?" I asked, trying to change the subject.

Her face took on a neutral expression, and she looked at Dylan, who looked back at her. "Not much of anything, to be honest. I know he's always glad to see us, but . . . he just gets this look on his face, like he wants to get back to thinking about something else. Or nothing at all." She wrapped a string of lights around her finger. "I mean, I under-stand. But I do sometimes want to point out to somebody that, well, they took my husband away, and they never told me who I'd be getting back at the end of everything. So, there's that." One of the lights was cracked, and she rolled it between her fingers. "Sometimes I wonder."

Dylan grabbed a fistful of blanket and raised it to his mouth, watching us.

"I think it's okay to wonder," I said.

She met my eyes and touched my knee without saying anything. I was struck by the heart-shaped face, the constellation of small scars from the chicken pox she had caught when we were sixteen, the fea-tures I knew so well. We were still young, I thought, and yet astonish-ingly, we were also old, well past the age our parents had been in our earliest memories of them.

"Oh, shoot, I forgot the cookies. Silly me." She pushed herself to her feet and disappeared into the kitchen, returning with a plate of sugary discs. "Although I really shouldn't eat these things. They'll make me fat again."

I reached for a cookie, letting the soft dough dissolve on my tongue. "No, they won't. You were never fat."

"Bullshit." She sank onto the sofa beside me and cast a look at Dylan. "I mean, bull malarkey." Reaching out her arms in a long stretch as she chewed, she tugged at the hem of my shirt. "Where'd you get this, by the way? I like the color."

"Yeah, I knew you would." I looked down at the loose hem and worn buttons. "It was my mom's, believe it or not."

I could remember when my mother had worn this blouse. It wasn't at Christmas—although she may have worn it then, too—but sometime later in the winter, back when I hadn't been much older than Dylan was now. We'd had a blizzard that night, and my father was somewhere out on the road. My mother would have just come home from her office job, the one she'd had for a while, a receptionist at a doctor's office or something, before she got fired for keeping a fifth of vodka in the filing cabinet. My brother was playing on the floor, ramming trucks into table legs, making a racket. My mother was holding me and watching the road from the window—or at least, what she could see of the road in the dark. I rested my head on her shoulder, gazing at her necklace of shiny black beads, something she'd found at Kmart or Woolworth's. Slowly—probably without realizing she was doing it—she began to sway back and forth, her hand on the back of my head. I pretended to fall asleep, closing my eyes and keeping as still as I could while she gazed out the window.

It was a shame, I thought, that everything had later unraveled. But things just happened that way sometimes.

Outside, I heard an antique-sounding engine start and a car drive away, followed by silence.

Beth cocked her head at me. "I have trouble picturing your mom in that."

"What? Oh—yeah, this was before the woodshop. And the denim-jacket phase."

"You think you'll see them tomorrow?" She stood, disentangling her feet from a pile of lights and ribbons.

"My parents?" I shrugged. "Who knows? They usually manage to stop by my grandmother's, though, so maybe. I'll probably make myself scarce just in case."

"Now there's the Christmas spirit," she said ironically, but I heard her laugh.

"Yeah, I'm kind of the Grinch."

"No, you're not. You try too hard. Real grinches are just like that naturally." Dylan coughed, and she hastened into the kitchen to retrieve a juice bottle. "Hey, there's a radio in here. Should we put on some Christmas music?"

"Sounds wonderful."

"Feliz Navidad" came on in mid-chorus, its long-dead singer chirruping joyously. Beth and I decorated industriously, bending and straightening. Her family used a cross instead of a star, and when we had placed it carefully at the top, we gathered the green wires of the Christmas lights and plugged them in, stepping back to admire our work. When we turned the lamps off, the tree glowed with that primal, half-hidden mystery, its pyramid of soft branches forming a veil over the points of light that shone through. It was a sight that always gave rise in me to a half-suppressed, childlike awe.

"I think we did okay," I said.

Beth bounced to her toes and threw an arm around my shoulder. "We did more than okay. We're amazing. What have I always told you?"

It was after midnight by the time I left. Standing alone on the smooth, paved driveway, I turned back in the darkness to gaze at the picture window, my breath rising in steam. The tree shone, majestic and solitary, seeming to hover protectively over the room before it. Rubbing my hands together and blowing on them, I regarded it, watching the string of colored lights pulse and flicker behind the ornaments.

Beth walked into the room, holding Dylan in her arms while he clung to her purple turtleneck. She kissed him on the forehead and held him out so he could reach for an ornament, her lips moving. When he had taken the shining ball from the tree, she swung him around in a circle. Through the window, I could see him chortling happily, looking up at her as her lips moved. It looked as if she were singing.

I felt a pang of a feeling I couldn't name, remembering the dreams I'd had when Amos and I had bought our own house, the scenes I'd imagined would take place there.

But it doesn't matter, I thought. *I'm happy. I don't mind.*
I don't mind.

After a few minutes, I lowered my eyes and strolled away, back to the solitude of my car, humming the song from the radio quietly, trying to remember the words.

The store was closed between Christmas and New Year's, a decision I disagreed with but that wasn't mine to make. There was a snowstorm the day after Christmas, and for two days my grandmother and I stayed in, her dozing in front of her game shows, me curled up on the sofa or by the window in my room, reading. The book unsettled me, the way it made me sympathize with the ragged Raskolnikov, the killer, and hope he would escape. I hadn't believed it was possible to feel such a thing.

When I'd turned the last page, I puttered around uselessly for a while, thinking, then drove into Carlisle. The town was a slippery grid of gray slush, low and gloomy. There was one nice street, however, that had old brick townhouses with shops on the ground floors. I parked and walked into one of the antique stores, keeping my hands out so they wouldn't think I was shoplifting, knowing I smelled like my grandmother's cigarette smoke and the bottoms of my jeans were frayed.

The first store didn't have the right thing, and the second and third ones didn't, either—just a bunch of heavy-looking brass and tarnished silver. I didn't even know what I was trying to find until I saw it: a glass bird, an open-beaked sparrow poised on a branch, its wings raised and tensed, caught in the moment just before it pushed off and lifted itself into the air. It should have been tacky, and maybe it was, but there was something in the energy of it, the sense of movement that saved it. Its neck was stretched, its white breast pushed forward, the wings strong and pointed.

I knew I couldn't afford to pay for it, but I did, cradling it carefully as I walked out.

Up on the mountain, surrounded by the fog that had descended as evening drew near, I knocked on the hostel's front door, lifting the heavy brass ring and tapping it against the wood. My other hand held the bird against my chest, trying not to put any pressure on the wings.

Martin must have been out, because after a minute had passed, I saw the curtains twitch in the breakfast room and the stranger himself opened the door.

"Oh, hello!" he said. "I didn't expect to see you today. How was your holiday?" He was wearing a different sweater, I noticed, cream-colored, probably something Martin had spotted at a church basement sale.

"Good, thanks. Here, this is for you." Pushing the bird into his startled hands, I took a step back and waved. "I'll see you."

"Oh," he said, surprised. "Yes, but wait—won't you come in?"

"Sorry, I can't. I have to go back and make dinner. Maybe next time." The car engine was still running, the Jeep spinning out a white thread of exhaust that blended with the gray fog. "I hope you like it."

"Yes, of course! It's lovely. I—I had no idea—I really wasn't expecting—" His expression suddenly turned to one of regret. "I'm sorry I have nothing to give you, myself."

"It doesn't matter—I don't want anything." I turned back and climbed into the car. "See you later."

He took a step forward, half raising a hand.

"Happy New Year," he called. His voice echoed in the valley, and he covered his mouth, his eyes wide.

I couldn't help but laugh. On an impulse, I rolled the window down. "Happy New Year," I called back, letting my voice echo as well.

It was one of the moments I thought about later, when they told me who he really was, or who they thought he really was. At the time, I simply watched him in my rearview mirror, a slender white apparition holding the glass figure to his chest and waving his hand, gradually growing thinner and smaller, evaporating into the fog that had spun its web around the mountain.

PART TWO

1

January always showed us the faults in our memory. There would be a week, or even two, of unexpected warmth, the sun shining and the snow melting, people wandering around looking half-blind and dazzled. It wasn't exactly pretty—brightly illuminated mud was still mud—and it was dangerous for the trees, tricking them into leafing and budding long before the winter had actually passed. Still, there was something about it, something that drew all of us outside, pointing at one another's light jackets, wondering if this had ever happened before. Of course it had; it happened nearly every year. And yet it worked its magic, the notes of it reaching into us like the Pied Piper's tune. It was enough to make a person wonder how much of human life still hinged on accidents of the weather.

I began spending my mornings on the porch, dragging a chair into a patch of sunlight and looking out over the mountains, shorn now of both leaves and snow. Sometimes, as I held a book in my lap, I found myself thinking about Amos. Not deliberately, of course—I never thought about him deliberately—but in brief snatches, like flickers of interference in a radio program, a strange signal cutting in when you're not expecting it. A look on his face, a phrase he had used, a fragment of a scene between us. I would glance up from the book and stare out at the trees, my mind momentarily caught up in these trailing wisps of the past.

I still had dreams about him at times, dreams that weren't quite nightmares but weren't exactly pleasant, either. Dreams in which we sat across a table from each other and I found I couldn't bring myself to leave. Dreams in which I opened a door with a sense of dread, knowing he would be in the room behind it. As in life, he never said much. For the most part he just seemed to stare, sometimes with an expression of sadness, sometimes without any emotion at all, as if he'd been drained of himself, like one of those decorative eggs that's pricked with a pin and eventually becomes hollow.

They said, after the accident, that I might not remember things, that there might be gaps in my memory big enough to swallow months or even years. They were wrong: I remembered everything. Nothing had become blurred, nothing was gone. Maybe I should have told them that, should have turned my face up to them when they were standing around my hospital bed and said: I remember every hour of every day. It might almost have been fun to spook them like that.

The way we met was so ordinary that later I was annoyed with myself for thinking there was anything special about it. It was a Saturday in September, just after I had turned fifteen. I had spent the night at Beth's house, and the two of us were perched on the couch in our pajamas, our feet propped up on the coffee table, watching a soap opera that I had always secretly found boring but Beth loved. Her older brothers were in the backyard with some friends, trying to train a basset hound they'd found by the side of the road and named, optimistically, Hunter.

Laughing and jostling one another, the boys came inside, Amos among them. He had a round face, sandy hair that fell over his forehead, blue eyes I noticed right away. Tall and ruddy, he looked at once older and more boyish than the rest, glancing around him with a thoughtful expression and saying little. When he did speak, it was with a deliberate drawl, scratching his face as if speaking were something unnatural to him, but I noticed that his eyes darted from person to person, object to object, as if he would someday be quizzed on everything in the house. "Hello," he said when I edged past him to take my bowl to the sink, and then seemed to lose interest when, surprised and shy, I mumbled a hello in return.

To my shock, he called the next day, and for weeks we talked almost every night, when I was home from school and he was back from his job as a mason's assistant in Mechanicsburg. I would sit on the carpet in my room, leaning against the closet door, the phone pressed to my ear, smiling as he told stories about his boss, the customers, life in a town that was big enough to have things like bars and traffic jams. When I hung up, my fingers would be stiff from gripping the receiver while I listened, trying desperately to think of something interesting to say in response.

"Amos Guttshall?" my brother said with disbelief when I told him. I was sitting on the edge of his bed, watching him stuff shorts and a

T-shirt into a duffel bag before basketball practice. We had the same dark hair and slender build, but it looked better on him; girls loved the way his blue eyes and black cowlick stood out against his skin, with an air of innocence and daring at the same time.

"Yeah," I said, pulling up my leg and picking at the rubber toe of my hi-top sneaker. "Why?"

"Nothing," he said.

I would think about it later, that "nothing." What was behind it, really? Why wasn't I supposed to know?

At the time, all he said was, "He's okay. Little bit funny, though. His parents are rich—I mean, not *rich*, but his dad sells houses and his mom's some kind of counselor. They're doing pretty well for themselves, but you'd think the guy didn't know his ass from a hole in the ground. Acts like he's the biggest born redneck who ever walked the face of the earth."

"I think he's smart," I said. At least, he sounded smart over the phone.

"Oh, he's smart enough. He just doesn't want anybody to know it." He waited for me to slide off the bed so he could turn off the light. "What's he doing now?"

"Mason," I told him.

He whistled appreciatively. "Ooh, my little sister's bagged herself a union man," he said, sauntering out of the room, ignoring my protests.

Before I knew it, my friend Melanie—a tall girl who ran track—was sewing me into a homecoming dress, a long black velveteen sheath she'd worn the year before. The hairdresser had curled our hair and woven primroses into it, and when I looked in the bathroom mirror at Melanie's house I was taken aback by the slightly sunburned but elegant brunette who stared back at me.

"I told you," Melanie said, leaning forward and applying a bright swath of red lipstick to her lips with practiced motions.

"Told me what?"

"That you could be pretty."

In spite of the cool fall weather, we drove into town to the ice cream place, the one that still looked exactly the way it had in the 1960s, and ordered vanilla milkshakes in lieu of dinner. I had never worn high heels before and was taking short steps back and forth across the parking lot, trying not to dwell on the thought that in a few hours I would be dancing in these things, turning in circles while pressed against the body of a man I barely knew. Melanie had struck up a conversation with a guy in a Camaro, someone she knew from track. I was beginning to worry that we would be late when I pivoted painstakingly and, looking up, saw Amos.

He was sitting in a truck that was parked across the road, leaning out of the window and beckoning to me. My stomach flipped; he wasn't supposed to see me yet, not until we met up at the school, where someone was going to have to sneak him in since he'd already graduated. I walked toward him, praying I wouldn't trip over the hem of the dress.

"Hey," he said. His eyes seemed luminous, and a warm, sweet odor of sweat mingled with cigarette smoke rose from his skin. He was wearing a gray work shirt with the masonry company's logo on it, and his hands and forearms were lined with the short scrapes I would come to know so well, the ones that came from the edges of stone. "Listen. Do you still want to go to this dance?"

"I. Well. Why?" I blurted out.

"I mean, we can if you want to. But I was thinking you might want to do something else instead."

"Like what?" Melanie had covered my eyelids with a vast amount of green powder, and I found myself blinking at him.

"I don't know." He tapped his fingers on the wheel and looked through the windshield. "Have you been up to Waggoner's Gap? I was thinking we could just talk. You know. Since we've never done that. Not in person, I mean." Although his sentences were fumbling, there was a sincerity in his face, a kind of intelligence that seemed to find difficulty compressing itself into words.

"All right," I said slowly, and shortly afterward found myself sitting next to him at the gap, on North Mountain, looking out over Carlisle's web of lights in the darkness while talking in quiet, halting tones about our lives. *I will remember this*, I thought at the time, and I did. The country station on the radio playing its Saturday-night classic songs, the towns below us glittering like scattered cinders. It was like the movies; it was, I thought, how it was supposed to be. Sitting there, I felt as if the whole thing were magic, something I didn't deserve, but I also felt like I'd achieved something. Like I should carry it forward so it could keep being the perfect story it was.

It's amazing, the power of a story.

We were married not long after I graduated, on a bright summer day a few months before I started classes at the state college in Shippensburg.

Amos kept his job in a town forty-five minutes away, his hands perpetu-
ally covered with dust, the scrapes gradually forming small, light-colored
scars. From the first, I decided I was going to be good, a good wife, that
the marriage was going to be a success. Even through the haze of my
nervous happiness, I had seen the glances at our wedding, at my pointed
seventeen-year-old elbows poking out of the frilly, adult-looking gown my
grandfather had insisted on buying for me. Amos's mother, for one, had
cried so much during the ceremony that I'd begun to be embarrassed. But
I was as sure about Amos as I had ever been about anything. To the extent
that I even acknowledged the glances, I was set on proving them wrong.

As I propped my feet up on the porch and thought about these
things—or tried not to—the stranger would usually appear, also with
a book in tow, scarf looped gently around his mouth and nose. If one
of the hunters showed up, he would quietly slip away, but often we sat
together for hours, the table between us, lost in our own thoughts. He
was mostly silent, but I could sense him, sitting there with his eyes
calmly lowered, occasionally turning a page. As the days passed, I
found that I didn't mind his presence, that in some way it helped to
keep the ghosts of the past at bay. Like me, he would sometimes look
up, his hand marking his place, and stare out over the mountains.
Maybe both of us, I thought, found each other's company useful for
the same reasons. I still wasn't used to spending so much time with
another person, but it didn't seem to hurt either of us to have someone
there who could keep us from sinking into the backwards pleasure of
tormenting ourselves, dwelling with astonishment and regret on the
hours that had passed us by and the people we used to be.

He found an old book of crossword puzzles and set about solving
them whenever he joined me, leaning across the table from time to
time to ask questions. Looking into his face, so open and somehow
sensitive, I could never bring myself to ask him about the bad thing he
said he had done. He was here illegally, I understood that much, but
I decided the rest didn't matter. It wasn't for me to ask questions, and
besides, the past was the past; if that could be true for me, then it could
also be true for him.

I failed to realize that the present had brought its own problems,
ones our mutual retreat into the depths of the woods wouldn't fix.

"Would you look at that!" he exclaimed one morning. "'Summering
for St. Petersburg,' five letters. It's a dacha! I didn't know Americans
knew any Russian words besides vodka."

"We don't," I said, and he slid his chair over next to mine, holding the book over my knees to show me. His shoulder brushed against mine.

"See?" he said, pointing. But I was looking up, watching a figure in a camouflage coat cut across the picnic grounds, treading slowly, a large gun I had never seen before dangling from one arm. It was Jerry.

"That's funny," I said, my eyes on the long black barrel, the powerful-looking scope. It was no longer rifle season.

Realizing that I wasn't talking about the crossword, the stranger looked up, too. "What?"

The figure had disappeared down the trail, the gun barrel leading the way before it. Before I could blink, it had vanished into the trees.

"Nothing," I said.

That afternoon, my grandmother collapsed facedown in her coffee while playing cards at the Friends of Eagles. The phone in the store still wasn't working, but somebody must have called the park rangers, because one of them came to find me. He took off his hat as he stepped through the door—something nobody ever did, except for the oldest hunters—and cleared his throat, looking uneasy. I put down the book I was reading, and we looked at each other for a long moment. He offered me a ride, but I shook my head.

The ambulance had taken her to the hospital in Carlisle. I sat in the waiting room on the strange pastel-colored chairs, my gaze periodically drifting to a TV without sound, trying to stop myself from imagining the worst. As the hours slid by, I tried to call my parents from a pay phone outside, but there was no answer.

The nurse, a squat blond woman bearing a clipboard, called my name just as I was opening a soggy-looking ham-and-cheese sandwich I'd bought from a vending machine. I hurried after her.

My grandmother was stretched on the bed with her eyes closed, a shining plastic tube leading from her nose to a beige machine. There were red lines around her mouth, where something—a mask, I guessed—had recently been pressed. Her brows were furrowed, as if, even in her sleep, she were skeptical of everything around her.

I sat next to her and waited, knitting my fingers in my lap. A different nurse padded in to adjust the pillow and check a small device that was attached to my grandmother's fingertip. While I watched, she smiled at me briefly, then padded out.

Another hour passed. When I had been in the hospital during the long months after the accident, I had tried to stave off boredom by watching animal shows on the television mounted on the wall, or, later, by playing private games, looking out the window and trying to think of as many words as I could that rhymed with a particular sound, my lips moving silently. At other times, I simply sat, letting my mind wander into dark crannies of the imagination I hadn't known existed. Sometimes, when I looked in the mirror, I was surprised to find that I was still who I had been before, the thin twenty-two-year-old. It was childish, I knew, to be so absorbed in my own daydreams. Yet, gazing out over the hospital's rolling lawn, I didn't really care if it was childish or not. The pills made it impossible to concentrate on anything important, anyway. There seemed to be no reason not to drift.

It was only later that I was sad, although I couldn't have said exactly what I was sad about. For whatever reason, it seemed to be worst when I thought about my brother, riding around in an armored car in some faraway wasteland. I pictured his Humvee from above, a square thing with a gun turret, like some bizarre kind of beetle making tracks in the sand. It seemed like such a useless, dangerous thing for someone as alive and human and real as my brother to be doing. I would cry then, without really knowing why. We had never exactly been close, but I couldn't bear the thought that he was out there, so vulnerable and exposed. Somehow, it seemed to strengthen the pain that had coiled itself so tightly around my bones, to make it burrow deeper.

Sitting by my grandmother's reclining figure, I was suddenly overcome by a regret I couldn't explain. She was, I thought, probably the person who cared most for me in the world, even if it was sometimes difficult to tell how she really felt about anything.

Just before visiting hours were about to end, she woke with a start, grasping the sheets.

"Grandma?" I touched her arm.

She opened her mouth, making a dry sound and looking around as if she didn't know where she was. The nurse had left a cup of water on the bedside table, and I raised it to her lips. She sucked on the straw, looking at me, gradually seeming to recover herself. As she sipped, she narrowed her eyes.

"You!" she said finally, spitting water onto the blanket. I hurried into the bathroom and returned with a paper towel, reaching out to wipe her chin. She turned her head away with a grunt.

"Yes, it's me. Here, let me—"

"Why are you here?" Her fingers clenching the blanket, she regarded me with a mixture of anger and embarrassment. I stepped back with a sigh.

"You got sick. Of course I'm here."

"Pah!"

I crossed the room as calmly as I could and threw the paper towel away. "You probably shouldn't talk so much right away. You'll get tired."

She made a face at me and turned her gaze to the window, where the two of us were reflected. Slowly, she lifted a hand and looked at it. A needle had been inserted into a vein on the back of it, held in place with white tape.

A minute passed. The sound of footsteps reached us from the hall, approaching and then fading. Far away, a door opened and closed.

"Are you going to take me home?" she asked then, in a voice that was more subdued.

"Yes, although I can't until the doctor decides you're ready. It might be a while."

Her eyes swiveled up to meet mine.

"I don't think it's going to be tonight," I said. "It's already late. How are you feeling?"

She gestured dismissively. "Old."

A light was pulsing on the machine next to her, in time with some unknowable part of the forces that were keeping her alive. The thought crawled into my mind that there might be something that interested me somewhere in the vicinity—a box of samples, maybe, or even a prescription pad lying around. With a grimace, I pushed the idea out of my mind. I was here for my grandmother, not myself.

"Do you want to go back to sleep?" I said. "I can go."

"I don't care. You do what you want."

I reached out and fixed her pillow. She let me do it, still looking at the window.

The light on the machine continued its pulsing. Drops of some unknown substance trickled from an IV bag into the needle on the back of her hand.

"I killed him, you know," she mumbled finally.

"What?" I started, looking down at her. "Killed who?"

She coughed, irritated. "Him. You know." An edge of defiance crept into her tone.

"Who? Grandpa?"

"Yes."

I stared at her, baffled. "No, you didn't. He had a heart attack on Thanksgiving, after dinner. Dad found him. Don't you remember?"

She glanced around her, confused. "Well, I wanted to kill him."

I sat back, rubbing my forehead, wondering if there could possibly be a good response to this. "That's not the same thing," I said eventually. "We've all had thoughts like that at times."

"You haven't."

I looked at her. For a disturbing moment, I thought she was alluding to the rumors, challenging me. Then, with an even bigger jolt, I realized she was sincere. It had never in my life occurred to me that she might look up to me, and I dismissed the thought immediately. It was simply too strange.

I straightened the blanket and pulled the sheet up to her chest. She lifted her arms compliantly, looking up at me.

"Never mind about that," I said.

I sat by her side, glancing up at the clock as the minutes ticked by. The thought of returning to the house alone, waking up there in the stillness in the morning, gave me a hollow feeling in my chest, a sensation I hadn't felt for a long time.

"I've never seen the ocean," my grandmother said abruptly. Her gray curls had fallen onto her forehead.

It sounded like a line from a movie, and maybe it was, but it gave me pause. "Well, neither have I." I forced myself to smile and shrugged. The farthest I'd ever been from home was to visit my aunt Jeanine in Pittsburgh, years earlier, when I was a child. "Not much chance of that in Pennsylvania, I guess."

Turning her head, she squinted and gave me a hard look. "You say that like this is the only place there is. Like they'll come and lock you up if you try to leave."

I closed my eyes. "I don't think that."

"Well, you must. Why else are you still here?"

I looked down at her, her meager form under the blanket, the needle in her hand, the cloudy eyes that shifted back and forth, unable to bring my face into focus even though I was no more than two feet away.

"Let's talk about this some other time," I said.

"You think I can't take care of myself?" she rasped. "Phuh. You're just stubborn."

"Some other time," I said again.

"I don't need anyone to take care of me. You think I got through seventy-five years of life without figuring out how to clean up after myself? You're just afraid of going anywhere. You're afraid of everything."

"No, that's not fair. And I'm sorry you're sick, but—"

"And another thing." She inhaled, evidently preparing to deliver the knockout blow, but was seized by coughing. Her face reddened as she hacked, glaring at me. I stood and watched her as she caught her breath, and thought that it was remarkably difficult to tell the difference between when she was irate and when she was frightened. Maybe, as I would understand much later, there was no real difference.

A nurse passing by in the hallway leaned her head into the room.

"Visiting time is over," she told us in a sing-song voice.

Outside the room, the nurses were beginning to dim the lights, rolling carts away with a clattering sound. I wandered slowly toward the elevator, turning corners, watching the white walls pass by beside me, the nurses' desk appearing and disappearing like an island in the sea. The place smelled the way hospitals always smell, the sharp scent of iodine and sickness, and I quickened my pace, wanting nothing more than to be home.

After a few minutes, I passed the nurses' desk again, unable to remember whether it had been on my right or left when I'd seen it before. Trying a different corridor, I did my best to pay more attention, peering around me, soon reaching a dimly lit row of rooms that had curtains instead of doors. Increasingly confused—I couldn't remember having passed this part of the ward on my way in—I approached a rectangle of light where one of the curtains was drawn back, thinking I might find a doctor who could tell me where to go.

Instead, I found an empty bed, a jumble of cardboard packaging, a glass cabinet filled with small white boxes and bottles. I almost turned around and walked back out, but something—probably no more than the working drudge's instinctive curiosity about places she isn't supposed to be—made me linger.

The labels on the boxes were small but distinct, black against white. As I read them, my eyes widened. Without realizing it, I raised a hand to my mouth.

It wasn't possible, I thought. This was some kind of joke. A trap.

There was no sound from the corridor. The glass panes of the cabinet reflected the fluorescent lights, bright and blank.

Reaching out tentatively, I touched the glass. The bottles that interested me were right in front of me, just above eye level, plain as day.

A strange sensation ran through me, cold and unsettling. For a moment, I had a feeling of suspension, of being genuinely unsure whether I was dreaming or awake.

I touched the lock with a fingertip, tracing it, tapping it gently with a nail.

The square of darkness behind me remained dark.

Looking around, I slipped my hand into my pocket and found a hairpin, straight and smooth against my fingertips. I closed my fist over it and drew it out, my stomach jolting. I was just testing, I thought, feeling the rough edge of the slot. It was almost like a game. After all, they couldn't really have left something like this where somebody could get at it. Not even in a two-bit town like this one.

I pinched the hairpin between my fingers, turning my body so my hip nearly rested against the lock, bowing my head so my hair shielded my face. The tip of the pin scratched the coppery surface; it wasn't an easy fit, but the thing was narrow, narrow enough to—

"Ma'am?"

I whirled around to find the blond nurse glowering at me, her clipboard dangling at her side, her mouth a straight line.

I yanked my arm back.

"Oh," I said, my voice strangely thin. "I was just—I was just looking. I thought you might have some Tylenol. I have a headache."

The obviousness of the lie seemed to irritate her further. "You can get Tylenol at the drugstore," she said flatly. Brushing past me, she rattled the door until the panes shook, making sure it didn't open. "There are police on the ground floor around the clock, ma'am. Don't do something you're going to regret."

I looked at her, swallowing, not knowing how to respond.

She turned and marched toward a staircase, and with a sick feeling I understood that I should follow her. That I had to. That she was escorting me out of the building.

When we reached the entrance, I turned to say something to her, my face flushing, but by then she was gone.

When I pulled into the driveway, it was profoundly dark, not a single light shining in the neighborhood except the bulb on my grandmother's porch. I cut the engine and sat, listening to the cooling motor tick in the silence, feeling the air around me lose its warmth.

Finally, I climbed out and leaned back against the Jeep. The stars were brilliant, piercingly white. I tipped my head back, feeling the cold metal against my scalp. My arm and hip ached, and the skin over my cheekbones seemed to draw tighter. I could see my coat collar tremble as my heart beat.

At last, I walked into the empty house, the same person I always had been, the same person I always would be. I sank into a chair by the dining room table, looking down at my hands. Minutes passed, and then hours, as I willed myself to dissolve into the darkness around me, to become simply part of the night.

2

The stranger and I were sitting together on the porch when the cars suddenly appeared, four of them, pulling into the park one after another. I had been fretting about my grandmother, who had come home with a shining gray oxygen canister in tow. My father had driven her, and when he'd attempted to carry her from the van to the house, she'd smacked his arm and waddled to the front door herself, looking from behind like an angry duck. She'd promptly settled into her usual place on the couch and, for the past two days, had been refusing to speak to anyone.

A small crowd of men came toward us across the parking lot, eight or nine of them, talking and laughing, pointing out over the view. Before I could even turn toward the stranger, he had slipped under the railing and disappeared around the corner of the building.

"Well, this is quaint, isn't it?" one of the men said as they came onto the porch, their steps heavy on the boards. They were a range of ages but all dressed similarly, in jeans and tough but expensive-looking coats, sturdy boots with logos on them. They moved the same way, too, arms crossed or hands on hips, as if they were evaluating the things around them, ready to recommend changes to anything that wasn't up to standard. Two had ponytails; several had wire-rimmed glasses that made them look like professors, or like the computer salesman in Carlisle who had acted as if he couldn't quite bring himself to notice me, years earlier, when I'd stopped in to see if I could afford to buy something.

"Yeah, I've always thought this would be a pretty comfortable place to do a dig," another one said. "It's got some great amenities. There's a campsite right over there with hot showers and electric hookups." He knocked the snow off his shoes, making loud thumping noises against the edge of the step.

"Hot showers on a dig site? I'm guessing the roads are paved with gold, too?" a third one said. He was older than most of the rest, and balding. His coat was a sleek, shiny gray-blue, and his feet were planted on the porch casually but firmly, as if no one had ever questioned his right to stand wherever he chose. When he spotted me, his smile widened.

"What do you think, girl? Look like a good day to be out in the woods to you?"

I turned toward him, too surprised at being addressed to react right away. Without replying, I moved automatically toward the door.

"Oh, you work here?" the same man said. "Maybe you could whip us up some burgers. You guys hungry?"

"I'm always hungry," one of the ponytailed ones said.

"Okay. Got any burgers here, girl?"

They milled around on the porch as I stood there, asking myself fleetingly if I could refuse, if they would drive away if I did. They weren't the cops, I could see that much, but something about them— the nice clothes, the colorless accents—gave off an authority that made me nervous.

"Yeah," I said, trying to sound neutral.

"Listen to that," the man in the gray-blue coat said. "'Yeah.' We're in luck, gentlemen."

I narrowed my eyes, fixing him with a silent, even look, but he didn't seem to notice. I had no choice but to go in.

"I've heard the site's almost untouched," the same man, who seemed to be the leader, said. "Which is pretty remarkable, when you think about it. It got turned into a church camp after the government was done with it, but nobody's really set foot in it since the seventies."

He was talking about the prison camp, I realized as I bent to pull pink rounds of meat from the freezer. It was just down the road, a collection of collapsed, rotted roofs and broken slabs of cement scattered through the forest, connected by a thin footpath that dwindled by an old swimming hole choked with branches. I sometimes went there to think, to gather myself, usually after some out-of-town hiker had started asking too many questions. I had never seen it in winter, but in the summer it was like a jungle, its ruins melancholy and mysterious, like some lost temple to a pagan god.

One of the men who hadn't spoken yet piped up as I put the meat on the hot surface, watching the ice crystals slowly break down. "I still can't believe it—it's so bizarre to think this happened, the War Department shipping a bunch of Axis guys off to some random place in Pennsylvania."

"I know," another one said behind me. "Eric tell you about the sweat box yet?"

"Yeah, I couldn't believe that, either—that's some straight-up *Bridge on the River Kwai* shit. I had no idea we did that."

"Well, you can do anything if nobody knows you're doing it. Look at those Abu Ghraib bastards."

My back stiffened, but I was careful to move normally, as if I weren't listening.

"Yeah, well, digital cameras. They should've known that would get out," the leader remarked.

"Still, though. Kind of sickening, the whole thing."

"What—that they did it, or that they took photos?"

"Well, both, obviously." The speaker's voice momentarily became louder. "Hey, could I get some onion rings with that? You got onion rings?"

I opened a bag and slipped them into the hot oil without speaking.

"Well, thank you very much, my lady," the leader chimed in. I could feel him watching my back. "You ever hear of an archaeologist? You know what that is?"

I remained quiet at first, hoping the others would start a different conversation so I wouldn't have to answer. But they didn't. They all seemed to be waiting.

"Yes," I said finally, not turning around.

"Oh, hey, how about that. What is it?"

"I beg your pardon?" I said.

"I said, what is it? Tell us what you think it means."

I looked up at the fan that whirred over the grill, sucking the smoke away, up through the ceiling. The handle of the spatula was splintered, and I could feel a sharp piece digging into my palm. The meat kept bubbling, collapsing outward, browning.

"It's someone who digs in the ground," I told the fan. "Looking for artifacts."

"There you go!" the man said, laughing and clapping his hands together, the gray-blue jacket making a slippery sound. "'Someone who digs in the ground.' Let's go see if we can do a bit of digging in the ground, gentlemen."

I handed them their burgers without a word.

When they were gone, I closed the front door and leaned back against it. My eyes began to fill, the ice cream case becoming a bright blur, the letters of the menu board indistinct. I wiped my face roughly and held my breath. This was stupid. I had no reason to cry, and I wouldn't.

I wanted to go back outside, to look that man in the face and tell him to fuck off.

But I didn't.

As I stood there, watching the last bits of meat on the cooling grill turn black, there was a knock. Reluctantly, I opened it to find Martin on the other side.

"Hey, what's up? Why's the door closed?"

"Nothing." I moved to my side of the counter and busied myself with cleaning up. When I trusted my voice, I said, "Could you find him and tell him it's fine?"

Martin was leaning on the Formica. "Him? Who, Danya?"

"Yeah."

"Well, sure. What am I saying is fine?"

"Nothing." I pulled out the mop and began swiping at the drops of oil on the floor.

"Oh, well, 'nothing.' Excellent—glad to hear it." He nudged aside the plastic display jar of Slim Jims. "Is something up? Did those guys bother you?"

"You saw them?"

"I heard them. Would've been hard not to—that was quite a commotion for our little neck of the woods." He reached for a napkin and began folding it origami-style, pressing the creases with his thumb, the tendons in his skinny arms twitching. "Seriously, though, did they do something they shouldn't've? You're looking a little edgy."

"I don't need to be told how I look."

He paused in place. A moment passed.

"Sorry," he said finally. "Well, if you need anything, you know where I am. And I'll pass along the message."

Patting the counter, he looked at me as if he might say something else, but he didn't. I heard his whistle and the creak of his steps as he crossed the porch, and then there was silence again. I pulled my hair back from my face, tugging until it hurt and holding it there, then let it drop.

A few hours later, at my grandmother's house, I held a sheet of paper with numbers hastily jotted on it. Even with in-state tuition, they added up to five thousand dollars per semester. My earnings at the store were barely above minimum wage, and even if I took a different job—I closed my eyes and slid the paper into a drawer, looking out the kitchen window at the deserted railroad tracks.

It would never work.

When the night came, I opened some soup and ate it standing up, spooning it directly out of the can, cold, while I gazed out the window. My grandmother was asleep in her chair, her head tilted back, her hair a gray halo around her face.

I tucked a blanket around her and turned off the TV whose muted images flashed in the background, reflected in the family photographs that hung on the walls. One of them was of my grandmother herself, her high-school graduation picture, sepia-toned and soft-focused, showing a girl with an open face and graceful smile.

Sometimes I couldn't help studying them, these images of the people who had come before me. Maybe one of them would have looked in my eyes and recognized something—whatever it was that was weighting my movements right now. Or maybe they all would have recognized it; maybe I was simply a link in a chain, destined to become just like the others and someday have children who were just like me.

I could never have foreseen, then, that everything I'd ever known was about to change so completely, that the stranger's arrival was already reaching into the future to alter everything I'd thought I understood, like cracks spreading through glass before it gives way, showing us something behind it we'd never expected to see.

———————

There was something I would always remember about the way the light had slanted through the kitchen of the house I'd shared with Amos, falling across me as I stood at the window, sometimes with the radio on but usually in silence. It was so warm, so solid-seeming, drawing out the essence of everything. It turned the wildflowers into stained glass, the dirt road into copper, the wheat fields into a rippling green sea. The house felt close and alive, not like the decaying box with dirty walls it really was. Every afternoon, I stood there, observing the small changes in the landscape, filling myself with the quiet before Amos returned from work. I couldn't have explained what I felt in those moments, or why I came to see them as so vital, a brace that held me up, reminding me that I was real, that I was there, that there was some part of my mind that no one else could reach, even if I myself chose not to go there just yet. I just knew that I treasured them, these minutes when I felt suspended in a beam of light, part of it, something more than myself and something less.

We were happy in the house, or so I told myself. It wasn't just the first place we'd owned, but also the first one where we'd ever lived together; I'd been at school with Beth until then. I'd never seen Amos as excited as he was when he held the deed in his hand, his signature still fresh. His smile had been broad and his face had looked as though it were lit up from within; he'd embraced me so hard he'd almost lifted me off the floor. Now, he murmured into my hair, we were finally a family. A real one.

He had never really wanted me to go to school. Even so, he had let me do it—something for which I'd been grateful, telling myself what a generous and understanding husband I had. I had liked college—loved it, even—although I'd never had more than a vague notion of what I was doing there. I'd taken a physics class in high school with a teacher I'd liked, a short, round man with a contagious love of his subject, who told me so many times I was good at it that I almost came to believe him. I let him talk me into sending off some college applications, writing that I would be a physics major even though I didn't actually have the faintest idea what that would entail. I was behind on the math; in Centerville, trigonometry had been the highest class we could take. Still, I had a dim sense that I should do what I enjoyed. So, after my first year was out of the way, I buried myself happily in darkened labs, calculating, adjusting, figuring the inner workings of the world. Thousands of others had done the same before me, I knew, but I didn't care. It was all new to me.

Somehow I fumbled my way through three years, directionless but awed, invisible to everyone around me but soaking it all in nonetheless. For me, these years were an adventure, one I would never have dared to hope for. I couldn't escape the sense that I didn't deserve it, but I did the best I could, naive and overwhelmed and, in my own way, terrifyingly in love with it all.

Meanwhile, Amos's silences grew longer and longer when I came to his rented room in Mechanicsburg, a cramped bedroom in a faceless house that was identical to all the others on the street. I was careful never to tell him anything about school; somehow, the sight of his dusty hands and tired slump made me understand that I shouldn't, that it would sound frivolous, or as if my life were moving on without him. Although he never said so, I knew he blamed himself for not having done well in high school, for having put himself in the position of being less educated than his own wife. He was intelligent but suffered from some kind of reading problem, something that had never been diagnosed but made his progress through even a short item in the valley newspaper noticeably slow. I did my best to show him that I not only respected him anyway, but very nearly worshipped him, that I knew the book smarts I was gaining were less important than the actual smarts that came from being out in the world the way he was, living the life he lived. The things he said seemed to me to have a kind of plainspoken wisdom, and I began to quote him whenever I was asked for an opinion about anything. When I was around him, my sentences ended with little laughs, as if to show him that I didn't take myself too seriously. The last thing I wanted to do was say something that angered him or made him think I cared about myself more than him.

I knew what was coming—I must have—even though I pretended I didn't. Still, when it happened, I was unprepared.

"I need a wife who's here with me," he said one day, sitting on the edge of the bed, his face turned toward the window. A plume of cigarette smoke uncurled above him, and there was sorrow in his posture. "I can't help it. I just do."

I stood looking at him, my backpack dangling heavily from one hand. My stomach dropped into my shoes.

"I need us—" he said slowly, "I need us to be a family." Leaning forward, he stubbed out his cigarette, studying the dead end of it before turning to look at me. His voice was gruff but vulnerable, determined but tinged with regret. "I'm sorry I feel that way. I know how much you enjoy being down there." The expression in his eyes was withdrawn, as if he expected to be hurt, had prepared for it. "If you really want to go on the way we've been going on, you might be better off without me."

"I'd never be better off without you," I said. Then, in a rush, "And I don't enjoy it. Not as much as I enjoy being with you, anyway."

"I'm not so sure about that." Resting his chin in his hand, he watched me, as if expecting to read something in the way I looked back at him, the way I breathed, the way I stood.

"If I asked you to leave that place, and come up here and be with me, would you?" he said finally. A moment passed, and he cleared his throat. "If it was important to me?"

A long silence followed. There was an unfamiliar sensation in my chest, a kind of tightening. As I gazed down at my hands, still gripping the backpack, I saw that the nails were white from pressure. But I knew there was only one right answer to the question.

"Of course," I said.

I threw myself into my studies for a few more months, hunching over a table in the library for hours, absorbing as much as I could, working on papers every night while Beth looked on, puzzled at this sudden, frantic activity.

"You're leaving," she said one day, in a tone of disbelief.

"Yeah," I said cheerfully, although I couldn't look at her.

"But you like it here," she protested. "You like studying. You love physics."

"Oh," I said, trying to sound careless, "I do, but the math's getting too hard. It was never really a good idea."

"What do you mean? You got a B+ in that linear algebra class."

"A B+ isn't really anything to rave about. Besides," I added, "what was I really going to do with a physics degree, anyway?" I was echoing the imaginary Amos who spoke in my head, and perhaps it was this that made her lose patience.

"Well, gee, I don't know," she shot back with uncharacteristic sarcasm. "Be a physicist?"

I laughed. "No way. You need a Ph.D. for that."

I had played my trump card. It went without saying that no woman whose husband only had a high-school diploma would ever dream of getting a Ph.D. It would be like castrating him.

She had looked at me, furious but helpless, unable to find her way around the solid walls of valley logic that encircled us both.

I never quite admitted to myself that I hadn't wanted to drop out, that whenever I thought about it, it gave me a strange twisting feeling that I was too young to know was regret. I couldn't have admitted that, because admitting it would have meant admitting other things, too. Instead, I pushed the nameless feeling away and told myself that I had done the right thing. That this was what love meant.

And so we moved to Centerville, not far from my parents, because it was the only area where we could afford to buy a house on Amos's salary. It was a drab little place on a back road, barely more than an old hired hand's shack, but I kept it neat and lined the shelves with books and trinkets we picked up at yard sales. Our lives came to resemble scenes from a play, a montage from one of those reassuring but dull daytime TV shows I sometimes watched when the cleaning was done. I packed Amos's lunch in the morning, sometimes standing in the doorway to wave as he pulled away in the truck, the only vehicle we owned. I washed the curtains and the walls; I settled into a chair to read; I made a cake—my first one— on the only occasion when Beth came to visit, glancing around her with a careful look, as if she were afraid I could read her thoughts. I vacuumed the carpet, humming to myself and stealing looks at the phone on the wall, vaguely hoping it would ring even though I could hardly imagine who would call. I sat on the sofa and watched the second hand make its slow turn around the clock; I slid casserole dishes in and out of the oven; I dusted the corners. The houseplants flourished, then died from overwatering. Amos would come home, sometimes happy, sometimes silent, always exhausted. I lived for the days when he would walk into the kitchen and put his arms around me, not saying anything, but sharing himself with me, burying his nose in my hair, making me feel as though standing there quietly with him was the best thing that had ever happened to me.

When we'd moved in, I'd slid my remaining textbooks and papers into a closet from which they'd eventually disappeared, although I never knew exactly where they'd gone. In the same way, I slid my memory of my time in school—that other place, the other Kathleen who had existed there—into a corner of my mind where I never had to look at it, just as if it had never been. Whenever I brought it out, it shone in my eyes, too bright, too hopeful. So in the end, I left it where it was, until finally it was buried so deeply under other things that I never even thought to look for it anymore.

I had become what I'd always expected to be: a wife. In the end, I found it hard to imagine what else I could have been.

And yet, I would stand at the window, feeling somehow as though the person I had been, some essential part of myself, were floating away, and that there was nothing I could do to stop it. It spun itself out from the center of me like the unwinding string of a kite, receding farther and farther, growing smaller and smaller against the sky.

Deep down, I knew I shouldn't let it go. But I never imagined how dangerous my life would become when it was gone.

3

The coffee machine hissed and burbled as I crumpled the new sheet of paper in frustration, tossed it into the trash can, and sighed. No matter what I did, I still couldn't make the numbers add up. Tuition, groceries, gas, car insurance. I didn't factor in the cost of the pills, since—no matter what the nurse in the hospital had seen fit to imply—they were temporary and I would be giving them up as soon as I was ready. Even so, I couldn't make it work. I could take out a loan, maybe, but I knew I didn't want that—to be a hostage to the government, or the banks, or whoever it was who was in charge of such things. Even if Beth paid the rent, even if I took a part-time job, there was simply no way to do it. Besides, what I had said about my grandmother was true. Whether she admitted it or not, she needed me.

There was a rapping sound, and I looked up to see the stranger's face on the other side of the door, surrounded by the early morning light. The knob twisted, and he stuck his head in.

"May I come in?" he asked.

"Well, obviously. Since when do you ask?"

The rest of him slipped through the crack in the door. I could see now that he was holding a wide, battered-looking gray box in his hands.

"What's that?"

He stepped forward, removing his hat, and slid the box onto the counter. After rubbing his hands together and blowing on them—it had grown cold again—he opened the box to reveal two jumbled rows of plastic figures.

"Chess," I said, surprised.

"Yes," he replied, suddenly beaming, as if he couldn't help himself. "I found it in the game room. Would you like to play? I thought you might enjoy it if I taught you."

I picked up one of the knights and held it in my palm, examining the proud, chipped horse's head. The white had yellowed to the color of ivory, and I ran a thumb over the mane, turning the piece over to look at the felt on the bottom. "You must really be dying of boredom up there."

"Not 'dying.' I mean, it's not terminal." Sorting through the pieces with his slim fingers, he darted a look at me to see if I'd appreciated his joke. "Really, I just like to play. We used to have a chess set in my office, in one of the back rooms. The other lawyers and I would play all the time. Some days, it was all we did."

"Okay," I relented, touching the folded game board. "You don't need to teach me, though."

"Oh—you know how to play?"

"Well, sort of. My grandfather taught me a long time ago."

"That's wonderful." His face was radiant. "Was he very good?"

"I don't know. He learned in the army. Good enough to win cigarettes off the other guys, I guess."

The stranger dragged the other stool out of the closet and began setting up the board. One of the bishops was broken in half, and a missing pawn had been replaced by a nine-volt battery. He pinched the heavy rectangular lump between his fingers and looked at it in consternation.

I took it from him and put it on the board. "Well, what did you expect? This is how rednecks play chess."

He gave me a surprised look, one that quickly turned to sternness. "You're not a redneck."

I laughed, wondering who had taught him the word. "Yes, I am, but I don't care. It's been a long time since I cared about other people's judgment."

He pursed his lips, looking, for a brief moment, not unlike my grandmother.

"You're not that thing," he said. "Here, you can be white and I'll be black. Do you know some good openings?"

"I used to. One or two, anyway. I'll have to see if I can remember."

After staring down at the board for a moment, I nudged a pawn forward. He did the same, and before I knew it, we were off. He beat me easily, but as we traded moves, the feel of the game—that way of thinking into the future, maneuvering based on invisible possibilities—began to come back to me.

"Again?" he asked when we'd finished.

For the first time since I'd met him, I thought, he looked genuinely happy.

"Yeah. I can't let you get away with that."

We put the pieces back in their neat rows and started over. It was all so quick, so absorbing, that I almost forgot how impossible the whole thing was: me, him, sitting together in this place as if there were nothing unusual about it at all. I looked up from the board at his lowered head, his expression of concentration, and was about to say something—to ask him, somehow, about the fact of his being here—when he broke in unexpectedly.

"Your grandfather," he said. "What was he like?"

"My grandfather?" I looked down at the black and white squares, caught off-guard. A laughing man with yellowed teeth, tall and slim despite his age, appeared in my mind's eye. "I don't know. Depends who you ask, probably. My grandmother would say he was—well, I can't repeat what my grandmother would say. He was a piece of work. Let's put it that way."

"I see." His knight advanced toward me. "So you didn't like him?"

"Oh—no, that's not it. I liked him very much, actually." I kept my eyes on the board, lifting a bishop and sliding it forward. "I saw a different side of him than most other people did. He was a nightmare of a husband, and a nightmare of a father, too, from what I can gather. But he wasn't too bad as a grandfather." After a moment of hesitation, I took my finger off the piece. "In fact, I'd even say he was pretty good."

He contemplated my move, scratching his nose. "So he changed as he grew older?"

I thought about it. My grandfather had been a difficult man, I knew, and yet a surprising number of my memories of him were gentle ones. Holding his hand as we walked to buy penny candy at the store that was now Miller's, listening to his jokes as he knelt to help me try on a pair of shoes, sitting beside him at the church organ and poking at the yellowing keys. He'd had a gift for music, and used to pick out tunes after mass sometimes, until Father MacIntyre politely asked him to stop. It seemed impossible that someone who had been so generally despicable throughout his life—and despicable was the right word, there was no doubt about it—could, at least at times, be such a doting grandfather. I had never been able to reconcile myself to it, the fact that these two radically different men seemed to live inside the same person.

My parents had been young when they'd had my brother and me, and for a time the four of us had lived in two of the upstairs rooms at my grandparents' house, next to the room where I lived now. One night, I remembered, my grandfather had climbed the stairs with a book of poems in his hand: Emily Dickinson. Smelling of the bar in Carlisle where he worked, he had sat down on the floor of the room my brother and I shared and read to us, coughing in his abrupt, guttural way every now and again. Rumor had it that he'd done terrible things in Korea, and I had seen him hit my grandmother more than once, at one point dragging her across the kitchen by her hair while she screamed. I had been both sad and relieved when he'd died.

"No," I said, "I don't think people really change. He was just kind of a complicated person. In fact—" I paused, twisting my hair in my fingers. "I might even go so far as to say he was a bad man." It felt disloyal, but it was, I thought with a surge of defiance, the truth, and my grandfather himself might even have been proud of me for saying it. "But he was a bad man with good aspects. He wasn't easy to love, but . . . I knew him for what he was. He never pretended to be anything else. It was confusing when I was younger, but by the time I got older, I'd accepted it. Mostly." I ran my fingers through my hair again. "It's harder when people don't turn out to be who you expect. Those are the ones that are . . . hard to take."

The stranger slowly moved his knight again, capturing one of my pawns. Holding the small piece in his palm, he looked at it, his hair falling forward over his forehead.

"I can see what you mean," he said after a long moment. "Although I think sometimes people become things they didn't expect to become."

I gave a small shrug, waiting for him to go on.

"And sometimes," he said, "they act as if they were good, because they wish they were. I think we all try that sometimes—pretending to be the person we would like to be." He put the pawn down with the other captured pieces. "It isn't a lie; it's more like a story. Even when we're older, we're not so different from children. We all have stories we wish were true. Wouldn't you say?"

"I suppose."

While I decided whether to move my queen, he sat back and rubbed his jaw, as if meditating on something.

"I never knew my grandfather," he said. "My father's father, I mean.

I used to see my mother's father all the time—he lived in a little flat in our neighborhood—but my father's father wasn't from there."

"Where was he from?"

"We don't know, actually. My father grew up in an orphanage in Moscow."

"An orphanage?" I looked up. "Really?"

"Yes. He made his way to Uzbekistan when he was older, maybe seventeen or so. There was an earthquake that destroyed most of Tashkent, and the government sent men from Russia to work on building sites. This was under the Soviets, of course. Someone told him to go, and he went. That's how he met my mother."

I looked up at him, studying his face. He was leaning over the board, his arms crossed, concentrating. The pose was so unself-conscious that it was almost like watching him sleep. I had never thought of him as having a family, although of course I knew he was married. For a moment, I felt it: the disorienting understanding that he was every bit as real as I was, had his own private world, his own secret thoughts and depths of feeling. Even the idea of it made me feel as if I were intruding somehow, treading in places that belonged to him, that he had a right to keep to himself.

I sat back. "You have brothers and sisters?"

"Yes, a sister. She has a couple of children, actually. Boys."

I absorbed this. "So, you have nephews."

"Yes. They're three and six." He stopped. "No. Six and nine. I keep forgetting that so much time has passed."

I touched a captured pawn to my lips, trying to picture these two children. "Is it . . . is life hard for them there, in your country? Not—I mean, not because of any special situation you were in. Just . . . in general." I closed my hand over the pawn and put it back down. "I keep meaning to learn more about what things are like there, but I haven't."

"Oh, I'd say life in Uzbekistan is much like anywhere else—it depends who you are. If you have good connections, if you're well-to-do . . ." He spread his hands out, as if the end of the sentence were obvious. "My father had his ambitions. He managed a con-struction operation for a while, and then after independence . . . things turned out well for him. For us. We were fortunate." His look grew distant for a moment. "So I think—I hope—they're all perfectly well."

Unconsciously, he crossed his arms, seeming to hug them together. Then he said, "I do miss them, you know. They were good boys. I—"

Behind us, the door opened and Jerry walked in, the black rifle hanging in the crook of his arm.

I had experienced panic—sudden, genuine panic—three times in my life. Two had been with Amos, and one had been during the fire, in the instant I realized the smoke I smelled wasn't coming from inside the store. The expression on the stranger's face was exactly what mine must have been in those moments.

In that instant, I understood for the first time that he wasn't hiding just because he didn't have some piece of paper he was supposed to have. He was hiding because someone was looking for him.

You can't stay, I thought, the truth of it entering me like a needle.

"Whoa," Jerry said gruffly. "Easy, son."

He stood with his boots planted squarely on the floor, his head tilted back, his beard gleaming blue-black under the florescent lights. My heart leaped into my throat, and I looked from the stranger to the gun and back again.

Something was wrong, I thought, even more wrong than I'd realized. It might be flintlock season, but Jerry's rifle was not a flintlock. Anyone could see that. I didn't know how the rangers could have missed it.

I had never seen a gun that large in my life.

The big man seemed to be appraising the stranger from under his cap.

"You're here early," I forced myself to say in what I hoped was a light tone.

"Yeah." Jerry cleared his throat and flicked his eyes at the stranger again.

I looked at him, too. "Would you excuse us?" I asked.

"Of course," he murmured, and left, brushing by the hunter with his gaze fixed on the floor.

I almost expected Jerry to say something about it, but he didn't. Instead, he simply followed the stranger with his eyes before turning back to me.

"Hot chocolate," he muttered, easing his weight from one foot to the other. The gun barrel dangled from his arm, pointing toward the floor.

"Sure," I replied as evenly as I could, ripping open the powdered mix and pouring it into a cup.

I could feel him watching me, taking in my movements. A few moments later, he took the steaming drink from my hand, and I began digging for my wallet.

"Hey, listen, Kathleen," he said.

My head jerked up.

He paused. "I'm gonna have to raise the price. It'll be three instead of two."

I stopped with the wallet in my hand, staring at him.

"Prescription got more expensive," he said.

"Oh." I stood still, looking from his face to the gun. It was still pointed at the floor.

"Yeah."

A deep apprehension seized me.

Say no, I told myself. But what would that mean? What was this?

"If we make it three," I said, as if to myself, drawing out the words, "that would be . . ."

"Sixty. For twenty of them. Yeah."

I stayed there, my hands resting on the counter. I couldn't afford sixty. I could barely afford twenty.

But there was something I didn't like about the way he'd looked at the stranger. Something that made my skin prickle, like an electric current.

On the other hand, refusing would mean either going without the medicine or getting it somewhere else. And getting it somewhere else would mean I wasn't just someone whose friend's uncle did her an occasional favor, one she didn't really need. It would mean I was someone else, someone I knew I wasn't.

I began pulling fives and tens out of my wallet, stalling for time as I counted. When I looked at him again, the money in my hand, I realized I was holding my breath.

I had enough. Barely, but I did.

When I held out the bills, our eyes met.

He placed the paper bag on the counter, resting his hand on it for a moment. His hat was pulled low, casting a shadow over his face.

"You take care, Kathleen," he said finally, shuffling toward the door, the gun still dangling from his arm.

When the latch clicked behind him, the air left me. I leaned forward over the counter, my legs feeling loose and unsteady, gripping my fingers together.

I waited, staring at the clock, until ten minutes had passed. Then I swept the chess pieces into the box and went out into the cold.

When I slipped through the hostel door, Martin was nowhere to be seen. I climbed the stairs to the second floor and wandered down the hall, trying to figure out which room was the stranger's. They were all dark.

Taking a guess, I knocked.

"Hey," I called.

I started tapping on doors as I passed them, touching them lightly with my knuckle. "Come on," I said. "It's me."

Finally a door to my right opened, and the stranger and I stood facing one another. As soon as I saw his expression, my heart sank. There was a sheen on his face, and his teeth were strangely gritted, as if he were suffocating as he tried to smile.

"Hey," I said, trying to convince myself at the same time that I tried to convince him, "Listen, that was—it was just Jerry. Someone I know. I'm sorry he surprised you, but . . . it's fine. I know him. It's fine." I took a deep breath. "It's got nothing to do with you."

"Yes," he said, his voice too thin and bright, like an echo of a sound someone else had made.

"Really. Please don't worry about it."

"Yes," the stranger said again.

I remembered that I was carrying the board game and held it out. He took it from me, and I could see how shallow his breathing was.

"I'm sorry," I said. "I should have kept an eye on the time. I didn't realize—"

"It's not your fault," he replied, giving a strange, jerking bow and turning away, closing the door.

The inside of the library was distinctly bluish, as always. My boots left tracks on the fading blue carpet as I wove between the stacks of black- and blue-bound books, past the librarians with their long blue skirts and pinched, blue-looking faces. The computers with their plain blue screens were in a corner, under a window. I scraped a folding chair toward one of them, ignoring the librarians' glances, and opened the browser. Outside, it was snowing again. Sometimes it seemed as if it would snow forever.

As I watched the flakes fall, I thought of Jerry with his gun, imagining him standing before me, his eyes following the stranger with that unreadable look. But I pushed the image out of my mind. My interaction with Jerry had had nothing to do with the stranger. It couldn't have, and I would simply be paranoid to think otherwise.

I pulled myself closer to the monitor but didn't know how to ask what I wanted to ask. *Uzbekistan*, I typed, but that didn't give me what I wanted—just statistics and weather and some pictures of buildings. I sat back and bit a hangnail. What I wanted to know, I thought, was something that almost couldn't be put into words: why the stranger seemed at once so worldly and so vulnerable, what was behind the look in his eyes when Jerry came in. I didn't really know him at all, I realized; or rather, what I knew was impossible to express. The way he spoke and gestured, the hesitation in his movements, his face as he looked out over the mountains on those mornings when we sat together on the porch. His patient resignation as he'd waited for the bus that would never come. His crossed arms as he'd sat behind the chessboard, talking about the place he thought of as home.

The cursor blinked.

Why people leave Uzbekistan, I tried.

That was somewhat better, although still unsatisfying. There were articles about a dictator, more or less what I would have expected for a place so far away with such an obscure-sounding name. Some of them talked about shuttered newspapers, tapped phones, children and elderly people bused out of the cities and forced to pick cotton. A few years earlier, it seemed, soldiers had opened fire on people in the eastern part of the country and killed a number that would never be known. Reporters talked to women who stood outside a hospital with pictures of their sons and husbands, waiting for news, their faces stoic but heavy with grief. There was an American military base that had been closed in the wake of the killings, I read, sitting forward as I did so and wondering if my brother had ever passed through there. But the thought was so unexpected, so incongruous, that I dismissed it quickly.

Then there were articles about the dictator himself, and even more about his glamorous family, especially the daughters. My hand on the mouse, I looked at them, the two women. They belonged to a world I could only imagine, and not only because they lived so far away. The oldest daughter, especially, seemed to skip across the globe, dressing in furs and dancing until dawn in places like Moscow and New York and London, shooting movies and singing in music videos, donning suits to speak at the UN.

I shook my head. Life was the same everywhere, I thought. Some people were born into a different universe from the rest of us, and they stayed there, floating around like angels in the heavens, their feet barely scraping the earth on which the rest of us walked. We could look up at them, but we could never touch them.

I kept clicking, almost aimlessly, beginning to give up hope of understanding the thing I was so clumsily trying to grasp.

Then, as if a shadow had fallen across the sun, I found the photographs. Page after page of them, in merciless color. Photographs I immediately wished I had never seen.

There were many things I had learned to face, to think about, after the accident. Blood, bones, nerves, skin and the various things that could be done to it. Even so, the images on the screen were so upsetting that my breath caught in my throat. I pushed the chair back, as if to distance myself from what had appeared before me. Inhaling, I placed my hands on my knees, looking away before forcing myself to look back again.

I had thought I understood most of the ways a person could inflict pain on someone else, most of the ways a limb could be twisted, flesh bruised or burned or broken.

I was wrong.

The images were from a place with bars, and the worst thing, I saw right away, was the eyes. Most of the photographs of the inmates, or detainees, or whatever they were, didn't show faces; they only showed torsos, backs, arms, the skin striped—the captions said—from whippings with electric cables, bruised from beatings, swollen from having been immersed in boiling water. Hands were missing fingernails; feet were broken or maimed. But the eyes, the eyes looked as though they belonged to dead people, even though everyone in the pictures was alive, at least when the photos had been taken.

Fighting a sense of sickness, I closed the browser.

I was taken in for questioning, I heard the stranger say.

Not the ordinary police, but a kind of special police. The police who do these things.

One year, when my brother and I had been very young, we'd sat at the Thanksgiving table and listened to my grandmother's brother babble. He'd looked even older than he was, white-haired and sallow, picked up and brought over from the hospital or wherever it was he normally lived. Over the pie, his run-on talk had turned to something that had happened forty years earlier, something on a grassy hill on an island, a kneeling Japanese prisoner with his hands tied behind his back, a knife between someone else's fingers, the cutting off of ears and nose, blood everywhere. Someone had gotten him to shut up, my great-uncle; the war hadn't been like that, as we all knew. It was sailors kissing pretty nurses, it was old men with medals sitting in the review stand at the town parades.

Lost ears, lost noses, burns, whippings.

I stood up, leaning against the back of the chair until the nausea had passed. The librarians turned to watch me as I walked out the door.

At the Joyride with Beth that night, I couldn't shake the sense that the world had spun off its axis into an alternate version of itself. *Your uncle,* I wanted to say, *is walking around with a .45-70 out of season. And I've spent the past five hours thinking about what people look like when they're boiled.*

We started a game of darts, but I kept getting lost in thought, standing in a shadow with my drink. The photographs seemed to hover in front of me.

I couldn't be sure this was what the stranger was afraid of, but something told me it was. Maybe it wasn't the whole story, but some part of what I had just seen was hanging in the background, I thought.

Beth, too, was unusually quiet. When I finally roused myself to ask her what was wrong, she shook her head. "Oh, you know. Just—the situation. Being without Mark; single parenting. That's all. I'm just feeling bad for myself, really."

I looked at her, and the images that were floating in my vision cleared for a moment. "Are you sure?"

"Yeah." Smiling lopsidedly, she reached for my hand and led me to an empty space. "Be my date? Maybe we'll both feel better."

We danced a few steps as we sometimes did when the bar wasn't crowded, leading one another through spins in a way that was mostly ironic, but our hearts weren't in it. I came to a stop, leaning against the pool table. When I focused again, she had already reached the other end of the floor. Tilting her head back, her soda spilling over her fingers, she swayed wistfully by herself, drifting away.

"You know," she said when she came back, "sometimes I'm not so sure about all this."

"All what?"

She leaned her head on my shoulder. "I don't know. All of it." She raised her hand in a helpless gesture. "The things we do. The way life takes hold of us. We think we've got it all figured out, and then—" I felt her sigh. "You know?"

The pictures still floated in front of me. I took a long sip from my glass, feeling the liquid burn on the way down.

"Yeah," I said. "I do."

4

For two days, the stranger didn't leave his room. Every few hours, I would find an excuse to wander onto the porch, dusting the tables and chairs, glancing up at the darkened window I thought was his. As far as I could see, there was no movement behind the curtain. I pictured him stretched out on his cot in the wan gray light, his hands behind his head, staring at the ceiling, imagining the things he feared most. Or maybe remembering them.

I waited, respecting his anxiety. There was no reason, I reminded myself, to think the situation—whatever it was—had changed. Jerry had just figured out that he could take advantage of me; I certainly wasn't happy about it and had no idea what I was going to do, but it had nothing to do with anybody else. All he would have seen when he'd walked into the store was two people playing a game, even if one of them was unusually jumpy.

I understood fright, though, especially fright that was rooted in the past and therefore harder to get rid of. And if there was one thing I truly grasped, it was the desire to shut out the world.

Finally, however, I began to lose patience. No matter what this deeply odd person was doing here, he couldn't possibly think he could stay hidden in some hole in the backwoods of Pennsylvania forever. It just wasn't practical. He was more intelligent than that—and, I told myself, so was I.

The next morning, I climbed out of the car with a newspaper under my arm, noticing that Martin's red station wagon was parked behind the hostel. I dropped the things I was carrying onto the hood of the Jeep and bent down to grab a handful of gravel. Mounting the hill, I positioned myself where the stranger could see me and cocked my arm back. The stones made a clicking sound against the second-story window, quiet but insistent. I kept flinging them at the

glass pane until I ran out, then stuffed my hands into my coat pockets and waited.

Nothing happened. Cursing quietly and biting a nail, I turned to go.

I was halfway down the hill before the door creaked open behind
me and the stranger stepped out, walking toward me, glancing out
over the landscape. When we met, he pressed his arms to his sides, as
if to gather himself, then looked away.

"I'm sorry," he said. "I've been rather ill, I'm afraid. I would have
liked to come visit you, but of course I didn't want you to become sick
as well. Fortunately, I think I'm better today, but—"

I cut him off.

"The people who brought you here," I said, looking him in the face.
"Are they ever coming back?"

He drew a breath.

"Nobody brought me here," he said finally. "I walked."

"Really?"

"Yes, of course."

"Because that's not what you said at the time."

For a long moment, he was silent.

"Come on," I said. "Don't try to pull this stuff on me. I thought we
gave that up weeks ago."

He shifted his weight, rubbing one of his shoes against the other.
"Yes," he murmured, clearing his throat. "I suppose we did. I'm sorry."

"Look, I don't want to pry into your affairs. But I do want to help
you." I pushed hair out of my face. "I may not know exactly what
you're doing here, but I know that whatever the plan was, it's clearly
gone wrong. You didn't mean to be here, or if you did, you never
thought you'd stay for more than a day or two. And this may look like
the ends of the earth to you, but it isn't. You're not invisible. I don't
know what you're hiding from, but . . . this isn't the place for you.
You're not safe here." I balled my hands in my coat pockets. "And if
you can't see that, then you're not nearly as smart as I've been giving
you credit for."

While I was speaking, he had lowered his eyes, seeming to draw
himself inward. When I stopped, he squinted silently into the cold,
looking off into the trees.

"All right," I told him finally, "I've said my piece. Your business is
your business. If you need me, you know where I am."

I turned back toward the store and walked briskly down the hill, keeping my head high and my back straight. I had almost reached the porch before I heard his voice behind me. "Wait."

I looked over my shoulder. He was still hunched forward, and for once, he looked small.

"They're not," he said.

"What?"

"They're not coming back."

I regarded him evenly. "Why not?"

He seemed to be speaking to the ground. "I don't know."

"Were they supposed to?"

He swallowed. "Yes."

Slowly, stiffly, I began climbing the hill again.

"Let me help you," I said when I reached him, making every word clear. "Tell me what you need. I can't make any promises, but between Martin and me, I'm sure—"

"You do help me," he said. "You help me every day."

I shook my head impatiently. "That's not what I'm talking about. Tell me where you need to go, and one of us will get you there."

As I said the words, I felt a twinge of something unexpected, a grain of reluctance that chafed under my skin like sand. But I ignored it and kept my eyes on him until he answered.

He looked up at me, taking a long breath. "No," he said at last. "There's nowhere for me to go."

I studied him. "What about New York? I've never been there, but if you really want to disappear for some reason, I'm sure that's a much better place. I could get you there in a few hours." I thought about it. "Okay, more than a few. But I could take you."

"You're a lovely woman." His eyes fell on the ruins of the furnace stack. "But I can't let you do something like that."

"What do you mean, you can't let me?"

For a moment, he said nothing, his face still turned toward the collapsed stones.

"You're very smart, of course," he said finally. "But you don't under-stand what you're offering."

Something in the way he said it—*of course*—made me step back.

"Oh?" I said, surprised and stung. "And what is it that I don't understand, exactly?"

"I can't explain it."

"Try," I said sharply.

He sighed. "I'm sorry. I'm not trying to make you angry. And anyway, it doesn't matter. As I said, there's nowhere for me to go."

Scowling, I scuffed a shoe against the ground and spat contemptuously to the side, the way I'd seen so many men do. "So," I said, "what's the plan, then?"

"I don't know."

"Yes, that seems obvious."

We faced each other. He twisted his hands together, the knuckles cracking.

"What happened to you, there?" I asked.

"Sorry?"

"In your country. What happened?"

He gave me a long look, as if trying to read what was behind my eyes. But his face was carefully expressionless, and he said nothing.

"All right," I said at last. "Have it your way." Turning on my heel, I walked down to the store without looking back. This time, he didn't stop me.

Inside the store, I scraped the already-pristine grill, and then, restless, stalked back outside. The Jeep needed to be cleaned, I decided, and went at it, dragging out the floor mats and striking them with a stick. When the worst of the mud was gone, I gripped the pieces of carpet in my hands and shook them hard, until my back ached and my shoulder burned. I saw myself reflected in the windows, with disheveled hair and a face set like stone, and turned away impatiently.

As soon as closing time came, I drove off, uncertain of where I was going but not caring as long as it wasn't home. I knew I shouldn't leave my grandmother alone for much longer, but, I thought, if she wanted so badly to be independent, she could survive by herself for another hour.

On an impulse, as I neared the plaque marking the site of the former POW camp, I pulled over and tramped up the path to the entrance. There was a lot of dead undergrowth, but I fought through it, my boots crashing through the bracken. The old cement foundations began to appear, ghostlike, about half a mile in, long blank patches that invited curious—or, perhaps, sinister—minds to imagine what the buildings that had once stood there had been used for.

I sat on the cracking ledge by the former swimming hole and wrapped my arms around my knees, staring down at the ice, its impenetrable mottled gray.

The forest was so quiet my ears rang. I imagined the swimming hole as it would have been sixty years earlier, when very different people would have sat in this spot, sunning themselves where I now shivered. American soldiers, men who would have swum here when not keeping watch over the prisoners, splashing one another, stripped to the waist. Young guards who were now old men. It was so easy to picture them, square-jawed and smooth-skinned, their blue eyes untroubled.

I hugged my knees tighter as a vision of Jerry's face and dangling rifle crowded the soldiers out of my mind. Who ever knew, really, the things we were willing to do to each other when no one else was watching?

The darkness was falling, turning the trees into black nerves that stood out against the sky. In truth, I thought, I had yet to find out what happened if you went south of South Mountain or north of North Mountain. I hadn't managed to get myself out of this place, even when I'd tried—even when my life had, in a very real sense, depended on it. I had failed. And now I was watching someone else fail as well.

But he wasn't failing, I reminded myself. He was refusing. Which was what made it all the more infuriating, all the more incomprehensible. It was true, I allowed grudgingly, that life had been more interesting since he'd arrived. But this was no place for him.

Why wouldn't he leave if he could?

I stood up, brushing myself off, and plunged back through the woods again. By the time I reached home, it was late, and I stood at the counter chopping onions, the knife knocking dully against the cutting board. *You are a lovely woman. But you don't understand.*

Bullshit, I thought. *You think I'm dumb? Is that what you've thought all along?*

The phone rang.

When I didn't pick up, it rang again. I wiped my hands irritably, threw the towel down, and grabbed the receiver.

"Hello," the guttural voice at the other end of the line said. "May I speak to Kathleen Guttshall, please?"

"Kathleen McElwain," I said bluntly. I had dropped my married name as soon as they'd let me. "Speaking."

"Oh, hi, Kathleen," the voice replied pleasantly. "This is John."

I was still absorbed in my thoughts. "John?"

"John McCullough. We saw each other—"

"Oh." I paused. "Yes. Hey."

"Am I interrupting something?"

"No, it's fine." I crossed my arms and waited for him to continue, staring through the window into the darkness.

"Not sure if you remember, but we'd talked about you coming over for dinner sometime. I was wondering if you might like to come down on Sunday. I gotta get my engine fixed, but after that, I'm around. I'd love to show you the place."

I held the phone against my shoulder, picturing him as he had been that evening, standing there solidly in his jeans and flannel shirt.

"Well," I said.

The stranger's face appeared in my mind, wearing that expression that was almost too patient, too compassionate, as if I were the one to be pitied and helped. *You are very smart. But not smart enough.*

My stomach tightened.

"Sure," I said into the phone. "Sure, I'd like that. What time?"

The face in the rearview mirror was one I both avoided and couldn't stop looking at. Beth had made me up in pinks: blush, lipstick, a blue shirt with pink trim she'd brought over to my grandmother's house.

"Ugh," I'd said as she'd perched on the bathroom counter upstairs, dusting my face with various brushes. "I'm really not a pink person."

"Baloney. It looks great," she'd said, her hands moving in swoops and circles as a large brush tickled my face. "You wouldn't want anything darker—it would wash you out."

My grandmother's voice had reached us from the living room. "Kathleen!"

Beth had jumped, and we'd looked at each other and laughed.

"How does she do it?" Beth had whispered. "I could be a drill sergeant and she'd still scare the crap out of me."

"Yeah, I know. Don't ask me how she can yell like that when she's on oxygen."

My grandmother had bellowed again. "Why isn't the remote working?"

I'd sighed, and Beth had smiled. Despite the expression on her face, I'd noticed, there were deep circles under her eyes and her skin looked strangely dull, although her voice was as cheerful as ever. Something was wrong, I'd thought, something beyond Mark's absence. I'd remembered something she'd once told me about one of his furloughs, how he'd spent every night in the car with the engine off and the radio on, staring out into the dark. She could hear the station changing, scanning from talk radio to music, over and over, as if he didn't know or care what he was hearing. Just voices.

"Remind me what I'm supposed to call your grandmother these days, again?" she'd asked me under her breath.

"Oh, who even knows?" We'd descended the stairs and I'd gently taken the remote from my grandmother's grip. "You're holding it upside down," I'd told her.

She'd taken it back in her claw-like fingers and looked me up and down. "Johnny McCullough," she'd said after a moment, and I hadn't been sure if it was a question or an accusation.

"Yes." I'd told her earlier where I was going and had somehow managed to fend off a longer interrogation. "Don't forget to take your prednisone. And there's leftover chicken in the fridge. I'll be back before too long."

"I'll be fine. I'm always fine. You go on."

The farm where John lived was close to Shippensburg, in a wide stretch of rocky cornfields and winding roads known as Quarry Hill. As I drove, I pulled on a sweatshirt, covering the thin fabric that showed a keyhole of flesh at the throat. I didn't want him to get the wrong impression—that I normally looked like this, which I definitely didn't.

Besides, I told myself, he was probably drawn by curiosity more than anything. If I showed up looking as if I were actually taking the whole thing seriously, he would probably just laugh about it later. I would give him the benefit of the doubt, I thought, but I wasn't going to let him think I was a fool.

There was no town to speak of in Quarry Hill, just a scattering of farmhouses and trailers that were all distant from one another, most of them as worn-out looking as everything else in the valley. But when I found the mailbox with John's address and turned up a long, rutted driveway, I was startled to see a small but comfortable-looking house, its outside done in a modern-cabin style and its windows glowing.

I parked and stood looking up at it. There were neat blue-and-white curtains, a flagstone walk. This couldn't be the place, I thought. But a truck cab, shining as if recently washed, was parked on the grass beside me.

The door opened. John emerged, thumbs in his belt loops, smiling.

"Good thing you got four-wheel drive," he called. "I was worried you wouldn't make it. Driveway's hell on smaller cars, that's for sure."

"Naw, I made it." I found myself echoing his drawl.

"Yeah, I can see that. I'm glad." He was still smiling. "Come on in."

Awkwardly, I drew nearer. Was I supposed to shake his hand? Let him embrace me? Do nothing? But he solved my dilemma by turning and walking into the house.

I wasn't sure what I'd been expecting; probably something like the inside of just about every other house I'd seen, with the old, mismatched furniture, the chipped mementos on the shelves, the blankets with twelve-point bucks and leaping bass on them, maybe a wind chime dangling from the ceiling. But the inside of John's house was much like the outside, simple but somehow appealing, with heavy carved furniture he must have gotten from the Mennonites. A large black dog that had been stretched out in front of the fireplace stood up and walked toward us, stopping at a distance and sniffing idly in my direction. Everything looked warm and solid.

I found myself wondering if his wife had ever lived there, had maybe given the place its atmosphere. But no, I thought; he'd said they'd gotten divorced down south somewhere. He must have done all this himself.

He turned to me, reaching out.

"Can I take your coat?" he said.

5

The next morning, I sat behind the counter shooting rubber bands at the wall. There was a calendar over the sink, one with pictures of rivers and sunsets and the address of Martin's church printed at the bottom. I took aim at the photo for February, a red barn in the snow, sending my projectiles smacking crisply against the paper. When I ran out, I walked over to the sink and gathered them up again, returning to my seat for another round. The empty squares seemed to taunt me; all I ever did was cross them out, marking them off like a prisoner in a cell or a castaway on an island. I hooked the rubber bands on my forefinger, stretching them back as far as they would go. *Smack, smack, smack.* After striking the photo, they scattered lifelessly onto the floor.

I was thinking about John, about John's house. The man who had sat across the table from me, lifting salad onto my plate, both was and wasn't the man I'd been expecting. The voice was the same, and the scruffy look, the slow grin, but he was, somehow, a settled person, one who was at ease with himself and moved through his home as if it were the most natural thing in the world. The divorce hadn't exactly been amicable, he'd told me—"She was a real spitfire," he'd said, with more than a hint of admiration—but it seemed to have made him thoughtful, given him a depth I hadn't suspected. There was a light in his eyes, an awareness, that made me think he noticed more than he remarked on.

The dinner had lulled me, almost. I had been wary at first; it had felt like a setup, somehow. There were candles, pork roast, pie for dessert: he was overdoing it, I thought, almost embarrassingly so. Yet, as the evening wore on, I had found it difficult to stay on my guard. It was the depth of the house, I thought, the warmth of it, the satisfaction it seemed to take in itself. It was as if it had created a space for me, was waiting for me to join it, to complete it, to sink into it.

Collecting the rubber bands again, I took aim at the stark row of empty days. *Smack, smack, smack.*

The conversation hadn't been bad; in fact, I had to admit, it had even been good. Thanks to a fondness for radio news programs, he knew more about what was going on in the outside world than I did; he'd had a lot of time to listen, driving up and down the coast, all the way from Maine to the Florida swamps. "Yep," he'd said, spearing a piece of meat with his fork, "been all over. It's true what they say, though—no place like home. That's why I bought the house." He chewed and swallowed, his stubble glinting in the candlelight. "Figured it was time to settle down, start making shorter runs, get back to all the stuff I've been missing. Sit down at the end of the day in my own chair, in front of my own fireplace. Put down some roots. Being out on the road is great and all, but it gets old." He'd patted the stomach that hung over his belt, smiling. "You get to an age where you don't roll along quite so easy anymore."

"Yeah," I'd said, knowing it was the right thing to say even though I wasn't sure exactly what I was agreeing with.

He'd asked me about myself, nodding and letting it drop when I gave short answers. Then we'd moved on to horses: he was thinking about getting a pair, and the people who had previously owned the property had, incredibly, left behind most of their tack, which was still out in the barn. He was thinking about going to school, too, trying out some classes at the community college in Harrisburg, although he didn't know how keen he was on the idea. Classes were a lot cheaper than a horse, he joked, but at the end of the day, he wasn't sure which he'd be able to ride farther.

Horses, I thought as I perched on my stool, gazing at the calendar and the mess I was making. When I was a child, my grandfather had once bought a horse, a racehorse that ran on the local track. It was sleek and brown and, no longer young, would give me long, wise looks when I fed it carrots and apples. When my grandmother had found out that that was what my grandfather had done with their savings, she'd refused to speak to him for nearly a month. My grandfather had kept it for a year and then sold it, but it had stayed where it was, running on the same track week after week and standing patiently in the same stall. I had visited it once or twice, and it had continued to look at me serenely, its face noble and untroubled. For all I knew, it was still there, older and stiffer now but still eyeing everything around it with the same expression, its passage from owner to owner momentous to everyone but itself, just pieces of paper changing hands while its life remained precisely the same.

Restlessly, I scooped up the rubber bands and dumped them into a drawer. Then I poured two cups of coffee and went out.

The cups steamed as I climbed the hill, taking pains not to slip in the mud. I must look like some sort of magician, I thought, moving slowly toward the hostel, plumes of white vapor rising from my hands. There was a sound, and I looked up to see the stranger standing in front of the building, his hand still on the door he had just pulled shut. He came toward me.

"I'm so sorry," he began. "I've been thinking about what I said. Somehow I always seem—that is, I really didn't mean to—"

I thrust a coffee toward him.

"Tell me," I said, "about Paris."

The hot drink spilled onto my bare hand, burning the skin, but I pretended not to notice.

"Paris?" he repeated.

"Yes. Tell me about it. What it looks like, what it smells like, what the people do there. I want to know everything."

He took the cup from my hands, and we stood looking at each other, his eyes seeming to search mine.

"It was a long time ago," he said at last.

"I don't care," I said. "Just humor me. If you don't mind."

"You're not angry about the other thing? Because—"

I waved a hand. "We can talk about the other thing later."

"Well, all right." He shivered in the cold. "Where should we go?"

"I don't know." I glanced around us. "I could stand to get out of that stupid box for an hour or two. How about the game room?"

"Sure," he said, and the word had such an unexpected American ring to it that for a moment I had to hide a faint smile. He was a mimic at heart, I thought, even if he wasn't an especially gifted one.

"We can play chess while we talk," he was saying. "I can teach you some new openings."

I was already passing him, climbing the hill, digging my feet into the mud. "Whatever you want," I replied.

That night, for what I had to admit to myself was the first time in weeks, I didn't take the pills. I'd put more wood in the stove before going to bed, but the house was drafty, and gusts of cold reached me from the window. There was an ice storm coming, the radio had said.

I lay on my back on the mattress, looking up at the ceiling I couldn't see. Unlike in Carlisle, the darkness out here was absolutely dark, the silence absolutely silent. After a time, I felt as if I were floating, hovering a foot or two above the ground, spinning lightly in the void. I didn't mind, and sometimes, on nights like this, I even sought out the sensation. My mind would come untethered, voyaging through the unknown, the things only I could see. Most of the time, they were benign, just shapes and colors and fragments of memory. Sometimes, though, they were sharper, words and scenes I preferred to forget. One of the many benefits of the pills was that they took away the odds this would happen by eliminating the game altogether.

Tonight, however, I had decided to play.

The house I'd shared with Amos had nearly always been silent, except during the few hours when he was both home and awake, when the main sounds had been the voices from the TV and our own forks scraping against our plates. His job exhausted him, and over time, I had learned to be careful not to do things that disturbed his peace—so careful, in fact, that when he was in the room I barely stirred. I learned to listen without responding, except for a nod or a sympathetic shake of the head, and to sit on the edges of things. In books, I remembered—especially those for children—characters would sometimes pinch themselves to make sure they were real, that they weren't dreaming. I would look into mirrors, touch my own face or the corner of a table, reassuring myself of my own solidity. Of course, it wasn't really as bad as that; I never truly had any doubt that I still existed. It was just that the quiet seemed to press in on me somehow, to wrap me in a layer of something I couldn't see, slowing my movements, making me wonder whether I'd said things aloud.

I didn't leave the small set of rooms very often—Amos brought us everything we needed, and anyway we only had one car—but when I did, I found that I was increasingly unsure of what to do or say. A checkout girl would say hello as she swiped my gallon of milk, and I would hesitate before answering. I didn't want to say the wrong thing, because I had learned that I often said the wrong thing; on the other hand, I didn't want to seem unfriendly either. I would look down into my purse, smiling shyly, pushing my hair behind my ears as I waited for the transaction to be over. Not long after they opened the Walmart in Carlisle, I overheard a cashier there say she thought I was deaf.

"I'm not surprised," Amos said when I told him. "Everybody always said you weren't quite right. That's what they used to tell me, when I first started seeing you."

He had looked up from his dinner and smiled, so I wasn't sure if he was joking, but maybe he wasn't. Maybe I had always been strange. Or maybe, as he sometimes suggested, I was starting to lose my mind.

"Crazy Kathleen," he would say, stroking my cheek with his thumb. "Crazy, crazy Kathleen. You know I've started hearing about you from other people? Maybe you should just stay inside."

Soon, the things Amos heard began to change. "Somebody told me they saw you at the café in Boiling Springs. What were you doing there?"

"Nothing," I answered, taken aback by his obvious displeasure. "I went there after I picked up the groceries. You know, just for fun."

"Boiling Springs is fifteen minutes away from the grocery store. You drove half an hour round trip just to have fun?"

"I'm sorry. I just always thought it was pretty—you know, with the lake and everything."

"Did you meet anybody there?"

"Anybody? Like who?"

"Like your boyfriend."

"What?" I nearly dropped the glass I was drying. "What are you talking about?"

"I don't know. Why don't you tell me?"

I gaped at him.

He laughed then. "Come on, I'm just pulling your leg." Even so, there was an edge in his tone, or so I thought. Things weren't going well at his job. It had become hard to tell when he was actually angry and when he wasn't. Each day, I wondered which one of him would walk in through the front door: the one who kissed me on the head and rubbed my elbow affectionately as I cooked dinner, or the one who sat sullenly on the couch for hours, seeming to watch my every move. Eventually, I came to understand that it would be better if I didn't leave the house.

So I didn't.

I never knew what it was that made me give in, really. He was stronger than I was—thanks to the masonry job, he was stronger than just about anyone around—but that wasn't it. He wasn't violent, at least not in the way most people think of violence. He was still Amos, the same man I had always known, but I began to discover that there was something deeper in him, deeper than I had ever suspected, like the water at the bottom of a marsh, dark and lurking, rushing in to fill my footprints before I even realized it was there.

This quiet and reflective person, I discovered, the one who noticed everything and kept his thoughts to himself, was someone who knew—instinctively, uncannily—how to make other people feel small. He knew how to say the thing you least wanted to hear, the thing you always suspected might be true about yourself but prayed wasn't. He would say the thing so softly, with such an absence of anger or expression, that you knew it must be right.

"You look like a boy," he told me one night, as we were falling asleep. "It's like fucking a boy, every time I fuck you."

I had turned to look at him, but he was facing the window, settling his head into the pillows, pulling the blanket over his shoulders. I curled on my side and said nothing, but later that night I got up and silently crept to the bathroom, looking in the mirror, taking in the angle of my jaw, the shape of my nose and eyes. I didn't cry. I simply returned to bed and curled on my side again, drawing my knees to my chest, staring at the wall until the sun began to rise.

Increasingly, he would brood, sitting in an armchair in a darkened corner of the living room, the light from the TV flickering over his face. I could sometimes feel him giving me sidelong glances as I read.

"You make me feel wretched," he said one day, fixing me with a hard, peculiar stare from his armchair as I looked down at the book in my lap. There was a hostility in his tone, an accusation, that caught me off-guard. He kept his eyes on me until I closed the book.

The moment was unnerving enough that the next day, I picked up the phone. My pride wouldn't let me call Beth, so after some hesitation—I realized I was no longer in touch with very many people—I dialed the dentist's office where my high-school friend Melanie was working as a receptionist.

"Wretched?" she repeated. A child was shouting in the background, and I thought I could hear the sound of her chewing something. "Is that some kind of slang, like 'wicked'? Like, maybe he means it in a good way?"

I looked out through the window, at the sun playing over the empty fields where, as I had been made to understand, I had no reason to go walking alone.

"I don't think so," I said.

One day, when I was washing the dishes, he crept up behind me, pinning my arms to my sides and holding a paring knife to my throat, a sharp, silvery blade with a short handle. I was silent, motionless, stunned. For some reason, as the edge of the blade touched my skin, I kept looking at the cans of baked beans on the counter, the ones that were waiting for me to put them away. Later, that was what I remembered: cans of beans. Everything else around me seemed blurred, dark.

I could feel him breathing behind me.

After a moment, he put the knife down. He seemed to think it was funny.

"You weren't really scared, were you?" he asked.

I reached for the dishrag, which had fallen into the water. "No," I said softly, beginning to rub hardened lumps of tomato sauce from a plate. The water turned a pale pink.

Looking back, it would be tempting to think of that moment as the beginning of the bad things. But of course, by then the bad things had long since taken root and begun to push their hard, blind way up to the surface. Years later, I would ask myself what I could have done differently, what I could have done to prevent the disasters. The question would come to me even when I knew enough to try to force it out of my mind, when I understood that there was, in fact, nothing I could have done. People are who they are, and he was who he was. There was no point in being angry with him—no point even in thinking about it.

But the thing about moments like that, as I was to learn, was that they were never truly over. Instead, they lingered just out of sight in the forgotten spaces of our own minds, wreaking havoc invisibly no matter how long or how determinedly we put them away.

6

"Oh, honey, he sounds *lovely*," Beth said a few days after I saw John, hugging my shoulders as we sat on the couch. Leaning forward, she handed a cup of bright red fruit punch to Dylan, who was kneeling by the TV, idly running a toy truck back and forth over the carpet while keeping his eyes fixed on the cartoon children who sang in front of him. His lips were open in an O, as if he were hypnotized.

"It was okay," I admitted grudgingly.

Beth was watching the back of the boy's head, her expression momentarily pensive, but turned her attention back to me. "Don't get me wrong—I'm not saying you should marry the guy. But you should definitely let him spoil you a little. And if it turns into something more, then great." She sat back and crossed her legs on the cushions. "You could use something to cheer you up. You know, get you out of that rut."

I frowned at her. "What rut?"

"Don't look at me like that. You know what I mean." She propped her head on her hand. "Not that relationships are a magic bullet, God knows. But still—I just want to see you happy."

I turned the toy truck upside down and spun the wheels with my thumb. "I am happy," I said.

"Are you?"

"Yes," I said flatly.

She looked at me and ran a hand through her hair, exposing a streak of gray that stood out startlingly against the black. I tried not to think about her uncle, his resemblance to her. "All right. I know better than to beat my head against a wall."

On the TV, the cartoon children were exploring a river, sailing through a dream world on their flying ship.

"So what's new with you?" I asked, trying to shift her attention away from myself.

"Oh, God, nothing. I'm in a rut, too, although of course mine's for the good of the country, et cetera, et cetera." She opened a soda that was sitting on the coffee table. "You know, everybody likes to run around saying it's a Very Important Job, being a military wife. But I don't see many of them rushing to sign up for it." She gestured around us at her parent's living room, the piles of toys in the corners and the heap of laundry next to us on the sofa. "I love my husband, and my kid's my whole world, but sometimes I wonder what people must really think of me if they're basically going to imply this is the best thing I ever could have done." She studied the can. "Are you scandalized that I said that?"

"Of course not."

"Well, good." She smiled. "But probably, you shouldn't listen to me—this poor guy was up three times last night and I'm just full of sour grapes today." Reaching across the table, she ruffled her son's hair. "Really, though, I think you should go on another date with what's-his-name. What do you have to lose?"

The characters on the screen held hands and began another song.

"I don't know. I just don't think it would work." The tune was beginning to annoy me slightly, although I tried not to show it. "Besides, I find it hard to believe he's anything more than a curiosity-seeker. I'm not sure what else he would actually want with me."

"Bullshit. He *obviously* likes—wait." Her eyes moved from the TV to me. "'Curiosity-seeker'?"

"Yeah." Internally, I scolded myself for having said it so openly. Deep down, I wasn't sure I really meant it, and anyway there was no need to go digging up things we both so carefully left unexpressed.

"What are you talking about?" she asked. "Curious about what?"

I gave a small laugh. "You know," I replied awkwardly.

"No, I don't know. What are you, a carnival? Why would you be drawing curiosity-seekers?"

I didn't understand why she was pretending not to know what I meant. But she was still waiting for me to go on.

"Because of what happened."

She still looked perplexed.

I searched for the right words. "Because people think I was . . . involved. You know that. I'm sure you do."

"Involved?"

"Well, I mean obviously I was 'involved.' But they think I'm responsible."

"What on earth are you talking about?"

"You know." I couldn't bring myself to say *for the accident*, but I knew I didn't need to.

She was staring at me.

"I don't think they've decided exactly why or how," I admitted. "I'm not totally self-centered; I know they don't just sit around thinking about something that happened all those years ago to somebody else. But they have an idea that it's my fault. That I did it. You know . . . on purpose. It's not very fair, but it is what it is. I don't blame them, but that doesn't mean I have to let them hang around and make a fool out of me."

"Kathleen," she said, and I was surprised by how upset she sounded. "That's crazy. Where did you hear this?"

"Nowhere, exactly. I just know. It's all right—I don't really care."

"But it's not true." Her words were almost breathless.

I put the toy truck down on the table. We both looked at it.

"Honey," she said. "I mean it. Go get the Bible from my parents' room, and I'll swear it to you. I see the same people you do, and I have never—never, never—heard anyone say anything even remotely like that."

"They don't have to say it. But like I said, it's okay. Really, I don't care."

She sat back and looked at me.

"Is that what *you* think?" she asked finally.

"What?"

"Do you think you're responsible for what happened?"

For a moment, I was left speechless. "Of course not. Why would I think that?"

She leaned toward me, folding her hands on her knees. "Because it would explain a lot."

I drew back. "I have no idea what you mean."

It was her turn to search for words that would somehow say what she wanted to say without actually saying it.

"You think I feel guilty about the crash?" My voice was higher than usual, incredulous. "Or the things that came before it?"

"It's occurred to me to wonder."

I sat still, feeling short of breath.

"The most frustrating thing," she said slowly, "for me, as your friend, as someone who loves you and thinks you're the smartest person she knows, is the way you've just sat back and let things happen to you ever since that time. That stupid store that takes advantage of you. Your parents who run around doing God knows what while you take care of your grandmother. All of it. You just let it happen and don't fight it. It kills me. And I do ask myself why that's happening."

"I don't know what you're talking about," I said, shocked and with rising anger.

She gave me a look that had miles of unspoken thought behind it. "I have trouble believing that."

"The only thing I feel," I replied forcefully, "is anger at that man. You have no idea how much. It burns me. It keeps me awake at night." Even saying these things made a feeling rush to my head, something swift and blinding. "It's the only thing I've ever felt and the only thing I ever will. I don't have room for anything else. I'm sure I'd be a better person if I did, but I don't. You don't know what I'd do to him if I ever saw him again." All those things I thought about at night, that I knew I shouldn't think about, that I imagined happening to him. The ways I would make him plead for forgiveness that I would never give. The ways I would make him suffer. "I've never felt guilty—not for a second. Because I'm not. He is."

She paused, clearly choosing her words carefully. "I know you say those things," she said. "Or rather, I know you think them. But you loved him. At one time. You did. I remember it." She searched my face, looking into my eyes. "And it was a loss, when everything fell apart. When he turned around and started doing all those things you think I don't know about. You were devastated. You *are* devastated. But somehow, he made you think it was all your fault. And somewhere at the bottom of all that sadness you're pretending isn't there, I think you still think that. That's what's so hard." She rubbed her eyes. "Sometimes, I think you still believe everything he ever said about you. And that you'll stay where you are, day after day, year after year, just burning yourself up, because of it."

The fury was so powerful I thought I would choke. "There's not a thing," I told her, "not a *thing* that man said that I believe. I hope he's in a place where he's paying for every word of it. *I* chose this. Everything you see me doing is *my* decision. I'm taking care of my grandmother because that's what a good person does. I'm working because I have to work. And I'm out doing what I have to do and what makes me happy. It's not for you to question that. It's not for anyone to say I'm such an idiot that I'm still under that—" There was no word for him. "—That asshole's spell."

"Take it easy," she said, reaching for my hands. "I'm not calling you an idiot. I'm just worried. I feel like I sit here watching you set yourself on fire day after day. You're too proud to admit you're in pain, so you're doing more damage instead. Like some kind of—well, penance, almost. Something that only hurts you over and over. How am I supposed to stand back and watch that?"

I pulled my hands away, scowling even as my body cringed away from her, as if it feared what she was saying.

"You have no right," I began, "no right—"

As I sputtered, trying to get the sounds out without losing control, Dylan upended his cup. The lid came loose, sending a wave of red juice over his arms and legs, the white carpet. Looking at it, and at us, he began to wail.

"Oh, shit," Beth sighed. "Shit, shit, shit. Sorry, hon." She touched my shoulder. "Just wait here, okay?"

But I didn't wait. As she hurried into the kitchen, I stood up and walked out the door.

It was inventory time at the store. I spent my days in the back room, holding a clipboard as I counted the boxes, making note of what had expired, what needed to be ordered, what we had somehow accumulated too much of, like gummy worms. Although I wouldn't have said so to anyone else, it was almost soothing, this responsibility for categories and numbers, for imposing order on the universe. I kept my mind fixed on the columns of handwritten figures, as if I were holding my breath, thinking about this task and only this task.

Most days, the stranger would invite me up to the game room to play chess during my lunch hour, and in that, too, I was brisk and resolute. I still lost, but my moves were crisp and decisive, and that counted for something, I thought.

Twice, I came home to find the light on the answering machine blinking. The first time I pressed the button, John's voice emerged, steady and cheerful, telling me he'd gotten the horses, two mares, and he'd be glad if I came over to try them out.

The second time, it was Beth. She was sorry; these things had been on her mind for a long time; she'd wanted to help; obviously the words had come out wrong. After I listened, I stood there for a moment, then erased the message. When I'd hung up, I could sense my grandmother hovering behind me like an owl, blinking, watching me with her watery eyes while she leaned on the walker my father had forced her to get. I turned away and ignored her.

In the store, I combed through the shelves, homing in on dented cans and torn packets, hauling them out to the dumpster until my hip ached and my face was covered with dust. First Loretta Lynn, then Patsy Cline sang out of the cassette player. I warbled loudly along with Patsy as I dragged boxes toward the door, refusing to acknowledge the stinging in my shoulder.

Eventually, I emerged to find Martin standing by the dumpster, eyeing the boxes and trash bags. "Dispensing justice with an even hand, I see."

"As always." I wiped the dust from my eyes with the back of my wrist.

"Mind if I bring some stuff down and work on the porch?"

I hefted a box into the metal bin and shrugged. "Do what you want."

I've got your memory . . . Patsy sang woefully. *Or . . . has it got me?* I hit the fast-forward button impatiently; sometimes, the woman sounded like she'd never had a moment of happiness in her life.

Martin's "stuff," it turned out, was a bag full of parts for the mystery machine. I paused on my way out the door with a full garbage bag, looking down at the jumble of metal.

"It's a bicycle," I said.

He moved down into a squat, holding a washer up to the light. "I'm not saying anything. You'll just have to wait and see." Reaching into his back pocket, he pulled out a pair of reading glasses I had never seen, pushing them onto his nose. They made him look worldlier, I thought, almost sage-like.

After watching him for a moment, I sighed and sat down, propping the bag against the wall.

It was the first time I had truly been still all week. I folded my hands and felt my back relax.

The stranger had found a guitar in the game room a few days earlier, and the sound of it drifted down the hill. I didn't want to tell him he could be heard, although I knew I probably should. The meandering tunes always made me imagine him as a student, just like any other,

WAYS TO HIDE IN WINTER

sitting outside a bar or café in his mysterious city and picking out a tune, surrounded by laughing friends, an admiring future wife, people smoking and drinking merrily around him, beckoning to passersby on the street. There was something about the vision that left me unable to shake the feeling that it was real, that this really had been him in earlier and happier days, the plucked notes floating through the night air, soft and invisible, like seeds from a dandelion.

"What are we going to do about him?"

Martin was glancing over the parts that surrounded him, looking contentedly mystified. "Who?"

I nodded toward the hostel. "Him."

He followed my gaze, then looked at me over the rims of the glasses. Picking up a bolt, he rolled it between his thumb and forefinger. "You know, I worked in a pet shop once, before everything. We didn't name the animals, because the theory was that that way we wouldn't get attached to them." He seemed to wait for me to answer. When I didn't, he said, "It didn't work, in case you were wondering."

I let this pass, partly because I was still taking in the words "before everything." Everyone knew about the stretch of years when Martin had left, although no one had ever asked him directly where he had gone during that time. I had been young then, too young to hear more than mutterings or understand what they meant. If anyone had ever tried to press him for details, he hadn't given any, and he and I had certainly never talked about it.

"I sometimes wish you weren't so smart," I said instead.

"And I," he replied, "am grateful every day that you are." Reaching for two hollow bars, he held their flattened ends together to see if the bolt would fit through the hole, but it didn't. He scratched his head and put the bars back down.

"I'm sorry," I said, looking down into my palms. "I feel like I haven't been as kind to you lately as you are to me."

"Well, I tend to agree with you, to be honest. But it's okay. We all have our rough times, I know." He sat back on his heels. "Anything you want to talk about?"

"No, I'm okay. But I do want to figure out what we should do about—"

"Danya. Yes, I know." He found a washer that matched the bolt, but closed his hand around it. "I don't think there's anything to be done," he said after a moment. "He's an adult, so it's not like anybody can force him to go anywhere. And I'm not going to kick him out. As far as I'm concerned, there'll always be a room here for someone who needs it. He's not much of a burden, and he's good about helping me out." He sat back and stretched out his legs. "Sometimes, I'm tempted to ask if he wants to take over the place so I can go riding off into the sunset."

"I'm serious."

"Yeah, I know. I just don't know what else to tell you. Wish I did." He folded his legs back under him. "We're all trying to do what we think is best."

The isolated notes continued to reach us, sliding by as the invisible presence uphill felt around for the tune. I imagined his bowed head and lowered eyelids, the concentration in his face. The pictures, the ones from my searching about Uzbekistan, appeared in my memory, and I found myself looking over my shoulder toward the hill that led to the road, the one that ran past the prison camp. A thought came into my mind, and I turned it over, pondering it without fully understanding its shape yet.

"Did you ever hear," I said eventually, "anything about a sweat box?"

Martin had resumed trying to fit metal pieces together. "A what?"

"A sweat box. Up at the old camp. Like . . . some kind of shed where they put people in the summer to punish them. To make them too hot."

"You mean that POW camp they had during the war? No, I've never heard anything like that." He thought about it, his expression puzzled. "Actually, I almost never hear anything at all about that place. Why?"

I looked down at the toe of my shoe as it swung above the boards. "Do you think it could be true?"

He scooped up a handful of screws and began sorting them into piles with a finger. "Well, I don't think I could say without knowing more about it." I watched him look up and think of something else. "Also, you know, this is America."

"And?"

"Oh, don't be so cynical. I mean, I'm as clearheaded as the next guy about some of the stuff we've done. My uncles were all in the 'Nam. But no, I'm not sure I could believe we brought a bunch of guys back here so we could stick them in some kind of torture device." Still holding the screws, he began arranging the bars around him, like a skeleton. "Doesn't that seem a little inefficient to you?"

"I heard there was one. And I think people will do just about anything if they think they have a right to do it."

He shook his head.

"I prefer," he said, "to have some faith in my fellow man. I assume people are good until I have a reason to believe otherwise.

I kicked a toe against the floorboards. "You must deal with a lot of disappointment."

"Nope—almost never. In fact, I've found it's not at all a bad way to go through life." Picking up a bar, he seemed to hesitate. "You know, I know sometimes things happen that—I understand life gets tough sometimes. Believe me, I get that. But no matter what happens, I think it's best to be able to trust other people. Without that . . . well, you lose yourself. You wind up doing things you regret. And I wouldn't want to see that happen to someone like you." His forehead wrinkled. "I think it would be something of a tragedy, actually."

He put the bar back down, and I walked to the dumpster, the bag dangling from my hand. Heaving it into the yawning gap, I stood there, knowing I should thank him, unable to repress a shudder.

One day, not long before the end, I'd lost my mind.

Things hadn't been so bad in the preceding weeks; it was early summer, warm, and the red, white, and blue bunting was still hanging in Carlisle where we'd gone to the Memorial Day parade a few days before. We'd sat on the sidewalk, watching the fire trucks and knots of Little League players and Girl Scouts go by, Amos holding my hand, people jabbering away happily in lawn chairs behind us, jumbo cups of iced tea in their hands. Some men in army and navy uniforms had gone by, waving, and Amos had waved back; they were his friends. "No one's ever gonna throw me a parade," he'd sighed, but when I'd glanced at him warily, he'd been smiling.

I'd smiled back, my lips closed, hovering above the scene in my imagination as I often did. Even though I'd left school, I couldn't quite bring myself to think of myself as just another woman in cut-off shorts watching the parade in Carlisle, one whose future was written in the faces and bodies of all the other women around her. The light glinted on the great brass curves of the tubas, the cheerleaders' pom-poms, the rows of children passing by, waving at people they knew in the crowd. Amos's hand was solid and warm, anchoring me to the earth. I'd leaned against him, unsure how he would react, and to my relief, he'd put his arm around me. When the cheerleaders went by, I'd expected him to make some remark, but he didn't, simply kissing me on the head. I'd felt myself relax. This was how I got through the days: by the hour, the minute, like a swimmer holding her breath. When viewed that way, things didn't seem so bad. I could get by, I thought.

Then he lost his job.

Even though I hadn't enjoyed being alone in the house all day, rattling from room to room, there had been a freedom that came with it, a freedom—at least within that small, closed sphere—to do what I pleased. With Amos home, sitting in the living room, staring out the window, I had to be careful all the time. I lost my moments of standing at the kitchen sink, looking at the fields. If I tried to do that, Amos would come up behind me, twisting my arm in a way he seemed to think was playful but hurt nonetheless. "What are you thinking about?" he would ask.

"Nothing," I would say, and it was the truth. At those times, I was doing my best not to think, especially about the moment with the paring knife. It lay within me like a cold weight, like a certainty, but I never wanted to think about it again.

I'd had a friend in high school, a shy, heavy, soft-faced senior with long dyed-black curls that hung over the Led Zeppelin and Marilyn Manson T-shirts she always wore. She wasn't my friend, really, although she might have been if things had turned out differently. She'd been in my gym class, and we'd always said hello to each other in the hallways; we must have sat together in the cafeteria a few times, too, because later I found that I could clearly remember her face, the way her eyes would crinkle as she listened to other people's jokes and drank her chocolate milk. She wore rainbow-patterned bracelets made of string and had dimples when she smiled and was in the special-education classes, the ones for kids who didn't exactly have anything wrong with them but were just slower than the others for whatever reason. We all knew she had a boyfriend, a stringy-looking guy in his thirties, and I must have met him at least once, at a party or something, because somehow I knew what he looked like even before they ran his picture in the news-paper. One night in the spring, he'd taken her into the woods, made her kneel by a creek, and shot her in the back of the head.

He had gone to jail—at least, I thought he must have gone to jail—and in the photos in the paper he'd had this look on his face, hollow-eyed and hunted and mean-looking, as if he couldn't believe he were being persecuted this way. Maybe it was just the way the photo was taken, but looking into his eyes, his open mouth, was like gazing into some kind of horrible void.

I began to get the same sensation when I looked at Amos some-times. Not always; until the very end, he had his days of kindness. But I began to think of my friend, to picture her sitting across from me in the cafeteria with her colorful bracelets and her chocolate milk, her elbows on the table, covering her face with her hand as she laughed.

He—her boyfriend—had shot her at the bottom of her skull, near the nape of her neck. The bullet had come out through the front. That's what the newspaper had said.

Her face would have been gone when they buried her.

I tried not to think of this, but found that I couldn't escape it. It often happened when I was looking in the bathroom mirror, lingering in the only place in the house where I could shut myself away and be alone. I would see her, and I would see myself seeing her, my eyes looking back at me from the glass. I would look away, but I could never quite escape it, that glimpse of myself that told me so much I would rather not have known.

"Why are you looking at me like that?" Amos asked once. Not angry, exactly, or at least not yet.

"Like what?"

"I don't know. It's sort of strange. You just look at me like I'm not even there."

"I know you're there."

"Yeah?" To my surprise, he walked over to where I was sitting and leaned down to kiss me on the forehead. "You still love me?"

"Yes," I said. "Of course I do."

If he heard anything odd in my tone of voice, he didn't let on.

One night not long after that, I had just pushed a casserole into the oven and was wiping my hands on a towel when Amos called to me from the living room.

"Come sit here," he said.

I perched on the couch next to him, the TV murmuring in the background. Reaching for me, he began kissing me, sliding his hand inside my shirt. I let him do it, and, a few minutes later, I heard the sound of him unfastening his pants. I stayed where I was, knowing better than to move away, even though I was already beginning to worry about the food burning.

To my confusion, he then slid his belt free of its loops and, as I sat there, put it around my neck, looping the end with the holes through the end with the buckle. Then he sat back and pulled.

The leather tightened around my throat, and I moved toward him involuntarily. He moved farther off, sliding across the couch and pulling again, as if I were a dog on a leash. I slipped my fingers between the belt and my neck, trying to loosen it.

"Don't," he said. Then he stood up and tugged harder.

"Stop," I said.

"Don't you tell me to stop," he replied, pulling again. I found myself on the floor, on my knees.

"It's sexy," he said. "I think it's sexy." Then he added, "You know I could kill you like this?"

I looked up at him, taken aback. Several long seconds passed while I knelt there, my hands at my throat, realizing for the first time—as if I had felt a tremor in the earth—what true fear was like.

After a moment, a strange expression came over his face, and he dropped the belt, walking away, shaking himself as if he too were disturbed by what he had done.

When I put the food on the table, we sat down and ate. Neither of us mentioned what had happened.

The next morning, something in me snapped. I didn't mean for it to happen, but it did. Amos was out, and I was cleaning the house, turning on the radios as I moved from room to room so I wouldn't be alone in the silence, not caring what was playing. Suddenly, the house was filled with a cacophony of voices from different stations, and I stood in the middle of it, a rag dangling from my fingers. Without quite knowing what I was doing, I moved down the stairs, putting one foot in front of the other. Then I was stepping into the sunlight and closing the front door behind me. I dropped the rag in the grass next to the house and began to walk, my hands still smelling of cleaning solution and my hair tied back in a bandanna. I didn't bring money. I didn't bring a change of clothes. I didn't bring anything.

I just went.

My feet took me to the county road, then the state one. I passed the fields, the old oak trees, the spring that ran under the small bridge by the railroad tracks. The fire company slid by on my left, then Miller's on my right, and then the mountain stood in front of me, imposing and green. I walked along the shoulder of the road, my eyes fixed ahead, my shoes leaving prints in the dust. My T-shirt began to cling to me, sticky with sweat, but I kept going, up the long ascent that flew by when you were driving. The sun was burning my forearms, my thighs—I was pale after so many months indoors—but I pushed on, into the shade of the trees. The cars and pickups would slow as they passed me, and finally one picked me up, carrying me to Gettysburg. I rolled down the window and let the breeze cool my face while the driver—an old man in suspenders, compact, with a face covered with white stubble—smoked a cigar. He didn't say anything, and neither did I.

When we got to Gettysburg, I stepped out, looking up at the other side of the mountain. The smoothly paved road, whose tar bubbled and fumed, took me through the canning towns, past the factories and the small knots of houses where, by and large, nobody lived. My knees ached, and I was thirsty, but the sun mysteriously seemed to have taken away my hunger, to have drawn it up out of me. I kept going, my canvas shoes beginning to fall apart, the left sole flapping when I took a step. For a little while, I stopped to rest outside an old schoolhouse, watching the clouds to the west begin to grow orange and red. When a car slowed in front of me, however, I waved it away and stood up, moving on.

It was long after dark by the time I reached Orrtanna. The light over the sign for the church was the only one for what seemed like miles; it shone by the side of the road, Father MacIntyre's name and the mass times seeming to hover in the blackness. Around me, the crickets and frogs sang, a soft but impenetrable backdrop of noise. There was no sign of life in the ranch houses and trailers that dotted the road, nor in the rectory, whose steps I soon mounted. I knocked on the door, holding my breath. The night air was chilly, and I wrapped my arms around myself, allowing my mind to form a complete, coherent thought for the first time that day: I wished I'd brought a jacket. And I would have sold everything I owned for a glass of water.

I raised a hand to my throat, where the belt had been. There weren't any marks there. Not that I had seen.

The priest opened the door in his undershirt, his hair—already white by then—drooping over his forehead and his eyes frightened and watery behind his glasses. He was stooped forward, his chin thrust out, but when he saw me he straightened in surprise and befuddlement. "Oh," he said. "It's Mrs.—Mrs.—"

"Kathleen," I said. I hadn't expected him to recognize me at all; I hadn't been to mass since I'd gotten married. I rubbed my bare arms, shivering slightly.

"Come in," he said, switching on a light in the hallway. "Come in, come in." Turning around, he beckoned to me over his shoulder, and I followed him. The corridor was narrow, the wallpaper a fading red and gold, and as he led the way with unsteady steps, I felt as if I were being drawn into a cave. It was only a sitting room, however: the same as any sitting room in the valley, with a pair of old reclining chairs, a flowered loveseat, shag carpet. A boxy TV sat on a table, its antennae casting shadows on the wall. The priest turned on a lamp. "Sit down, sit down. What brings you here? Actually, if you'll forgive me, I need to excuse myself for just a moment, but do have a seat."

I perched on the edge of one of the reclining chairs, embarrassingly aware that he had excused himself to use the toilet. While he was gone, I looked around the room, fidgeting. For some reason, I expected that when he returned, he would be wearing the robes in which I'd always seen him, but when he sat down across from me he was still in the stretched white undershirt. He leaned toward me, clasping his arthritic hands together.

Amos would have been looking for me for hours by now, I realized dimly. He would be frantic.

"What can I do for you, Kathleen? What's the matter?" The priest pushed his glasses up his nose, fixing me with a look that was sympathetic but wary. Before I could go on, he looked down. "Goodness gracious, you've hurt your feet."

I glanced down, too, and saw that blood was soaking through the toe of one of my shoes. "I'm sorry," I said quickly, pushing myself out of the chair. "I—"

"No, just stay there, it's all right. Let me get you some bandages. Do you think you need a doctor?"

"No, I'm sure they're just blisters." I looked around, more embarrassed than ever. The only thing in the room that would reveal this to be a priest's house was a painting of the Virgin that hung in a corner.

There were some dusty spider plants, an ashtray with a coating of gray on it. The priest hurried off again, and I heard the clicking of a light switch, followed by a rustling and clinking in what I assumed was the kitchen.

I leaned back in the chair, gazing up at the painting. It was ordinary, just the Virgin by herself, blue-robed, modest, grieving for the world. I looked away and closed my eyes. The smell of stale cigarette smoke that clung to the chair was vaguely comforting, and I rested my head against the upholstery, breathing deeply, listening to the indistinct murmuring that came from the kitchen.

When I opened my eyes again, there was a glass of water on the table beside me, along with a dusty box of Band-Aids. The priest was seated across from me, reading a book. He had put on a sweater.

"Thank you," I said, reaching gratefully for the water and draining the glass. "How long was I asleep?"

"Not long. Just a short nap. You've obviously had a bit of a walk." He rose to fetch another glass of water and settled in again. "Now, tell me how I can be of help."

The day came back to me.

"My husband," I said.

"Yes?"

"I just—" I didn't know what to say, and I found myself stumbling into the truth before stumbling back out again. "I ran away. Not really. I just needed to get out for a day."

"I see." He adjusted his glasses, crossing his legs and wrapping his hands around his knee. "And what brought you here?"

"I don't know." Then I said the thing I had never admitted to myself before. "I—I'm afraid. Sometimes."

Picturing Amos behind the wheel of his truck, furious, worried, searching for me, I felt a quickening of guilt—of panic—but pushed it aside.

"What are you afraid of?" He squinted at me with a look of concern. "Does he hit you?"

"No, it's—well. Not exactly."

"Not exactly?"

"He does other things. It's hard to explain."

"What kinds of things?"

I shook my head. My feet hurt, and I stretched them in front of me, looking down at them.

The priest peered at me, his head seeming to bob slightly. The skin of his neck hung in folds over his Adam's apple, as if it, too, were tired. He steepled his fingers in front of him.

"You're Howard's granddaughter," he said.

I looked up, unsure if this was a question. "Howard and Lydia. Yes."

"I see."

I didn't see, but I stayed quiet, watching him watch his fingertips.

"Is your husband happy?" he asked finally.

"No. Yes. Sometimes." I toyed with the box of Band-Aids. "He lost his job."

"Ah," he said, as if he'd discovered something. "Yes, yes. Of course."

"But I don't think that's it," I hastened to add. "Not really."

"Men are at their weakest at times like that. Most prone to err." He nodded, as if he were agreeing with me.

"Well—yes. But even before—"

"He must be very unhappy," he went on, as if he hadn't heard. "Very unhappy indeed. You know, as Christians, it's our duty to love those who are suffering, and help them see the right path."

He paused.

"Um," I said.

"Just think of Christ on the cross," he continued. "The pain he bore in order to redeem us. He's an example to us all. There are times when we all have to endure certain things in order to remain true to God's will. That's what love means."

I found myself watching his face, something within me slowly seeming to break off and fall away, a cliff sliding into the ocean.

"Be patient," he continued, his tone growing easier. "Many marriages go through difficult periods. But with time, and love, we can all grow and change." He coughed into his palm and shifted in his seat, sitting up straighter. "Just be patient and have faith. God united you with your husband, and if you obey him"—I blinked, unsure whether he meant Amos or God—"if you obey him, you'll find that you grow and learn together. I've seen it happen with many couples in my time. Go home, forgive your husband, and ask for his forgiveness. That's the only thing to do."

The lamp made a pool of light on the floor. I looked at him, his face that was half in shadow, my mind searching for words and finding none. It was warm in the room, and I suddenly realized a smell hung over the place, something artificially floral, sickening and heavy.

There was a sound outside, the unmistakable crunch of tires in a driveway, someone pulling in and hitting the brakes hard. My head jerked up, and I shot a stunned look at him, the shriveled old man in the chair across from me, my eyes asking a question he didn't answer.

"Everyone is capable of change," he said. "Everyone can be redeemed. That's the very premise of our faith, isn't it? What can we believe, if we can't believe that?"

There was a second crunching, the sound of motors, car doors. I pushed myself to my feet, staring down at him, terrified.

"Wait," I said. "Let me stay. Don't send me back. I'll go tomorrow, I'll—"

There was a knock on the door, knuckles against the glass, loud and sharp.

"That must be your father," the priest said, pushing himself to his feet. "I called him while you were resting. I do hope I haven't—"

The door opened, and Amos strode in, enormous, seeming to fill the hallway. His head lowered, he looked at me from under his brows. His breathing was uneven, as if he were trying to keep himself from shouting, or weeping.

"Let's go," he said to me, not acknowledging Father MacIntyre.

Paralyzed, I glanced from him to the old man, gripping the arm of the chair. The priest was standing uncertainly, looking from one of us to the other.

Amos grasped my wrist, turned, and marched out. I followed him, my steps stuttering, emerging into the night air behind his broad back.

Outside the house, as if in a dream, my parents were sitting in their truck, staring at Amos, at me. They looked confused, frightened. They got out, their mouths open, but they seemed to have lost their voices.

Amos passed by them, not turning his head, dragging me after him as his fingers dug into my arm. I glanced back over my shoulder and saw them standing there like statues, my mother's hair fluttering in the night breeze, both of them pressed back against their truck as if pinned there.

They let me go.

Amos's pickup rumbled down the mountain, bearing us back, back to the house where the rag I'd dropped still lay in the yard. Later, all I would remember about the ride would be the sharp smell that seemed to rise from my own body, a mingling of sweat and fear.

"I'm sorry," I said as he turned off the engine. He nodded and opened his door, getting out with the solid sound of steel-toed boots against asphalt. I looked quietly through the windshield as he made his way to my side. The door next to me opened with a creak.

He helped me down. I looked up at him, but he turned away and walked into the house.

In the kitchen, there was a cup of coffee on the table, cold, next to the cordless phone. The creamer had formed a skin on top. The chair in front of the cup was pushed back, and I pictured Amos sitting there, hunched over, staring at the phone, waiting for it to light up.

He sat down heavily and unlaced his boots. I stood by the sink, waiting without being sure what I was waiting for. A dim, grayish glow was beginning to appear on the horizon. The grass outside was wet with dew.

Finally, with a sigh, he stood, pressing his knuckles into the table. Rubbing his face with his hands, he moved toward me, seeming to look past me, through the window. Then, with a gentleness that surprised me, he took my elbow, turning me and steering me back toward the door. We walked into the garage, the empty, oil-stained space where the truck was usually parked. As my eyes adjusted to the dark—taking in the same rows of shelves and boxes as usual, the saws and wrenches hanging on the wall, a bag of nails on the workbench—he released my elbow. I felt him look down at me. Then he walked back into the house, closing the door behind him.

I stood still for a moment, bewildered. There didn't seem to be anything I needed to clean up, any boxes to pack or unpack. In my confusion, I almost forgot my exhaustion, my throbbing feet.

Glancing around, still finding nothing unusual, I approached the door and turned the knob.

It was locked.

"Amos?" I whispered.

There was no answer.

Outside, far away, I heard a rooster crow on one of the Mennonite farms, its sound in the distance a thin wail.

I rattled the knob again, harder this time. Gathering my courage, I called more loudly. "Amos?"

I heard his footsteps as he left the kitchen and mounted the stairs.

Just then, I looked up at where the automatic garage door opener should have been. Instead, I saw only a splaying set of wires, jutting into space.

Fear rising in my throat, I stepped backward, lifting the doormat, looking for the house key, feeling for it in the dark.

It was gone.

I stood there alone, disbelieving, miles from anyone.

Locked in.

7

My assault on the disorder of the storage room continued. I tracked the mud of midwinter in and out, swabbing it away every evening, restoring it with stamping boots every morning. With a sponge and a ladder, I washed the walls, ignoring the possibility of slipping. I let my humming fill the cavern-like space until I was making enough sound for two people, sometimes drumming my hands against the metal safe that stood in one corner as I passed.

The stranger watched my movements from the hostel porch, his eyes peering out above his scarf. Finally, he came down.

"You know," I told him, "you're not making yourself any less conspicuous, standing around up there all bug-eyed. Especially with the scarf."

"You have a very pretty singing voice," he said.

I looked at him and snorted, flinging a box into the dumpster.

"What are you doing?" he asked.

"Penance," I replied, striding back into the dusty cave. "Apparently."

He followed me to the doorway, concerned. "What?"

"Nothing. Never mind. It was a joke." I wiped my face, feeling a passing tightness in my chest. "Sort of."

With a carpet knife, I ripped open another box, rifled through its contents, and hauled it off the pile.

"What's in there?" he asked.

"These?" I looked down. "Swedish Fish."

"Do Swedish Fish actually go bad?"

I sighed. "That's not the point."

"I see."

I threw the box away, but somehow, as I hoisted it into the bin, I felt the energy begin to drain out of me. I wiped my palms on my jeans and looked at him. He had turned to take in the view of the park, the endless swells of rock and tree, the bare limbs that almost looked as if they'd given up, given in, turned to stone. '

It was still beautiful, in its way.

I walked over and stood beside him.

"If this were the last thing you ever saw," he asked, "would you be happy?"

I was quiet for a moment, wondering what had prompted him to ask. Whether he somehow knew that I had once stood here asking myself the same thing.

"It's not like that," I said at length.

"What do you mean?"

"When something actually happens. When you think the end is coming. You don't even notice what you see."

He looked at me. I returned to the dumpster and pulled out the box I'd just tossed in.

"Have some Swedish Fish," I said.

He took a packet from my hands. Before he could say anything, I launched myself back into the storeroom, tearing into another box, and by the time I came back out, he was gone.

It had been almost three months since I'd gotten a postcard from my brother.

On a Sunday, I finally called John back, holding the phone for a long moment before pushing the buttons. When he picked up, his voice had the same pleasant tone it always seemed to have.

"You said something about riding?" I asked.

He laughed. "I reckon I did. You want to come over?"

When I got there, I followed him up the hill to his barn, where we saddled up. Dust and bits of hay filtered down from the loft above, floating in the cold, bright light as I helped tighten the girths. They were good horses, not too old and not too young, trotting effortlessly over the swells of the fields to the line of trees where we picked up a trail. John sat heavily in the saddle but held himself straight, one hand on the pommel and the other on his hat. I tucked the reins between my fingers the way I'd been taught when I was little, feeling the horse's sides under my legs as she exhaled and snorted, smelling the unmistakably animal odor of her sweat, listening to the creaking and clanking of the leather and stirrups.

On our way back to the barn, she started to canter and I let her, nervously at first, but then holding myself up so I was taut, poised above her, flying. She picked up speed, stretching her head forward. I'd forgotten what it was like to move so quickly, to feel so weightless, hooves pounding under me and a mane whipping my lowered face. Clods of mud flew up behind us, but the horse's legs were steady, her fixation on the food and warmth to come giving her a certainty that carried us both. When she finally slowed, we were both panting. I let myself fall forward and patted her neck.

John trotted up behind me, bumping along instead of posting.

"I didn't know you were gonna do that," he said.

"Me either." I knotted my fingers into my sweaty hair, pulling until it felt good, then dropping them.

We looked over the land. From here, the farm looked immense, the fields stretching away, interrupted by looming oak and elm trees. I preferred being on the mountain to this sense of space, but, I thought, this wasn't so bad.

I closed my eyes and then opened them, feeling as if a heavy hand had removed itself from my head.

John was watching me.

"Thanks," I told him, twisting around to look him in the face. "Really."

He smiled widely, resettling his hat on his head.

"Any time," he said.

On my way home, I sang along with the radio, tapping the wheel, cracking the window so my hair blew in the wind even though it was cold. At a convenience store, I reached up with my good arm and piled things into the basket, my clothes smelling of horse sweat, my muscles satisfyingly weary. When I swung my things onto the counter, I did it as if they weighed nothing.

As I approached my grandmother's house, though, I saw a strange car parked in the drive. Its purple hood glinted in the sun, the fields of patchy snow and broken cornstalks reflected in its windows. Cradling the groceries in one arm, I pushed through the door to find my aunt Jeanine—the one from Pittsburgh—sitting at the dining room table with my grandmother and my parents.

My stomach sank.

"Oh," I said, looking from one face to another.

Except for my grandmother, they looked startled, as if they'd forgotten I lived there. Two tall, clear bottles sat at the center of the table like shrunken monuments, and my parents and Jeanine had shot glasses in front of them. Jeanine's face was brown and battered-looking, her hair a neglected gray pulled back in a bandanna. My father was leaning forward on his elbows, half-slumped; my mother, I noticed, looked pink and disheveled, as if she had just come in after walking very far in a brisk wind.

"Kathleen!" she crowed, focusing vaguely in the direction of my face and blinking. My grandmother glanced away and smirked.

Sighing through my nose, I left the bag of groceries at the bottom of the stairs and trudged up to my room. At the bottom of the closet, there was an old cardboard suitcase that had once been my grandfather's, olive-green and smelling of cigar smoke. I had nearly filled it when I heard my grandmother's slow, labored step on the stairs.

"You're not staying?" she asked, not sounding surprised in the least.

"Nope." I shoved a last pair of socks into the suitcase and closed it.

"Suit yourself," she said, a phrase she had learned from TV. A thin, shining line of mucus on her upper lip showed where she had recently been connected to the oxygen tank, which I assumed was downstairs by the table, near her cup of cooling tea. Tea, too, was something she had lately been inspired to take up by the television. Apparently all the older women on there—all the contented ones, anyway—drank it. In my grandmother's hands, it was like a wish for a happier fate.

I bent down to search for an extra pair of sneakers under the bed, and she clumped away toward her own bedroom, a place she had rarely gone since she'd begun sleeping downstairs on the couch. A few minutes later, she returned, clasping a faded piece of paper and holding it out to me. It was a twenty-dollar bill.

"What's this?" I asked, staring at the note as she forced it into my palm with fingers that were surprisingly strong.

"What does it look like?" She turned toward the stairs.

I stared at her retreating back, the crooked coral dress she had gotten at a yard sale. "I don't need your money, Grandma."

"So?" She began lowering herself down the stairs, back toward the sounds of the party in the dining room, where glass was clinking and thumping against wood. "Go leave and do something fun. It'll serve them right."

I left with a nod goodbye to my aunt, who watched me with surprise and seemed to be asking a question of my grandmother. My father looked up at me, a pack of cards in his hands, and we held each other's gaze for a moment. Then his eyes flitted away uncomfortably and he began to deal.

"Make sure she takes her meds," I ordered the table in general, pointing at my grandmother. "If anything goes wrong, it's on you and I'll never forget it."

The door closed solidly behind me as I walked to the car.

At the hostel, Martin looked at me quizzically. I dropped my suitcase on the floor in front of the reception desk and reached for my wallet.

"Are you crazy? You're not paying for anything." He pushed my money back at me. "It's not like we've got any big crowds tonight, anyway. We're still just the Two Musketeers up here, me and him."

"Thanks. I'll just need some sheets and stuff then, I guess."

He examined me before turning to the linen closet, my mud-spattered jeans and tired posture. "Everything okay?"

"Yeah," I said. "It's fine."

He handed me a room key, and I accepted it with a gratitude I was torn between expressing and hiding. Then he handed me something else, a white card that had been sitting on the polished wood of the desk.

Tyler MacDougal, it said. *Pennsylvania State Police.*

I turned it over; the edges of the card felt sharp in my palm. "What's this?"

"They were here earlier today. I thought you should know."

I stared at him. "What for?"

"I'm sure you can guess."

"What did they say? Why didn't you tell me right away?"

"Well, you weren't here, and I didn't see any sense in worrying you." He closed the ledger. "Someone," he said, "thinks I might be harboring an illegal immigrant, it seems."

I looked at him and swallowed, the specter of Jerry's face passing through my mind.

"I'm sure it's one of the rangers," he added. "I don't know who else would know or care what I do up here. I could be running the biggest murder-for-hire operation east of the Mississippi and nobody'd be the wiser."

"So what happened?"

"Well, nothing, in the end. They came, they asked a couple of questions, and they left. Which is exactly as it should be, since nobody's doing anything wrong."

"What kind of questions? Was he here?"

"He was down in the game room. They didn't see him." He toyed with his pencil. "They wanted to know if he was working for me. I said no, I hadn't paid him a dime, he just helped me out with chores sometimes. They then very kindly explained to me what 'harboring' means." He scratched the back of his arm. "I reminded them that I'm running a hostel. Harboring people is what I do."

"That's it? They didn't go looking for him?"

"They didn't have a warrant. I'm not as dumb as I look—I know how these guys work. I asked them to leave, and they did."

I imagined Martin face-to-face with the police, saying those words, and was struck with a mixture of awe and apprehension. "You said that?"

"You bet I did. If you let them mess with you once, they get the idea they can do it forever. It's a gamble—if they decide to come back at you, they're probably gonna do it pretty hard. But I don't see how they have any kind of leg to stand on—they're just doing something somebody told them to do. And at the end of the day, I'm willing to bet they have better things to do than drive all the way up here again to chase some rumor. Nobody gets promoted over something like this."

I was still watching the scene in my mind with amazement. "I would never have known to do what you did."

"Yeah, well. One of the many things I learned in my misspent youth." He smiled lopsidedly. "Anyway, I don't think there's any call to panic. Besides, panicking is how bad decisions get made. No sense in doing that here."

"Does he know?" I lifted my chin to indicate the floor above us, where the stranger's room was.

"Yeah, it would've been pretty hard not to hear the guy stomping around here like he owned the place. I think Danya's upstairs now, if you want to talk to him. Here, let me carry that suitcase for you."

"No, I've got it."

I climbed the stairs as quickly as I could and made my way down the darkened corridor.

There was no response when I knocked.

"It's Kathleen," I called.

There was a pause, and then a sound like the shuffling of papers. The door opened a crack, showing a cautious eye and wet hair. He must have just showered.

"Oh," he said. "Yes, it is." He opened the door until I could see his face perched on its white neck. "I thought you had gone home?"

"I did go home." I put the suitcase down. "Now I'm back. Are you okay?"

"Yes, of course. Come in," he urged, opening the door to reveal a darkened room lit by a single lamp. I saw that he was naked from the waist up, a towel clutched around his hips. Averting my eyes, I saw a book on the bed, a pile of papers, a pen. His shoes were aligned by the dented folding table that was meant to serve as a desk, his clothing folded neatly and stacked on the broad windowsill, the guitar propped in a corner. He raised the blind, but the room became no brighter, late as it was. There were long pink lines on his back, I noticed, faint but discernible against the pale skin, like the creases that come from sleeping on a wrinkled sheet, but deeper and darker. Embarrassed, I looked at the floor.

He turned to face me, and I caught a glimpse of other pink marks on the inside of his arm as he reached for a sweater. These were small and round, not much bigger than a dime, and quickly disappeared from view as he pulled the shirt over his head, catching the towel awkwardly with one hand before it dropped. "Please sit," he said, gesturing toward the metal chair by the desk, then caught sight of the suitcase in the hall. His eyes widening, he looked back at me. "Are you staying here?"

"Yes. I mean, not here in this room, obviously. In another one."

"But you live very close to here. Or at least, that's what I've always thought." He remained standing, looking like an absurd scarecrow in his sweater and towel. Close up, I could see that he looked fatigued, but there was nothing in his face of the shock or terror I had expected to find.

"Yeah, I do," I said. "My grandmother's just having guests, so I decided to clear out for a while."

"Clear out?"

"Leave." I watched his movements. "You're sure you're all right?"

"Yes, yes. Let me bring your suitcase in." He stepped to the doorway and reached down, touching the brittle sides of the case, its rusted handle. "Oh, my. This is an old one."

"Yeah. It was my grandfather's."

"It reminds me of the one my father had when he was young and traveled from Moscow to Tashkent. He still has it somewhere, but I never even thought of trying to use it." He placed the suitcase carefully by the desk and closed the door.

I wasn't sure whether to be relieved or alarmed by his seeming serenity. "You're a lot calmer than I expected."

"You mean about the police?"

"Of course I mean about the police."

"Well," he said. He sat down on the edge of the bed, looking away as he gently smoothed the covers with his hand. His thin legs dangled from the towel. "When they first came, it was—of course, I was upset. But it's a bit like a fire, being frightened in that way. It burns very terribly all at once, and then it's gone and you're only rather tired."

Water trickled from his hair onto his neck. He looked exposed, vulnerable, like a man dropped into a hostile wilderness.

Yes, I thought. I knew that kind of fear, the one so sharp it left only exhaustion in its wake, a kind of indifference to fate. It was dangerous, that feeling. It led to a certain kind of decision-making, like a sleepwalker choosing to leave the doors unlocked when she goes to bed.

"I don't mean to sound like a broken record," I told him, picking at a streak of mud on my thigh, "but I'd think the obvious thing to do would be—"

He raised his hands and then dropped them. "Martin says they will not be back right away. In the meantime, I'll think about what would be best."

For a moment, I felt a shadow of what I suddenly understood Beth must feel whenever she tried to make me see reason. Exasperation mixed with pity.

"All right," I said finally. "I'm going to dinner. But I'll knock when I come back—if you're still awake, maybe we can talk then."

"I'll go with you."

"What?" I did a double take. "No. No, no, no. That's not happening."

"Why not? I would like to."

"No," I said again, shaking my head. "Absolutely not. I've watched you spend all this time trying to make yourself disappear up here. I may not think that was the world's best idea, but I'm not going to help you fling it away on an impulse. No."

He laughed self-consciously. "You're a good friend. And I'm grateful for your concern. But . . . well, it seems to me that it makes no difference. If I stay here, I'm a sitting duck, as they say. Besides . . ." He glanced around the small, square room with the bare floor and gray furniture. "If I sit in here, you know, I just . . ."

He didn't finish, but he didn't have to. I could picture him sitting there, gazing at the blank white walls, thinking the same thoughts over and over. Jumping at every sound.

"I understand that," I said. "I do. But it can't be a good idea."

"I'm not certain anything I do is truly a good idea."

"Yeah, well, that may be, but—"

"Please," he said softly.

The word hung in the air, delicate and suspended, like a moth that had flown into a web.

I let my head fall back and looked up at the ceiling. "All right," I said at last, trying and failing to quiet my better judgment.

"Thank you. Just—if you could—maybe somewhere—"

I understood. "Yeah, I could take us to the twenty-four-hour diner up on the interstate. They get a lot of travelers. They'd probably be less likely to notice us."

It had begun to rain, and the drive was a slow one. The stranger sat in the passenger's seat in silence, watching the road as it unfurled in front of us, turning his face every time we passed a house or a barn even though it was impossible to see anything more than shadows. He smelled like soap.

As we pulled onto the highway, he looked at me. "You seem troubled," he said.

"I'm driving around with a crazy person. How should I seem?"

"No, I mean it looks like it's something more than that."

"Oh." I glanced at the headlights in my mirror. "No, it's nothing."

I slipped into the traffic, not that there was much. This stretch of the highway was usually empty at night except for the trucks, eighteen-wheelers that barreled down the interstate on their anonymous way to Allentown, Scranton, New York. Elsewhere.

"These guests at your house," the stranger went on cautiously. "You don't like them?"

"I can't believe that's what you're worried about right now."

"Well, I'm not worried, exactly. You just look a bit—"

"No." I gave in. "It's not that I don't like them. They're my family. We're just different people."

"How are they different?"

"It's not important—they've just done some things I wouldn't have done. Or that I hope I wouldn't have done." I flicked my turn signal to pass a slow pickup.

"Yes, families can be like that. Believe me, my father—well, that's another story for another time. And of course it isn't good to disrespect one's parents. Not that I'm blaming you," he added quickly.

I smiled briefly at his politeness. "It's fine," I said.

"What did they do, if I may ask?"

"It was a long time ago. It doesn't matter." We passed a rest stop, its entrance lined with parked trucks, the drivers probably sleeping in their cabs. Several of the rigs had shapes on their grills done in what looked like Christmas lights, mostly crosses. The stranger turned in his seat to look at them, but within moments the trees that lined the highway had cut off the floating apparitions, and we were left in darkness.

The diner's neon sign shone down on the parking lot. A strip of bells clanged when we pushed open the door, and the stranger jumped, stumbling into me. I felt him go tense. "Careful," I murmured, and asked the hostess—a pert, sharp-looking woman with a pen in her mouth—for a table in the smoking section. She nodded and plucked two menus from a pile, pen remaining pressed between her lips.

"I didn't know you smoked," the stranger said as we slid into a booth. He curled forward, his hands in his pockets, looking around him.

"I don't. Well, not usually. But apparently nobody else does tonight, either." I lifted my chin at the empty booths and tables around us. "We can talk without worrying about who's listening."

"I see." He opened the menu, glancing at it doubtfully. "I'm actually not very hungry, I'm afraid."

"Pick something anyway," I advised. "Otherwise they're more likely to remember you."

I watched him think about this. "All right." He stared at the menu again as if it were written in hieroglyphics. "What should I choose?"

"Well, none of it's exactly fine cuisine, but the roast beef's not bad. In my opinion."

"Okay. I'll get that." He closed the menu and leaned back against the booth. Whatever it was that had been buoying him up seemed to be draining away now that we were here; I watched him cast his eyes over our surroundings, doing a very poor impression of someone who wasn't nervous.

When the waitress came, I ordered for both of us, the beef for him and an omelet for me. Two coffees. A lifetime ago, when Amos and I had been dating, we'd come here often, ordering scrambled eggs and hash browns late at night for no particular reason. Like the teenagers we were, I thought, and then pushed the memory from my mind.

"So," I said when the waitress had put our food on the table and left. "What are you going to do?"

He turned his fork upside down the way British people did on TV, nudging at his meat. "Do?"

"You can't stay. Not if you're worried about someone finding you. You have to know that."

All at once, the skin around his mouth seemed to sag. "As I said, I—there's nowhere I can go."

"But you came here. To the park, I mean."

He took a sip of coffee and looked at his plate. "Yes. I was lucky."

I found myself looking at his frayed cuffs, the tarnished buttons of his coat, all the small things I had come to know so well and that cried out, in their own way, with an unmistakable desperation. I pushed my plate aside.

"I'm not going to beg," I said, "but I really could take you somewhere. Even another rural area, if that's where you want to be. I don't care how far we have to drive; I'll do it."

He spread a layer of mashed potatoes onto his fork and examined it without answering. His hair had fallen over his eyes. Maybe it was something about being in a new place, I thought, but I had never seen him look so fragile or so worn.

I took a deep breath, bracing myself.

"What exactly did you do that was so bad?" I asked finally.

His head jerked up swiftly. "That's not why the police came."

"I'm not talking about why the police came."

He looked me in the eye for a long moment. We had never exchanged such a look, not in that way. His irises were dark, the darkest I'd ever seen, and I was suddenly, almost dizzyingly reminded that I was talking to a man who was twelve years older than I was, who had traveled the world, whose simple words were probably meant to soften an intelligence that would otherwise be overwhelming; who would, in the ordinary course of life, never have been sitting here, never have ventured anywhere near here, never have found himself in this place having a conversation with someone like me.

I dropped my gaze, tucking my hands into the front pocket of my sweatshirt. Despite his absurdity, his awkwardness, I was in awe of him. There was no denying it. And even though there was still something unreal about the fact that the two of us were sitting here, facing one another under the slowly revolving ceiling fans and dim lights of a highway diner, I had to admit that he had brought something to my days, something that had been missing. I was fine on my own; I had long ago learned how to make do with my own company. But it was true that his arrival had thrown the previous months, and even years, into a different light. I would never have told him so; I would never have told anyone. And yet when I thought of those days, I now felt as if I stood on the edge of something. They hadn't been a wasteland, I told myself. They hadn't been barren. But they had been different, and, if I were being honest, I wasn't so sure I was ready to go back to them. Not just yet.

"I betrayed people," he said softly, breaking into my thoughts.

I looked back at him with a start. He was gazing at the empty place in the middle of the table.

"You what?"

He didn't reply.

"I don't understand," I said.

He started to speak again and then stopped.

"You mean you think you let someone down?"

Clearing his throat, he wrapped his fingers around his mug. "No." He considered his words. "I mean I betrayed people. That's what I did."

The fan spun overhead.

"I'm sorry," I said. "I don't know what that means."

"Of course," he sighed. "I keep forgetting that you've never left this place."

I must have winced, because he added quickly, "I mean to say you live in a place where these things don't happen."

He fell silent for a minute, then two. The waitress appeared, refilled our coffee cups while he stared at his plate, and disappeared.

"I can explain," he said eventually. "But I need you to understand that these are things I wish I hadn't done."

I reached for my mug and held it.

"Okay," I said.

He coughed, leaning forward.

"In my city, in Tashkent, about ten years ago—not quite ten years, but nearly—there were bombings. Six car bombs in one day. It was horrible. So many people were injured. I was at my office, and I felt one of them. I came down to look and there was just . . ." He opened his hands. "Pieces of metal and glass. Blood everywhere. It's impossible to describe—you see things like that on the news, but when you're there, you see the people, you hear screaming, you smell—" He shook his head, as if to clear the memory away.

"Most people in Uzbekistan—I mean the Uzbeks, not Russian people like me—are Muslim. Not the kind who pray a lot; usually more laid-back. When I was younger, during Soviet times, the government kept a close eye on things—not just mosques, but churches and everything else, too. It controlled the kind of religion people could have, more or less, so nobody was very religious. Not really." Briefly, his face took on an exasperated look. "Things were so much better then, let me tell you."

I opened my mouth to argue, but let him go on.

He sank slightly in his seat, focusing on the fake flowers in the middle of the table. "When the bombings happened, the government blamed the Muslims—the religious ones. So, of course, a lot of other people did the same thing." He made a helpless gesture. "I believed it. Almost everyone believed it. It was only later that people started asking questions. Asking whether the government itself might have . . ." He drew a breath and let it out. "Well. It doesn't matter. We'll never know."

For a moment, he paused. Then he said, "I was a lawyer, as I mentioned."

"Yes, I remember."

"I had—" He faltered. His hair had fallen in front of his eyes. "I had clients, of course. People told me many things. And I knew a lot of people from my university. I was . . . always a friendly person."

Fingering his coffee spoon, he wiped it on his napkin and began scraping it lightly against the edge of the table.

"All right," I said.

"One day I received a call on my phone, my mobile phone, telling me I was invited."

His eyes were fixed on the spoon.

"Invited?"

"That's what they call it. They 'invite' you." A corner of his mouth twitched into a dry, fleeting half-smile. "As if it were a dinner party."

"'They'? The—the secret police, like you said before?"

"Yes, but a different kind of them. A more serious kind." He leaned back against the orange vinyl cushion of the booth.

"Of course, when you're invited, you can't refuse. So I went." He glanced up at the light that hung over our table. "I took the bus, and I still remember everything about it, that ride. The people around me seemed to know where I was going. No one would look at me. It was very strange.

"When I arrived, there were two of them, just like in the movies. One of them was tall and strong-looking, and the other one was shorter and rather fat. Their faces were similar, though, like they could have been cousins. They were both very light, as if they didn't spend much time in the sun.

"I came in, and they poured some glasses of vodka, one for me and one for each of them. They made small talk with me for a while, about my work, my family, a class I was teaching at the university. Then they asked." He paused. "They asked me what I had heard."

Taking a breath, he let it out slowly. "You have to understand," he said, "that I was frightened, and angry about the bombs. Many of us were. And I believe in a—what would you call it?—a secular society. After independence, many of us were already worried that things would change too much, that everything around us would become unrecognizable. And I . . ."

He looked down into his cup.

"I was persuaded," he said. "I started . . . giving names. Not just anybody, but the people I knew, or had heard of, that were activists. Those were the ones I mentioned, at first. In most cases, they were names I was sure the government already had. I thought I couldn't be doing any harm."

His voice grew softer.

"The thing about that kind of police is that they know more about you than you do about yourself. It's not that they're especially intelligent. In fact, they're often the men who didn't do well in school. But they know what to say." He glanced at me briefly. "They kept wanting . . . well, they wanted to know what I'd heard. What people were saying. More names.

"And I wanted to leave," he said. "They knew that. They knew I'd studied languages at university, that I wanted something different for myself." He swallowed. "And of course, there's always a threat hanging behind what they say, even if they never actually come out with the words. I'd been in prison once before, like I told you—my father was trying to get someone to pay a debt, and he made the wrong kind of people angry. I didn't want . . . I couldn't bear to go through that ever again. When people go into prison in Uzbekistan, things sometimes happen . . ."

He left the sentence unfinished. "And so," he continued instead, "eventually, I agreed to work for them. I knew a lot of people. My clients, my friends. Students I had once taught, when I was a professor's assistant. They trusted me, they told me everything." He paused. "And I betrayed them. Every week, I went to that building, to the officers who had invited me. And I betrayed them."

He rubbed his eyes with the heel of his hand, although he wasn't crying. More than anything, he looked exhausted.

"There was one young woman, a painter. I remembered her because she used to wear these silk flowers in her hair. She was bold—she was never afraid of saying anything. I used to get so frustrated with her. I thought she was wrong about everything." He seemed to draw in on himself, his shoulders curving. "They took her. I told myself she must have expected to be taken, since she'd said such bold things in front of other people. I . . ."

He trailed off.

I was too stunned to speak. We sat across from each other, the smoke from the kitchen wafting over us, the fan blades endlessly paddling the air.

"Let's go," I said finally, and he nodded. We slid out of the booth, walking to the register.

In the darkness of the car, I put my hands on the wheel. The stitching in the leather felt rough under my skin. I stared straight ahead.

"So what happened to them?" I asked. "Those people you . . . told the officers about?"

He seemed to speak with difficulty. "Well, they would have been questioned."

"In prison?"

"Yes." He'd taken a toothpick from a cup by the register when we'd walked out, but he wasn't using it, just turning it over in his hands, pushing the points against his skin. "Some of them . . . I don't know. I didn't see them anymore. Maybe they were suspicious of me, or maybe they . . ."

He didn't finish the sentence.

I started the car. As we drove, the vision came to me again, those happy faces bobbing in a candlelit circle in a café, listening to the stranger tell jokes and play his guitar. Slowly disappearing, one by one, like the Cheshire Cat, until even the smiles were gone, leaving just a trace of a glow lingering in the darkness.

I thought of the photographs from the prisons, distress rising in my throat.

"Eventually, I came here," the stranger continued, as if he felt he had to finish the story now that he had started. "I—I knew the right people. To arrange things so I could leave." He looked down at his palms. "When I first arrived, I was a student for a while—I went to a university in Virginia with my savings. I had a visa. Then it ran out." He bent the toothpick until it broke. "I asked for asylum, but somehow, they knew what I had done."

"Who did?" I forced myself to ask.

"The Americans. The judge. I was told I couldn't get asylum. There's a rule, you see. You can't get it if you've done certain things. And they said I'd done one of them, because I'd worked for my government. Because I had," he drew a breath, "informed on people."

My stomach cramped. As he spoke, I was overcome by a vision of the day Amos had locked me in the garage. The smell of it, the darkness.

He'd left me in there for three days.

There was no food and no water.

"There's another rule, however," the stranger was saying, "that even if you can't get asylum, you can't be sent back to a place where you're going to be—well, if certain things are going to happen to you. But the judge said, 'You worked for your government. Why would they now hurt you?'" I could hear the disbelief in his voice, as if this exchange had just happened. "He didn't understand how angry my government would be—will be—when they find out I talked about what I did. What they asked me to do. It makes them look bad." He gave a short, humorless laugh. "Obviously."

I saw myself calling out in the dark until my voice was gone, pounding and clawing at the doorknob until my hands were bloodied and my nails torn loose. Finally, I'd curled against the door, noiseless, so thirsty I was sure I would die.

There was a cold sweat on my palms, the back of my neck, as I listened to him.

"So you didn't get asylum," I said.

"No."

"And you came up here. Or your friends brought you here."

"Yes," he said. "Eventually."

Much of my screaming—more than I cared to remember—had been for my parents. I'd kept picturing them standing in the priest's driveway. It was clear what had happened: the priest had called them, and then they had called Amos. They must have realized their mistake. They'd seen the way he'd charged into the rectory, the way he'd wrenched me out, taken me away. They would be worried. They would come to the house. They would hear me.

They didn't.

They were, if anything, even more terrified of him than I was. But with far less reason.

"How many?" I asked as we turned off the highway.

"Pardon me?"

"How many people did you . . . turn in?"

He turned to me, surprised.

"I don't know," he said. A gust of wind blew through the tops of the trees as we passed through Centerville, pelting the car with water. "Maybe a hundred. Maybe more."

A chill ran through me, a literal feeling of cold making my skin draw toward itself.

"A hundred," I repeated.

"Maybe. I really don't know. It was a long time before I could escape."

"How long?"

For a moment, I thought he wouldn't answer.

"Five years," he said quietly.

Turning on my emergency lights, I pulled over onto the shoulder of the road. The tires crushed the leaves and gravel.

The stranger looked at me. I kept my eyes fixed ahead, on the point where the black asphalt merged with the darkness. The emergency lights clicked softly as they blinked.

Before me, I saw the pictures, the limbs that had been boiled, the burns from shocks, the vacant eyes. The hopelessness.

"Did they die?" I asked.

There was a long beat while he seemed to struggle to decide what to say.

"Some of them confessed," he said. "I know that. People will say many things, when they're . . . under pressure." He shifted slightly under the shoulder strap. "And in my country, a confession is a serious thing. It's hard to undo it, once you've said you did something. Almost impossible, really."

I squeezed the wheel.

"So, they're dead," I said.

He didn't answer. His face was turned away, his throat long and white.

I unfastened my seat belt and opened the door.

"Wait," he said, but I didn't listen.

Outside, in the cold, I walked behind the car and leaned against it. The taillights throbbed red, pulsing into the night. I gazed down the empty road into the darkness. A cold drizzle had begun to fall, sticking to my face. As I stood there, it soaked into my jeans.

In the hospital, Amos had explained that I'd gotten sick, I'd refused to go to a doctor, I was a bit unbalanced, I'd tried to move a heavy load of firewood and it had fallen onto my hands.

When it was time for me to be discharged, they'd sent me back. He'd stood at the front desk and taken my arm. And we'd walked out.

I wiped the drizzle from my face. Slowly, almost calmly, I bent double and threw up. When it was over, I straightened. Then I put my hands on my knees and did it again.

When the feeling of sickness finally passed, I slid down and sat on the crust of snow. The rain dripped into my eyes, and I let it, leaning my head against the warm fender.

It was a long time before I stood up and walked back to the open door on the driver's side. The stranger was as I had left him, looking down at his hands. My seat was flecked with rain.

I lowered myself onto it and closed the door.

"Your wife," I said in the silence.

I could tell he was looking at me, but I refused to look back.

His voice was small. "Yes?"

"You left her there."

His gaze shifted away. "Yes." The word seemed to catch in his throat. "It was dangerous to leave. And she didn't know. About . . . any of it." His hands gripped together in his lap. "I thought that would protect her."

The rain spattered the windshield. "Did it?"

He looked down at his thumbs.

I turned the key and reached for the gear shift, flicking my turn signal even though no one was there. We pulled onto the road.

"Are you angry?" the stranger asked as we pulled into the lot and confronted the silent brick hulk of the hostel.

"Angry's not the word," I said. "Let's let it go for tonight. We can talk tomorrow."

"Are you sure? I—"

"Yes. I'm sure." I turned off the engine. "I need some time."

The room Martin had given me was dark and cold. Mechanically, I stripped, pulled on my pajamas, brushed my teeth in the harsh light of the bathroom, lay down on the hard mattress. There was no moon outside the window, just the rainclouds. The first two pills didn't work, and the second two didn't, either. I couldn't stop seeing the photographs with their raw, broken skin. The blue eyes of the doctor as he'd bent over me. The priest with his frightened face and rumpled sweater, standing alone in the light of the bulb that hung over the rectory door, realizing his mistake much too late.

Finally, upending the paper bag into my palm, I swallowed a handful of the white ovals without counting them. Gathering myself into a knot, I shivered, breathing in the slight wild-animal smell of the blanket. When the blackness hit me, it hit me hard, sending me sailing off into a place where there was no thought.

And I was grateful.

8

In the early afternoon, I awoke slowly, rising into consciousness like a diver floating toward the surface of the sea. There was a sharp, repeated sound somewhere in the distance, hard and regular, like marching. *The prisoners*, I thought groggily, imagining them emerging from the mist in the uniforms they would once have had, the fabric in tatters, their hands behind their heads. But no, it wasn't them. It was knocking, someone knocking on the door of the room that it took me some time to realize wasn't my own.

"Hey," Martin called.

I sat up and walked unsteadily to the door. The light from the windows was blinding.

"Are you all right?" He looked me up and down. "I just realized you weren't down at the store."

"I'm taking a sick day," I said, or tried to.

He was still looking at me, worried and uncertain, when I closed the door.

By the time I stepped out of the shower, I felt steadier, although I seemed to be having trouble grasping things and it took me a long time to get dressed. I sat on the edge of the bed, feeling as if I were outside my own body, struggling to pull my thoughts from circles into a straight line. Gradually, the previous evening came back to me.

At one point, there were footsteps that paused outside the door, soft and rubbery-sounding. I didn't move, and eventually they went away.

I drank a glass of water, gazing into it between sips. Then I reached for my keys and left.

The drive down the mountain passed before I quite knew it, the car seeming to float over the road. I pulled into the gas station and parked by the pay phone, my stomach empty and my hair still wet.

The phone wasn't in a booth; it was just mounted on top of a short pole. I stood and looked at it, fingering the coins I had found in my pocket.

I picked up the receiver, hearing the dial tone.

Then I let it drop again.

Massaging my forehead, I drifted into the convenience store and bought a pack of Marlboro Reds. There was a line of long parking spaces for tractor-trailers on the other side of the lot, and I moved the car there, in a corner, up against the grass. I climbed onto the hood and sat back against the windshield, pulling on a cigarette, my legs stiff from the horse ride I could hardly believe had happened just the day before. The sunlight flashed on the door of the convenience store as it opened and closed, admitting the stream of men and women who were going about their days.

The cigarette burned down to the filter. I stubbed it out on the sole of my shoe and got back into the car. There were too many people here; I needed somewhere quieter, more alone. It was like a deep internal itch, like the hard-edged restlessness I got when I didn't take the pills.

I remembered where I'd been when I'd first seen the other photos, the ones the archaeologist had mentioned while I was cooking hamburgers in the store. It was spring; I'd been in my own empty kitchen, sitting by the table, a few days before I let the bank take the house. Almost all the other furniture was already gone, either moved to my grandmother's basement or—in most cases—sold. I myself had already moved into the room at my grandmother's and almost never came back. There were cobwebs in the corners, dust in the sink, newspapers piled on the front step in their orange bags. I'd brought the papers in and, already fatigued from the effort of walking, dropped them on the table. As I sat there, I'd grabbed the one that looked the least faded. And there they were, on the front page, the pictures. The worst ones were on the inside, so children wouldn't see them. Naked men in pyramids. Men dragged at the ends of leashes, threatened by dogs, forced to touch themselves, hooded and strung with electrical wires. I'd sat there and absorbed the colors, the grinning people in uniform, the terror of men who flattened themselves against a wall. Then I'd looked out the window for a long time.

Abu Ghraib. In other places, where the TV was on, I heard people talking about those pictures—the newscasters on those shows where the men always wore suits and the women wore bright short dresses, as if they were flowers. I heard the men on the radio talk about them, too, the men who always shouted, who were always so sure they were right.

They all seemed to assume they knew what we—people like me—thought, because of who we were. It didn't seem to occur to them that we could think differently. That we could look at something through different eyes. That we could stay up at night, imagining or remembering, asking ourselves questions.

They'd sold us a bill of goods; that's what I thought. All of them. They sold us the army and sent the people we loved off to die awful deaths for reasons that didn't hold up. They sold us pain and said it was fine. They had such contempt for us, and they thought we didn't see it. Just because we lived where we lived and were who we were. They didn't think any of us could look at such horror and see something in it that looked familiar, something that made us recoil. They didn't have those kinds of imaginations.

And I faulted them for it. I blamed them in a way that was clear-eyed and hard.

They thought I was stupid and gullible, that I moved through life like a block, full of anger at the things they told me to be angry at and unable to feel anything else. They thought I didn't know when something was inhuman or unjust.

They were wrong.

There was a rest stop along the highway, a patch of grass and trees with a small shelter housing the bathrooms and vending machines. I pushed my way through the door, approaching the phone in its shadowed corner. The floor beneath it was strewn with candy-bar wrappers, crushed paper cups, black clots of mud.

I stood there for a long moment, seeing myself as if from the other end of the room. My mind still felt as if it were suspended by threads, but also, I thought, had a clarity it seldom had.

I held this other receiver in my hand, feeling its weight.

Then I pushed my coins into the slot.

I didn't know the number for the police, I realized as I looked at the keypad. But I could call the park office, where the rangers worked. That would be enough; after all, the park was their territory.

I pressed the numbers and waited for the ringing. There was a click as someone picked up.

"Hello," a woman's voice said on the other end of the line.

I gathered myself. "Hello," I said.

"You've reached the office of Pine Grove Furnace State Park in Gardners, Pennsylvania," the voice continued. "Please leave—"

I cursed under my breath and hung up. After a moment, I tried again.

"Hello," the same woman's voice said.

I sighed.

"Excuse me?" the woman said.

"Oh—" I gripped the receiver with both hands. "Sorry. I, um . . . is there someone I could talk to about . . . uh, somebody in the park?"

"Somebody in the park?" she repeated. "Are you having a problem at the campsite?"

"No, it's—something else."

"Well, tell me what you need and I'll tell you if we can deal with it." Her tone was impersonal and professional, her accent slightly southern.

"It's kind of hard to explain. I wanted to . . . to report someone." The word "report" had a jarring sound as it fell from my mouth, and I squeezed the cord in my hand.

"Okay," she said, apparently unfazed. "What are they doing?"

"Well, it's not something they're doing, exactly. They did something before, in the past." As I spoke, I saw the stranger's face, with its hollow cheeks and fine lines. "People are looking for them."

"I see."

I could picture her leaning back in her chair and tapping a pencil, as if she had just realized she was talking to someone who had a screw loose.

"What I mean is . . ." I paused. The metal keypad was covered with fingerprints, traces of other people who had wound up here, using this thing in a trash-strewn corner as the cars outside rushed by. The broke and broken-down.

"Ma'am?" the ranger said.

"Yes—sorry."

"Can you tell me what this person looks like?"

I steeled myself.

"Tall," I said. "Thin. He has black hair."

"Caucasian?"

I had never thought about it. "Um . . . yeah. I guess so."

"How old is he?"

"Thirty-nine. Maybe forty by now."

"And how much would you say he weighs?"

The stranger hovered before my vision again. Hat in hand, eyes calm and gentle. A distinct feeling of self-loathing began to creep over me.

On the other end of the line, the ranger sighed. "Listen, ma'am, if you're not—"

I hung up.

There was a picnic table outside, and I sat down on one of the wooden benches, listening to the roar of the traffic. Car after car, truck after truck. Other lives.

The ground shook as each of them passed, endlessly.

I looked down the hill, where a muddy path led nowhere, ending at a barbed-wire fence and a row of trees.

The lines in the photographs, I thought. The ones that came from whipping. If they had been less vivid, if they had healed, they would have looked just like the pink lines on the stranger's back.

I tried to remember exactly what I'd just told the ranger, how much I'd given her to go on. It hadn't been much, I thought. There was still time to reconsider, to decide what to do. Tall, thin, dark hair, about forty. That could be anyone. They wouldn't pursue this; they'd think I was just some crank. Wouldn't they?

My mouth and nose burned with the fumes from the interstate. I pressed my hands against my knees, looking down at them, feeling the table tremble. *I am the wrong person for this*, I thought. *Every time I think I understand it, every time I'm sure, it slips away from me. Tell me what to do. Tell me what to do.*

The traffic rushed on.

PART THREE

1

I woke up the next morning with my jaw aching, having clenched my teeth together as I'd slept. The buggies went by on their way to somewhere. My grandmother poured herself a glass of water. I sat up slowly and pushed aside the afghans.

I'd retrieved my suitcase from the hostel the day before, slipping in and out without anyone seeing me. I hadn't told Martin what I'd done. I hadn't told anybody.

I showered and tied my hair into a knot, noticing that I was losing weight. The scars stood out as starkly as ever, but I ignored them, pulling on my clothes and lifting the hood of the sweatshirt over my head. I didn't bother with a coat as I walked to Miller's, the small grocery store that stood in a dirt patch by the Centerville intersection. The wind bit at my legs under my jeans, and the fields and pastures had a vacant look, as if the end of the world, Judgment Day, had come and gone.

The morning after the fire had been like that. When it had happened, a few months before the stranger had come, I'd been at work as usual, washing the accumulated grease from the insides of the windows and listening to the wind. It was whistling around the sides of the store in bursts, bearing leaves and twigs that brushed against the stone walls. As I'd kept listening, I'd realized there was something unusual about it, that it couldn't seem to settle on a direction. There was an awfully strange storm coming, I'd thought.

By the time I'd smelled the smoke, looking around at the grill and the heater with increasing panic, the rangers had shown up, their tires screeching as they'd pulled into the lot. I'd left the store the way they'd demanded but found myself transfixed when I got outside, frozen by the sight of thin tongues of smoke wafting from between the trees. The rangers were already racing down toward the town's firehouse;

when I thought about it later, I realized the phone lines that connected the park to the outside world must already have gone dead. Finally turning away, I'd run as best I could to the car and begun my own drive down the slope, but the day seemed to be growing dim and it was increasingly difficult to see. The trees along the side of the road were distinct enough, but behind them was a deepening screen of gray, one that continued in a vault overhead, as if I were driving through some kind of cathedral in a grim dream. The smoke slowly began to edge across the road, a patch here, a patch there. I'd turned on my head-lights and held a sleeve to my mouth, breathing through the fabric. In the rearview mirror, almost nothing was visible: just a few yards of asphalt, a curve of floating ferns and jagged boulders, and then an unearthly blankness.

All the familiar landmarks had been hidden from view, and I'd reached the valley floor suddenly, emerging from the corridor of thickening darkness to find that I was about to run the stop sign at the foot of the mountain. I'd slammed on the brakes and found myself staring at a herd of Guernsey cows that had backed up against the barbed wire on the other side of the intersection, their faces turned ominously to the sky, bellowing and stamping. A helicopter had whirred overhead and disappeared, followed by another. I'd driven home, pausing at the railroad crossing to take another look at the mountain in the rearview mirror. It was burning, all right: you could see it. The normal autumn mosaic of green and gold on the north face was overhung with thick patches of gray, billowing slowly and broadly toward the sky.

The next day, I'd driven up to find the forest like lace, untouched pockets of maples and beeches interspersed with ghostly stands of burned trunks, charred javelins surrounded by layers of smoldering ash. I'd parked and walked through the ruined terrain in my boots, the ground crackling and still smoking under my feet. Later that day, I'd heard the park buildings had been spared, but hadn't found the news as reassuring as expected. I'd thought I'd known what this place was, thought I'd known its every rhythm, but I'd been wrong. It was so much greater, so much more powerful, than I was. And I barely understood it at all.

I strode into Miller's and glanced around at the shelves. The shop was dark, giving off the smell of newsprint and candy and the metal of the guns they sold in the back. The woman behind the counter looked from the TV to me without changing the angle of her body.

I approached the counter.

"I need a map," I said.

"Pennsylvania?" the woman asked without interest. "Maryland? Eastern U.S.?"

I thought about it. "Eastern U.S.," I told her. On the TV, there was a burst of laughter. Two women in an apartment in some city, thin and elegant even in their jeans, with pretty, swingy hair, were having an argument. The camera lingered on their faces as they circled around a coffee table, pointing at one another with manicured fingers.

I put my money on the counter and left.

Back in my grandmother's kitchen, I dug for the box of tea I knew was lurking there and put the kettle on, watching the flame dance under the metal, losing myself in my thoughts. Then, leaning against the counter, I spread out the map—Florida Keys to New Brunswick, it said on the front—and traced the roads with a finger.

For a long time, I took in the patches of green that were forests, the hard-edged gray blots of cities, the brown dots that were mid-sized towns. Sipping my tea, I traced the roads with a fingertip, thinking without any resolution.

Then I folded the map and carried it up to my room, where I slid it under the mattress.

That night, I made shepherd's pie for dinner but found I couldn't eat it, dissecting it with my fork while my grandmother dug in. If nothing else, she had a healthy appetite.

I watched her for a time.

"Grandma," I said finally.

"What?"

I fiddled with the silverware next to my plate. There was something I wanted to ask her, but I didn't know how to ask it, or even exactly what it was. It had something to do with a sense that I was being watched, tested, judged for what I did in these hours. To my surprise, it came out as "Do you believe in God?"

She glanced up, a streak of mashed potatoes trailing along one cheek. "Do I believe in God?" Her tone was suspicious, as if she smelled a trick. She was wearing the flowered dress she only wore when I forgot to do the laundry.

I decided to stick with it. "Yeah."

She considered the question, her mouth opening slightly as she chewed. "No, I don't think I do. Why?"

"Did you ever?"

She pinched a corner of bread from the slice on her plate, pushing it through the pool of meat juices. "I guess so. At one time."

"But you changed your mind."

"Yeah." She thought about it, the powdery skin of her brow crinkling. "I must've."

"Was there a reason?"

"I don't know."

I studied her from across the table. "You still go to mass, though."

"Yeah." She shrugged her thin, bird-like shoulders. "Got to go somewhere. Why?"

"I don't know. Never mind."

We lapsed into silence. I imagined the stranger sitting on the edge of his cot, tense and worried, afraid to leave the room but just as afraid to stay in it. Standing up, pacing, fixing his gaze on the door, waiting for someone. The police. Someone like Jerry, with his long black gun. Me.

I closed my eyes.

"Your father had a sister," my grandmother said suddenly.

I looked up at her. "Sure," I said, wondering what had brought this up. "Aunt Jeanine."

"No."

I looked at her. She blinked back at me in her tortoise-like manner.

"Different sister," she said. "Lulu."

I eyed her warily. "I don't have an Aunt Lulu."

"You did. Before you were born. Long time before that." A streak of gravy had found its way into her hair, causing one curl to droop. "She had problems."

"What do you mean?"

"Problems," she said again vaguely. "She didn't develop right. She had problems in her brain. Seizures and other things."

I knitted my fingers together, uncertain of what to say. "I . . . didn't know that."

She shook her head. "They talked me into giving her up. The county. They took her away. She died when she was three." She looked down, aligning her fork and knife along the edge of her napkin. "Three years and five months. She never said a word. That's what they told me." Coughing, she covered her mouth. "That kind of thing used to happen back then. It's not like now, when they can fix these things.

Everything was different." She coughed again and reached for her glass of milk.

"After they told me she died, I was just so tired. That's when I stopped thinking about things like God, I guess. I just didn't have the energy. It takes energy to believe in that kind of thing, that's what I found out, and I didn't have it. I was busy taking care of your dad by then. He was almost two.

"The priest told me my faith would come back, but it didn't. I never told him that, though. I didn't feel like arguing about it." She crumbled a piece of bread.

I opened my mouth, but she went on. "I just didn't see the point of it—living. I did everything I was supposed to do. I did what I thought was best. I thought it would help her when I gave her up and it didn't. I thought it was the right thing." Her eyes flicked up, and she peered at me. "You looked a bit like her, when you were little. I always thought so."

I shifted in my chair. "Do you have a picture of her?"

"No." She closed her eyes and shook her head. "No pictures. We didn't have a camera back then." She took a long sip of milk. "I'm the only one left who remembers what she looked like." Then, with a wry look, "Me and God, I guess."

She began to pull the dishes and silverware toward her, stacking them in a careless pile. When that was done, however, she became still.

"I did what I thought was best," she said again. "To this day, I wonder if I was right or wrong. I never meant to hurt her. I never wanted that." She stopped, seeming to reconsider what else she had been going to say.

The kitchen sink dripped in the silence.

"For the life of me," she went on finally, "I don't know how it is that we wind up doing bad things at the exact moment we think we're doing good ones. That's one thing I've never been able to figure out."

We sat together. It seemed to me, as I absorbed her words, that the house was watching us, as if we were characters in a play.

"Can I ask you a question?" I said eventually.

She grunted, crumpling her napkin and dropping it on top of the plates.

"If you knew someone who had done something bad—I mean something really, really bad . . . What do you think you would do?"

She pursed her lips, eying me suspiciously. "Like who?"

"Just someone. Like a friend."

She raised her shoulders. "I don't know. Was it something they did to me?"

"No."

"Well, then," she said, bracing herself against the table and pushing herself up, "I don't see how it would be any of my business. But I don't know—I don't sit around and think about these things the way you do." She looked around. "Where's that thing your father got me?"

I retrieved her walker from the living room, watching her as I gathered the dishes until she was safely settled onto the sofa. She turned on the television, raised the volume, and lit a cigarette.

You still think about her, I thought. *Lulu*. Then, abruptly, I realized that I was looking at a woman who had never stopped thinking about her, a woman for whom the past wasn't past and never would be. Who was seized on the inside by doubt and regret.

Who was any number of things I suddenly and powerfully recognized.

"I'm sorry," I told her that night before I went to bed.

"For what?"

"For what you told me. Aunt Lulu."

"Yeah," she replied, in a voice that was somehow not her voice—the voice of a younger woman, a woman who was not yet sitting before me and smoking her life away, the woman who had stood in this same place some fifty years earlier and watched her children play on the rug. "Me, too."

2

I turned the key and pushed on the wooden door, which had begun to stick in its frame. The lights came on. The ice cream case and the grill showed their blank, shining surfaces.

I didn't think I needed to tell the stranger what I'd done. I'd hardly given the ranger who'd taken my call anything to go on, and anyway, I doubted she'd written any of it down. Even if she had, as far as she knew, I was just a crazy person who could barely manage to string a sentence together.

Still, I felt uneasy. When I opened my book, I found I couldn't read it and pushed it aside.

I had just unwrapped my sandwich and was gazing down at it, struggling to work up a desire to eat, when the door opened and the state troopers walked in.

There were two of them, a man and a woman. The man was lanky and awkward-looking, the woman petite and focused, her frizzy red hair pulled back in a knot.

I stood as they entered, my mouth dry.

As much as I'd been agonizing, I hadn't truly expected them. Not here. Not in front of me.

Not at all.

"Ms. Guttshall?" the woman said, taking a step toward me. She was remarkably compact, like one of the women wrestlers they sometimes showed on TV.

I took a deep breath that I hoped they wouldn't notice. "McElwain," I said.

She checked some papers on a clipboard. "Ms. McElwain. We were wondering if we could talk with you."

I rested my palms on the counter, as if to show I had nothing to hide, even though something within me had gone cold. "Sure."

"You know Mr. Landis? Up the hill?"

She meant Martin.

"Sure," I said again, attempting to shrug.

"You seen anything unusual going on up there lately?"

I sucked in my lower lip, trying to put on a puzzled look while my mind raced. "Unusual," I repeated.

"Yeah. Like, anybody going in or out at odd hours, for example. People maybe you don't know."

"Well," I said slowly. "I mean, it's a hostel."

"I'm talking about people who don't look like hostel guests."

I looked down at the counter, gripping my hands together and studying them for a moment. Then I looked up, my pulse thrumming in my ears.

I had to choose.

And I chose.

"No," I said. "I don't think so."

"No?" The woman raised her eyebrows. "Are you sure? One of my colleagues was up there the other day, but unfortunately Mr. Landis wasn't very cooperative. We thought you might be able to help."

I forced myself to meet her eyes. "No, ma'am," I said. "I'm sorry."

"It's a criminal offense to lie to the police, ma'am." She said it without anger, but with firmness. "Did you know Mr. Landis spent three years in the federal penitentiary up at Lewisburg?"

I stiffened, trying not to show the surprise I could tell she wanted me to show. Her partner was watching me keenly, my discomfort apparently rousing him from his boredom.

"No," I replied.

"He did. Aggravated assault. Heroin deal gone bad." She paused, as if for effect. "Victim suffered severe spinal injuries. He won't be able to walk again."

I crossed my arms. "I didn't know that," I told her, keeping my voice even. "And I don't care to know it now."

She sighed. "Please, ma'am. Don't make this hard. Where's your friend?"

"My friend?"

The man spoke up for the first time, with an authority I hadn't expected.

"Yes, your friend," he said, his tone so dispassionate it almost gave me chills. "The Russian guy. Rangers've had their eye on him for weeks."

I glanced from one face to the other. A deep, churning pit seemed to open in my chest.

"I don't know anyone from Russia," I said finally.

The woman looked as if she planned to stare me down. "Do you know what 'aiding and abetting' means?"

"Yes, ma'am." I set my face in a mask. "And I've never met anyone from Russia."

"You haven't?"

"No, ma'am," I said. In a bizarre way, I was almost tempted to laugh. "I haven't."

"You don't have any idea who I might be talking about?"

I had just opened my mouth to reply when the stranger himself appeared on the other side of the screen door, his expression hopeful but anxious. His lips stretching into a nervous, apologetic smile, he was glancing to the side, checking for unwanted visitors in the wrong places. Horrified, I watched him reach for the doorknob.

"I don't know any Russian guy," I repeated loudly, the sound of my voice so harsh and strange that the policewoman took a step back.

Behind the screen door, the stranger's face changed as he registered my words, emptying in shock. Then he opened the door.

"I believe you are looking for me," he said.

The two figures in uniform turned around.

"You stay here," the tall officer barked at me as the woman reached for the stranger's elbow.

They moved out of sight and I rushed to the door, leaning over the porch railing as they moved up the hill. The stranger's foot slipped, and he dropped to his knee in the mud. The tall officer grabbed his sleeve and yanked him up, pushing him forward. The hostel door closed behind them.

"That was so foolish," I told him.

We stood next to each other on the cold, pale sand at the edge of Fuller Lake. The moon was so full and close-looking that it seemed like it could sit in the palm of the hand. The tapering fingers of the pines jutted into the sky, reflected in the water below along with the few stars that were visible alongside the moon's light.

The stranger carefully unscrewed the cap on the bottle he was holding, the one I had brought from the cache I'd long ago found at the back of the storage room, and took a sip. "I had to do it. You couldn't see yourself. You looked—" He wiped his mouth with his sleeve and shook his head, handing the bottle back to me. "Besides, it was better for them to hear it from me. If I show I'm not afraid of them, maybe I can gain just a bit more time."

"You don't have time," I said.

He copied my pose, gazing at the lake, and didn't answer.

We weren't supposed to be here after dark; no one was. I listened for footsteps in the sand behind us, the breaking of a twig. But we were alone.

"What did they ask?" I said finally, twisting the bottle open and swallowing a mouthful of the honey-colored liquid. It burned my throat and traced a warm, slow trail to my stomach.

"Oh, this and that. What's my name, where did I come from, how long have I been here. They asked to see my passport, and I showed it to them. They made some phone calls, and then they went away."

"They saw your passport?"

"Yes."

"And nothing happened?"

"No."

There were small bits of quartz in the sand, rough, rectangular pebbles that glinted in the moonlight. It had been years since I'd seen the lake at night. I tugged the hood of my sweatshirt over my head until the water, sand, and trees were all I could see. It was cold, and my skin tingled, but the alcohol warmed me.

"Does that mean maybe nobody's looking for you anymore? I mean, no one important?" I asked.

"It means nobody's looking for the person in the passport," he said after a moment, tracing a line in the sand with the tip of his shoe.

The silence descended again. Slowly, I folded myself and sat down.

The lake was no longer frozen, not entirely. Islands of ice loomed on its surface, looking as though they were suspended in the darkness.

"Is your name really Daniil?" I asked.

Looking out across the water, he opened the bottle and took another sip. The whiskey had begun to go to my head, and as I watched him, it felt as though the ground had begun to revolve gently beneath me.

"No," he replied quietly.

I nodded, closing my eyes.

"Everything else I told you is true," he said, adding after a pause, "For better or for worse."

I waved a hand at him. "It doesn't matter."

After a moment, he sat down next to me, and I felt the sand shape itself around our bodies. The shore curved before us, and I remembered the day I had run out onto the ice, tempting fate. Or simply needing the danger in order to feel alive, to feel as if I were still myself.

"How long is it going to take them to figure that out?" I asked. "That the passport is fake?"

"The passport is real—it's just somebody else's. The people who brought me here, they arranged for that. They put my photo in it somehow." He touched his forehead and tugged at a strand of his hair. "Those officers said they didn't have a reason to arrest me. But . . . I've never been very good at telling lies, I'm afraid. I think they could see that. Maybe they'll forget me, but I think maybe they won't. They went away, but they never actually said they were finished."

I'd lent him one of my other sweatshirts, and his wrists stuck out of the sleeves. I looked at them, the fine black hairs on the backs of them. There was a feeling pressing in on me, warm in the wrong ways, agitating, rising inside my chest. Guilt. I shouldn't have made that call, shouldn't have tried to judge what wasn't mine to judge. But this wasn't a useful emotion, not now. I tried to press it back down.

"One thing I don't understand," I said carefully, "is why you've always seemed to think somebody was hunting for you. From the beginning, I mean. I just don't see why anyone would be so interested in you, especially if nobody tried to . . . arrest you, or whatever they could have done, after you went in front of the judge. Unless we just hunt for everyone we think is here illegally, and I don't know it."

He looked down at the bottle he still held in his lap. "Well," he said, with the same gentle, slightly regretful tone as always, "partly, I worry about people from my own country." He raised his palms. "But the other thing, the police . . . I don't know. It's a mystery to me, too. I'm Russian; maybe they think I'm some sort of spy."

I knew it was meant to be a joke but found it impossible to laugh. I let myself fall back, resting my hands on my chest and nestling my head in the sand.

The stranger drew a breath, as if he would speak, but stopped.

I waited. When his words did come, his voice was thick.

"I wish," he said slowly, "that things had been different. That I had done things differently. Of course I do."

I kept still, watching the back of his head.

"You know, I grieve about the things I did. That might not be how I should say it, but it's the best explanation I can give. I grieve as you do when someone dies. It's . . . somehow, it's a loss within me. As if, when I made the decisions I made, someone came and started taking the thing that was me out of my body. I walk around and yet I'm not myself." He paused, and I heard him exhale slowly. "I'm a coward, I know. If I weren't, I would go back and face . . . well, face what would happen. In my country, the authorities don't look kindly on those who have talked about what happens there. If I went back—if I were sent back—I would be punished. Wherever they took me, I would not walk back out again." He fell silent for a moment. "But then, there are those who would say I deserve to be punished. And I can't say they're wrong."

I watched him pick up a handful of sand and let it run through his fingers.

"This will sound absurd," he said, "but sometimes I feel so angry that . . . that there's nothing in human life we can ever take back. I don't believe in a God, but whatever it was that arranged things so we only experience time one way, moving forward, just forward . . . there are moments when that seems truly unfair. But I try not to lose myself in self-pity."

He stopped playing with the sand and rested his chin on his arms. Then he lay back as well.

"That's probably what forgiveness is for," I said, groping toward an idea that seemed faint but real. "It's a way of letting other people erase the mistake. Isn't it?"

"I'm not sure who would forgive me. And I'm not sure I would ask that of them. Just think, if—if it were you, would you forgive someone who had done what I did?"

Something deep in my body constricted. I started to speak, but my throat was dry from the liquor, and I coughed. Rocking forward, I rose slowly and walked to the edge of the lake, stumbling as my feet sank into the sand. Where the water met the shore, I bent down and cupped my hands, raising them to my face to drink. The water numbed my fingers; it tasted of leaves and stone. Looking up, I saw myself walking out onto the ice, my head high, so angry, so proud. So obviously distraught, as I understood now.

"No," I said when I sat down again. "I don't think I could. And in fact, I would probably be tempted to want to hurt you." I pulled my sleeves over my wet hands. "But I don't think anyone deserves that, either. You know, all our lives, we get told there's some person or some group of people out there who deserve to be killed or put in pain, because of what they did or how dangerous they are or whatever. And some people think other people are just . . . lower. Like they can be hurt, and it doesn't matter." I let out a breath, shaking my head. "There was a point in my life when I saw through all that. I'm not saying I'm especially smart; I'm not. Things just lined up in a way that let me see it. And I was pretty furious when I did. I felt like . . . like we were all getting tricked. Or even like we were made to become just like the thing we all thought we hated." I hugged myself tighter. "It's hard to keep sight of that, sometimes. Believe me. But I do think it."

The chill from the ground was reaching up into me, making my body feel as if it were gradually turning to stone.

"So, no, I'm not much for forgiveness, really. I think things should be fair. But hurting people isn't fairness. And I know that." I raised my shoulders, then dropped them. "Maybe that's what forgiveness means—maybe it's just that you're able not to want to hurt someone anymore. But I'm no priest. What do I know?"

I took a long swallow of whiskey.

"I think you know a lot," he said.

A twig fell into the water, creating ripples. Together, we watched them.

"Tomorrow," I said then, "we're going. You can decide where. But we're going. You can't stay here. In fact, I don't think you should even stay in your room tonight." The surroundings were beginning to spin, and my thoughts seemed to be running together, but I pushed on. "I'll take you as far as I can and then I'll—I'll see what I can do."

He opened the bottle and drained the last of it, wiping his mouth with his hand.

Looking out, it was still possible to see the ripples spreading.

"All right," he said.

We sat together, looking into the darkness side by side.

"Thank God," I replied after a moment. "I was getting sick of arguing with you."

His lips twitched, almost a smile. He planted the empty bottle back in the sand.

An owl called softly in the woods, its sound reaching us once, then twice.

"I would say 'thank you,'" he said. "But that wouldn't really be enough."

"You can thank me by picking a place to go. That's one thing I can't do for you. Believe me, I tried."

He looked down at his fingertips. "Whatever you think is best," he said eventually. "Just not a city. I don't want—it wouldn't be good for anyone to recognize me."

"Recognize you?" I looked at him, unsure whether to laugh or yell. "I don't understand how to get through to you. If you don't want to be recognized, then a city is exactly where you want to be. Not a place like this. You have no idea how much you stand out by hanging around in places that have a population of basically zero."

He laughed, although it was somehow a sad sound. "I do have some idea. And yes, I'm aware that you disagree with my current choice of residence. Maybe you're right." His gaze swept over the silent tableau around us. "Still," he went on, "there are many things about this that I don't regret. I have felt, in these past weeks—I don't know. There's something about being in such a place that reminds a person he's alive, in a way I probably couldn't explain." He rose to his knees, pushing against the sand. "And of course, I could never have imagined I would be shown such kindness."

I shook my head.

He stood and dusted the sand from his palms, bending over to brush off his jeans and extending a hand to me. I felt the ground tilt beneath me, and he caught my elbow as I stumbled forward.

"I'm fine," I said.

"I think maybe you shouldn't drive anywhere."

"Probably not. It's okay—I'll sleep in the car. I can check on things at home in the morning."

We left the beach and followed the path to the parking lot, the trees hovering over us and blotting out the sky. I concentrated on following the faint trail, lifting my feet over roots that suddenly seemed to be moving and shifting deceptively. It was several minutes before I realized that he seemed to be slowing behind me.

Finally, just as we reached the end of the trail, he stopped.

I sensed that he was gathering himself to say something, but for a long moment, he kept still. We both stood at the edge of the parking lot, the small clearing hemmed in by the pines that towered so steeply on all sides.

He looked at me. Putting his hands in his pockets, he seemed to pause, as if he were unsure of something. It wasn't until I heard the breath rushing in and out of his lungs that I realized he was shaking.

"Hey," I said. "What's wrong?"

Even as I said it, I knew. His fear filled the air around us, surrounding us in something metallic and cold.

"Come on," I said softly. "Come on. You're all right."

He nodded with a jerking motion, biting his lip, but the short, jagged breaths continued. He raised a hand to his face. "I know. I'm sorry."

"Don't be. It's just the whiskey. We're going to get you out of here—you're going to be fine."

He was looking at the ground, rubbing his wrist briskly across his eyes.

I reached out and touched his sleeve.

"It's all right," I said again.

He didn't answer. Slowly, he let out the breath he'd been holding, wiping his face with his fingers.

"Here, come on." I gestured for him to follow me, leading us toward the path that ran back to the store and the hostel. "Can you find your way back? If not, I'll walk with you."

"I can find it," he said. "I'm sorry. Thank you."

"There's no need to be sorry. But listen. We're going to get you out. Tomorrow, I promise. I'll open the store so nobody notices anything, but the minute I've done that, we'll go."

He swallowed. "Yes. Okay."

We looked at each other. The terror seemed to be draining from his face, leaving exhaustion in its wake. The gravel crackled under his feet as he shifted his weight.

"You know," he said, "if anything ever happens to me, I . . ."

"Nothing's going to happen to you. Go on, you just need to sleep it off."

We stood together, looking down the path, its entrance barely visible in the dark. Then he said goodnight and set off. I watched him walk into the woods, my eyes following his stumbling figure until it was gone.

In the morning, I walked into the house to find my grandmother sprawled next to the sink, her lips parted, unconscious. A shattered glass sparkled at her fingertips.

"No," I whispered.

I called the ambulance and sat next to her, holding her hand and brushing the hair out of her eyes, talking to her even though I knew she couldn't hear me, rocking back and forth as I held her. She opened her eyes briefly, looking at me without recognition, then closed them again.

I leaned against the cabinet, pressing my head against the wood, praying for the scene not to be real until the ambulance came and bore us away.

3

The hours passed with a torturous slowness. At the hospital, the nurses and doctors moved efficiently around my grandmother's motionless body, like insects that swarm over an object only to lose interest and be replaced by other insects. She'd had a stroke, they told me—something I'd already known without putting it into words. To all my other questions, including the most important one, they would only answer "maybe."

By the time I tore myself away from the gray cube of the building, the sun was high overhead. I stopped at the lights and made the turns automatically, moving like a machine, doing everything I could not to think or feel. Crocuses had begun to raise their heads through the snow, a scattering of violet along the roadside, but I barely noticed them. I barely noticed anything, even the through-hikers who had suddenly shown up at the hostel, the first of the season. They lounged on the porch and took it over, drinking the warm beer they'd lugged with them, but I didn't actually see them, not really. They were just a strange sort of human furniture.

Martin, I learned, had hidden the stranger in a kind of hole in the hostel basement, a bizarre crawlspace beneath the game room. I'd never seen it or even had an inkling it existed; it was accessible only by passing through the maze of the old root cellar and pushing aside some rotten boards that led to creaking steps, an airless room. The darkness there was absolute.

"What is this place?" I asked Martin as I followed the beam of his flashlight, taking in the damp earth of the floor, the moldering bricks of the walls.

"Underground Railroad," he said shortly.

"Oh." My eyes roamed over the dank, close space, the long cracks running through the ancient bricks. "Right."

"Either that or an old icehouse that got filled in. At any rate, it's nobody's idea of a good time, but it'll keep him out of sight until I can find a way to get him out of here." He looked more closely at me. "You okay?"

"Yeah. No. I'll tell you later."

Hearing us, the stranger emerged from the space in the wall, brushing dirt and cobwebs out of his hair.

"Welcome," he joked feebly, blinking in the light. "It's not the Ritz, as they say, but I suppose it will do. I'm afraid I've gotten spoiled by the first-class accommodations upstairs."

I tried to answer, but the words caught in my throat. Standing in front of the crevice in the wall that led to the crawlspace, his shoulders hunched and his hands in his pockets, he looked like a hunted animal.

Quietly, Martin left us, handing me the flashlight.

"I'm sorry," I said. "This is—it's—"

"Don't worry about me," he interjected. "I'm fine."

A hollow pain rose within me. "We'll still go," I said. "I'll get you out of here as soon as I can."

"Really. It's all right." There was a tension in his voice, an echo of the previous night's fear, but he did his best to hide it, smiling. Even as I watched his face, I couldn't bear to see it.

By the evening, there was no change. My grandmother seemed to be losing her shape, fading into the bed, but the doctor—a new one—talked about her "vitals" and said she was hanging on, if only by a thread. I pictured her unconscious form caught in a spider's web, coming loose, dangling over space.

There was a cheap restaurant in the middle of town, the Greek place, and I took refuge there that night, hunching over oyster sandwiches and French fries I barely touched. The dining room was jammed, waitresses nearly running up and down the aisles, couples and families jabbering in the booths while the man at the grill sweated over rows of hot dogs and hamburgers. I watched them from my table in the corner, stupefied; I couldn't remember the last time I'd been around so many people, all of them talking at once. The laughter, the noise, the tumult wrapped themselves around me so densely I kept staring around and blinking. *I must be getting strange*, I thought, but couldn't stop watching these unfamiliar people with their unfamiliar voices and gestures, finding myself astonished that the world still had so many other human beings in it.

Looking around at the booths and the rush of diners in and out, I thought of my grandfather, his loud laugh filled with false teeth. The last time I had seen him, a few months after the accident and just weeks before he died, he had taken me out for ice cream at a restaurant much like this one. Sitting upright had still been painful then, but I had tried not to show it, listening to his happy banter and doing my best to smile at his jokes. He had ordered a double cheeseburger while I'd asked for a scoop of vanilla. "You be sure and put a cherry on that," he'd told the waitress, giving me a wink.

Halfway through the meal, he had reached across the Formica tabletop and patted my hand. "You're gonna be all right, sweetie."

"Thanks, Grandpa."

"You will. I know it. After all, you're just like me."

I must have given him a wary look, because he'd laughed. "Not the bad parts. The good ones. You and me—" he had gestured at the other tables around us—"we're not like these people here. We've got brains in our heads. At least, we've got the brains to know there's something else out there, right?"

"I think everybody knows that," I'd said.

"No, sweetheart." He'd shaken his head ruefully. "They don't. You might think they do, but they don't."

After that, he'd seemed to watch me for a long moment.

"I'm an old man, you know," he'd said finally, then thrown his hands in the air. "God! Look how old I am. I look just like those old bastards who sit around bullshitting at the gas station all day. Somehow, I never thought this would happen." He'd been smiling, and I'd managed to smile back, although rays of pain were beginning to spread through the bones on my left side.

"And yet it still seems like just the other day you were a little thing riding around on my back like I was a horse." He'd picked up a cold French fry. "You remember that?"

"Yeah. Of course I do."

"Your grandmother hated it. We'd keep knocking things over in her living room and it'd drive her nuts."

"Yeah."

"Oh, well. We had fun, didn't we?"

There had been an odd note in his voice, and I'd looked up from my dish. His eyes had been almost too bright, his smile slightly uncertain.

"Sure, we did," I had answered, thrown off-guard.

He had reached over and patted my hand again. "You're a good girl," he'd said.

He'd begun talking about something else then, a car he'd bought the week before, the first one he'd ever had that was foreign-made. When we were ready to leave, he'd held my jacket for me, helping me as I cautiously slid my arms through the sleeves.

"You all right, honey?" he'd asked when he dropped me off at the house I had until recently shared with Amos, and which I hadn't yet relinquished. "Want me to walk you up to the porch?"

"No, I'm fine. Thanks for taking me out, Grandpa."

He had reached over and hugged me, kissing me roughly on the cheek the way he always did. "Sure thing, my girl. Like I said, you're gonna be all right. You just remember that."

I had walked into the house, pushing my way through the heavy door with its flaking paint. Inside, as I'd struggled to take off the jacket, I'd realized that the car's engine was still running outside. Through the picture window in the living room, I'd caught sight of my grandfather slumped in his seat behind the wheel, his eyes closed and his hand over his mouth. He'd rocked forward, his shoulders seeming to shake. Just as I was about to go back outside, he had straightened, seeming to compose himself, and driven away.

I missed him. To this day, I regretted not having gone out to him, telling him that everything would be all right. That I loved him, which, in spite of everything, I did.

The nurses let me spend the night in my grandmother's room, curled in the armchair in the corner. When the dawn came, her condition still had neither worsened nor improved.

"If she pulls through, she's going to be in pretty rough shape," one of the early-shift doctors said. "She'll need somebody with her around the clock. You folks thought about how you're going to take care of that?"

On the drive up the mountain, I kept hearing his voice. *If she pulls through. You folks thought about that? Around the clock. If she pulls through. If.*

"I don't know what to do," I told the stranger at last, standing before him in the dark pit where I could see him shiver even though he tried to hide it. "We have to get you out. But I can't leave her."

But by then, he was calm, almost strangely so. I didn't know where it came from, this eerie tranquility, nor was I sure I wanted to. I didn't let myself imagine what he thought about, alone in the blackness hour after hour.

"It's all right," he said in response. Then, to my surprise, he gave a small laugh. "It's the way of the world, isn't it? Nothing is ever as we expect."

That afternoon, Jerry came into the store. There was no gun this time, but the look in his eyes made me uneasy anyway. I moved mechanically but warily, fixing his food.

"Thanks," he said when I gave it to him.

I waited for him to put the bag on the counter, but he didn't. Instead, he lifted his cap and resettled it on his head, looking away. His face, I realized, looked as though it had aged, marred by deep lines that I couldn't remember having been there before.

"Hey, listen," he said.

His tone made my back stiffen.

Not again, I thought. *Not now.*

He slid his thick hands into his pockets.

"I'm gonna need an advance," he said.

I looked at him. His beard had grown longer, nearly reaching his chest.

"An advance," I repeated.

"Yeah."

The electric heater on the wall hummed.

"I don't know what you mean."

"Five hundred," he said.

I looked at him. Between us, his drink was cooling.

"Five hundred?" I echoed, although I knew I'd heard him right.

"Yeah."

We locked eyes.

"I don't have five hundred," I told him.

"Yeah, I know." He straightened and looked away. "But you're gonna have to get it anyway."

"Well," I said after a moment, "I can't."

He licked his lips, seeming to prepare himself.

"You're gonna have to," he repeated. "Or else I tell my niece. About you."

For a moment, the world stopped. I imagined Beth as she might have

looked at that very moment, pursing her bright-pink lips as she listened
to a customer attempt to banter with her. The way she'd leaned toward
me on the couch the day we'd fought. How she'd held my hand when
I'd been recovering on my hospital bed for all those months, barely
speaking to anyone. The hope in her eyes when she'd tried to talk me
into going back to college.

I looked at him, and then I began to laugh. A long, rolling laugh
that filled the store.

"Go ahead," I said. "Tell her. In fact, invite me when you do."

His face tightened.

I kept laughing, trying to stop but unable. For a second, I worried
I would lose control and slide into hysterics, but eventually I slowed
down.

He waited until I was done. Then, leaning forward, he put his hands
against the counter, bringing his face inches from mine. From inside
his clothing, there was the clank of something metallic. I could smell
motor oil, sweat, wood smoke.

For a long moment, he didn't say anything. I stayed where I was,
seeing the redness of his eyes, a scratch that ran down the edge of his
mouth.

He was thinking about something, something other than the scene
that was playing out between us. I could see it.

He wanted me to see it. To know that he knew.

There was no laughing now. He had the look of someone who,
no matter what else he might be, fully understood his own size and
strength. Who had the advantage.

"Don't be a fool, girl," he said quietly. "I know every inch of this
place. You think I don't know where he is?"

A cold sensation ran down my arms and legs. I stared him in the
face, but inside I quavered.

He looked me up and down. Then he pushed himself back from the
counter, shrugging.

"Have it your way," he said in a low, flat tone, and turned away.

I watched him take a step toward the door.

"Wait," I said.

For a moment, I didn't move.

Then I opened the register, taking out the tens and twenties. My
fingers seemed to thicken as I counted them, putting them in slim
piles.

There wasn't enough.

With quick steps, I moved past him. Through the door, outside, into the storage room, to the safe in the wall. I spun the combination lock and reemerged.

"Here," I said, holding out the bills.

We stood facing each other on the porch, squaring off.

He counted the cash, keeping half an eye on me as he did so.

"Okay," he said finally.

I looked at him, the money in his fist. The bills seemed abnormally green, as if they'd been transformed, as if they were shouting to the world that something had happened here, something for which someone should feel guilty. I felt my skin prickle.

He folded them and put them in his pocket.

"Next time," he said, "don't say 'no' to me. It don't suit you."

His boots made heavy sounds as he walked across the porch. He looked back at me for a moment, then vanished around the corner of the building.

I only realized then that there was still nothing on the counter. No bag.

I locked the store and climbed the steep embankment behind it, sitting down on the shoulder of the state road and looking out over the park. The trees hadn't begun to bud yet, but the snow was disappearing, and I knew the great thaw wasn't far off. I reached out to pluck a crocus, then wrapped my arms around my knees, picturing my grandmother in her hospital bed, the empty house, my room, the paper bag under the mattress, the trodden earth as I'd followed John on his horse, the great stretch of the valley, the mountains that bounded the world.

There was only one thing to be done, I thought. About the stranger, about everything.

And I would do it, I knew then.

I would do it.

Still carrying the crocus like some kind of talisman, I slipped into the hostel, glancing around to make sure I wasn't being observed, although by now I knew I probably was. I made my way down to the basement, then the crawlspace, feeling my way in the darkness until I reached the bottom of the ladder.

"Hey," I said, my voice sounding strange in my own ears.

"Oh," a voice replied. "I wasn't expecting you." There was a click, and the stranger appeared, holding the flashlight Martin had given him.

"We'll leave first thing tomorrow," I said. "I just have to do something first. It's important, but I'll . . . I'll take care of it as quickly as I can."

There was a layer of dust on his skin, but his eyes shone out at me.

"You look so terribly sad," he said.

I gestured the words away. "Let's not talk about it. I had some decisions to make, and I've made them." I reached out to touch a loose brick in the wall. "I'll probably still open the store in the morning so no one gets suspicious, like we talked about." There was a twisting in my gut, but I didn't tell him who "no one" was. "I'm not sure how we're going to get you out of the building without anyone noticing, but I'll talk to Martin and we'll figure out something."

He hesitated, then nodded. His look was vague and thoughtful, as if his mind were far away. Glancing around at the cracked walls, he looked back at me as if he might say something, but he didn't. If he hadn't nodded, I would almost have wondered if he'd heard me.

"What's that?" he asked finally, glancing down at my hand.

"What? Oh. It's a crocus. First sign of spring. Here, take it."

I gave it to him, his dusty fingers brushing my palm. He raised it to his face.

"Don't be afraid," I said, as much to myself as to him.

He didn't respond. Instead, he held the flower in front of him, turning it in his fingers, taking in the deep violet color that was even more striking in the dim light.

"I brought your bird down here," he said, sounding almost shy.

"Bird? What bird?"

He knelt and reached behind him, then held out a glass figurine. It was coated with dirt, but still whole.

"Oh," I said, taking it in my hands. The glass was cold.

"It makes me think of better places. If you understand what I mean." He smiled, looking down at his shoes. Then he looked back up. "You know," he said, "truly, you are very good. I've met few people who would be so generous."

My throat constricted, and I looked away. "I'm not as good as you think I am. Believe me. I wish I were."

"You've made all the difference to me."

I grimaced. "No," I said with difficulty. "I've made things worse for you. You don't realize it, but I have."

He shook his head. Then, reaching forward tentatively, he brushed the hair away from my face, taking care not to graze my skin, as if he were afraid I would run away. Surprised, I looked up at him.

He put his hand on my face then, his palm curving gently around my chin and his thumb resting on my cheekbone. His fingers were cool against my skin. As I stood still, he moved toward me, putting his mouth against mine. I felt the pulsing at his throat, the soft edge of his collar, realized I knew his smell.

He let me go, and I stepped back, stunned.

I found myself unable to look at him, caught by the sensations warring within me. Instead, I stood there, holding myself still, staring at the circle of light on the ground.

"I was thinking maybe northern New York," I said finally, my voice sounding disconnected even to my own ears. "Along the river. From there, you can decide what's best. I mean, heading down toward the city or up to the border or something. If that's what you want."

A silence filled the small space.

"All right," he said.

We stood wordlessly for a moment, the light shining between us.

"I should get going," I said then, holding out the figurine. "There are things you're—we're—going to need. For the trip."

"Yes," he replied. "Of course. Go ahead."

"All right." I stuffed my hands into my pockets. "I'll see you then."

Turning, I began to walk away.

"You know," I heard him say, his voice trailing off.

I stopped, my foot on the ladder. But he didn't finish the sentence. "What?"

Even in the dim light, I could see his face turn a deep red.

"Only that if you want to come back . . . I will still be here." He gave a small, embarrassed laugh. "I mean, of course I will. But . . . it's just that you mean very much to me. That's all."

Behind him, the blackness was so black it looked infinite. I could hear my own breathing.

I lifted my hand to the rung.

"I'll see you tomorrow," I said.

I mounted the ladder, choosing not to see him still standing there.

In the car, I shook myself, blowing on my cold fingers and gazing through the windshield at the steep wall of forest in front of me. It hadn't happened, I told myself. It simply hadn't happened.

I started the engine.

In town, I drove up to the ATM and left minutes later with my life savings—a pathetically small bundle of green—folded inside my fist. At the Walmart, I stuffed a wire basket with water, sandwiches, two sets of men's clothing that didn't look as if they'd come from some backwater Salvation Army, a pair of off-brand sneakers, a baseball cap that could be pulled low over the eyes.

Then, at the hospital's back entrance, I joined the knot of people who always seemed to be there, drawing on their cigarettes and looking up at the setting sun. I asked my question, quietly, and after a moment of hesitation one of them told me where to go.

In an alley that ran between the courthouse and the bar next to it, near a warren of two-story houses that had been turned into apartments for the very young and the very old, I found a scraggly-looking man in a black jacket and told him what I wanted.

He looked me up and down suspiciously. Something about him looked familiar, as if I might have gone to school with him. I probably had.

"Twenty," I said, opening my hand slightly to show him the folded bills there.

He still looked reluctant.

"You can search me," I told him.

He moved away with a slouching but still alert walk and a few minutes later was back with a larger man, who did search me, patting me up and down as I stared up at the slice of waning light between the buildings, keeping any expression from my face.

When he was finished, the larger man looked at me. Maybe he recognized me, or maybe there was simply something in my look that he'd seen before.

"Give it to her," he said to the smaller man.

I left with the bag in my pocket, walking alone back up the alley.

In the hospital lobby, I asked the receptionist if I could use the phone and dialed Beth. When she picked up, I suddenly found myself struggling not to cry.

"I'm sorry," I told her, my voice threatening to break. "I can't talk long. But I'm so sorry. I just want you to know that."

"Oh, hon," she breathed on the other end. "Don't be. I'm the one who's sorry. I should have known better than to say those things. You're doing what's right for you—I know that."

My breathing became uneven, and I turned away from the waiting room, trying to hide my face in my sleeve.

"Honey," she said. "Do you need me? Where are you?"

While I waited for her, I sat by my grandmother's side, holding her hand and listening to the sound of her breathing. Her hair was a tangled cloud, and I washed it, running a cloth carefully over her face, the crown of her head. When I was done, she didn't look any more like herself; she still seemed empty, just another old woman in the hospital. But I talked to her anyway, straightening her gown over her shoulders, telling her things she would have scoffed at if she'd been awake. At last, moving around the machines, I kissed her on the cheek and held her palm, keeping it in mine for a long time.

Eventually, there was a rustling sound in the hallway, then a child's fussing. "Kathy?"

I walked out, closing the door behind me.

Beth had Dylan on her hip, her purse slung over her other arm, an expression on her face that was almost like fear. She drew me into a hug. "Is she . . ."

"No, she's still alive."

"Oh, thank God." Dylan's face was red, as if he'd just been crying, and she ran her fingers over his cheeks. "What's going on?"

"I have to go somewhere," I said. "For a while. I'm sorry to ask—you don't have to, but could you . . ."

She put the child down, and he clung to her leg. "Check up on her? Sure, when do you need me?"

"I'm . . . things are a little unclear right now. Maybe—maybe you could call my parents tomorrow? If it's not too much trouble?"

"Of course, hon."

"You're wonderful." The words felt inadequate, but they were the only ones I had. "Thank you."

Dylan pulled at her jeans and began making thin sounds, as if he were considering crying again. As she moved his hands away, something about the way the artificial light of the corridor struck her face showed me a thing I hadn't seen before.

"Are you . . ."

She gave me a long, sad smile. "Yeah. I'm pregnant."

My mouth opened, but I couldn't do anything more than look at her.

"Yeah." She looked away. "When Mark was here on leave—we really didn't want this—I definitely didn't—but—well." She ran a hand through her hair, lifting her shoulders. "I'm due before he's even back. Isn't that—well, it's crazy. So, our big back-to-school dream wasn't going to work out anyway, I guess."

"I'm—" I was too disoriented from the speed at which everything was happening to know what to say. "I'm sorry. I mean, congratulations. But also I'm sorry."

She gave a laugh that wasn't a laugh. "Yeah," she said. "That's just about it, isn't it?"

I wrote down some numbers for her, and she took them, already looking older and more tired. Reaching for me, she wrapped me in a hug again, her hair pressed against my cheek.

"Do I need to worry about you?" she said. "Don't get mad at me for asking, but have you gotten mixed up in something you shouldn't have? Where exactly are you going?"

"No, I promise. And I'll tell you everything in a few days."

"All right, baby girl." She rubbed my arms. "You go enjoy your freedom."

At the gas station, I filled the tank, then began the drive west, back to my grandmother's house. The sun was almost down, the clouds black and low on the horizon, edged with a last tinge of heavy blue. The mountains loomed in the distance, and I looked up at them. The car radio was playing, but I turned it off, watching the long chain of peaks pass by in the silence. When I got to the intersection in Centerville, I stopped, sitting with my headlights cutting swaths of light across the road.

There was something in the air, something that came with the changing of the seasons, leading a person to have thoughts that would normally be unthinkable.

I looked down at the glowing panel of gauges, the clock. The fields outside were vast, open, looking somehow new. I drew the night air into my lungs, letting it slowly back out again.

Then I turned away from home and kept driving, back up the mountain, toward the brick building that loomed in the darkness, lost among the trees.

4

The next morning, the telephone in the store rang.

The dawn had brought a clear day, the light extending its first fingers through the windows of my grandmother's house as I'd roamed through it, quietly stuffing clothes into plastic bags, making the bed, putting away the dishes. The gravel had crunched under my feet as I'd walked to the mailbox, the sun illuminating the red flag that stood proudly above it. Reaching into the box, I'd pulled out a pile of bills and junk mail. Perhaps superstitiously, I had thought there might be a letter from my brother, but there wasn't.

Back in the house, I'd placed the bills on the table, unopened. Then I had left, turning a key in the front door that, in my lifetime, had never been locked.

I was calm, much more so than I'd expected to be. Returning from the hostel to my grandmother's house very early that morning, watching the headlights pass over fields that were otherwise swathed in darkness, I hadn't known what to think—about the stranger, about any of it. In some ways, I didn't want to think about what had just happened at all—the way his face had looked when I'd reappeared; the drawn curtains in the upstairs room; the silence; the way he'd run his hand over my skin, the smooth places and the scars. It was something too strange, too enormous to be looked at. So I didn't. I put it away in the back of my mind, like a mysterious object I'd found in the street, to be taken out and considered later.

Thankfully, no one had been waiting for me at the store; it was still early. Shouldering my purse, I'd pushed my way inside, turning on the lights. I still had enough cash for another two or three tanks of gas, a bit more for a sandwich here or there. I didn't think about what would happen after that.

The sound of the telephone tore through the air like an electric shock.

I stared at the receiver on the wall next to the ice cream case. How long had it been working? Why hadn't anyone told me?

"Hello?" I said uncertainly.

"Kath, it's Martin." He sounded breathless. "Could you come up here for a minute?"

I hung up and hurried out, letting the door slap shut behind me.

Martin was standing behind the front desk, face devoid of expression, back hunched like a question mark. With him were two police officers I didn't recognize, both men.

"Is this her?" one of them asked Martin. He had sandy hair and tanned, smooth features, like a high-school track coach. Martin, by contrast, looked haggard and shriveled. There was a hammer on the desk, and he was turning a long, shining nail over in his hands, not looking up.

"What do you want?" I asked, with a feeling of deep dread.

"We just took your friend into custody," the other officer said.

I looked from them to Martin, who looked back at me, his face empty and devastated. The room seemed to close in on itself, the air suddenly cold.

"My friend?" I forced myself to say, my voice sounding flat and far away.

"Come on, don't play dumb," the sandy-haired one said. "The foreigner."

I glanced from one of them to the other, struggling to hide my shock.

"We're aware of your relationship with the minister," the same cop went on. "We'd like to ask you a few questions about him, if that's all right."

It took me a moment to absorb the words.

"The minister?" I echoed, confused. Martin lowered his head again.

"We'd like to ask you a few questions," the sandy-haired one repeated.

"No, I don't think so." I took a step back. "I don't even know who you're talking about. I don't know any minister."

"I'm talking about your friend," he said patiently, as if talking to a small child. "The, uh . . ." He pulled a leather-bound notepad from his pocket and consulted it. "The Deputy Minister of the Interior, or whatever he is. We picked him up here about half an hour ago. Somebody called in with an anonymous tip this morning. Seems he's been hiding out here for a while."

"He's in a whole lot of trouble," the other cop said. His trooper's hat was pulled low over his eyes; I couldn't see his face clearly, although it looked round and pink. "They've called the FBI in for this one," he went on. "They've called in the State Department. Our phone's been ringing off the hook all morning. People from Washington. Whoever this guy is, he's somebody's big catch, that's for sure. And that's not gonna make things any easier for you if you decide you don't feel like cooperating."

My legs began to bend under me, although I managed to step sideways and sit in one of the chairs that were pushed against the wall. "I still don't know what you're talking about. Deputy minister? What is this?"

"This guy, lady." The same cop, the one with the face like an Easter ham, reached into an envelope and held out a photocopy. The black-and-white picture showed a serious, thin-lipped man with a puffy face and neatly trimmed hair, staring straight at the camera with long, narrow eyes. He wore a suit and tie, and was holding a briefcase in one hand, a sheet of paper in the other. There were tables in the background, a patterned carpet, as if he were in some sort of fancy restaurant or ballroom. A shining clip held his tie in place over his rounded stomach.

"I don't know who that is," I told them, pushing the photocopy away.

"Look again." The cop held it out in front of me. "He looks different now. He's obviously lost a lot of weight. But you know him. He's been here for months."

"I don't know who that is," I said again. "I'm not lying."

"That man is responsible for a lot of things, ma'am. At least that's what we're told. He ran the detention centers in Uzbekistan. He oversaw—"

I rose to my feet, bracing myself against the wall.

"You don't know what you're talking about," I said harshly. "And frankly, I don't either."

"Come on, don't bullshit us," the Easter-ham cop said.

I rounded on him. "You don't know the first thing," I said, my voice forceful. "You don't even know where Uzbekistan is. I'd bet money on it."

They looked at one another.

"I'll be in my store," I said. "If you want to talk to me, bring me a piece of paper that says I have to."

Without looking at Martin, I left and walked briskly back down the hill. Inside the store, I locked and bolted the door, closed the shutters, and sat down on the stool. My fingers pressed to my lips, I kept still.

The hours passed. Someone knocked, hesitant and hopeful-sounding, before giving up and going away. I stayed where I was, watching the squares of light from the windows as they crept across the floor, leaning and elongating as the sun moved west.

After a long time, the knob twisted, and I heard Martin calling.

"Kathleen," he said.

I remained motionless.

"Come on," he urged, more loudly this time. "Don't scare me. I know you wouldn't do that to me. Open up."

Slowly, I slid one leg to the floor, then the other.

I thought he might have given up by the time I appeared, but he was still there.

"Come on," he said. "Come out here with me. It's better than sitting alone in the dark."

I gave in. He sat on the bench on the porch, and after a moment, I lowered myself next to him.

The minutes passed.

"Do you think it's true?" he said, just when I'd decided neither of us was going to say anything, that we were going to just sit there forever.

"Do I think what's true?"

"This deputy minister stuff."

I looked away. "It doesn't matter."

He kept his eyes on me for a long moment.

"It didn't look much like him," he said finally.

"What's it to me, whether it was or wasn't him?"

"Come on, Kathleen. It's not like I'm not upset, too."

My shoulders sagged, and I turned my head away. "You're right. I'm sorry."

We lapsed back into silence, gazing down at the ruins of the furnace stack.

"We did our best," he said eventually. "We did what we thought was right. And it *was* right. No matter who he was. Is. I don't doubt that."

"Yes, you do."

"No. I don't."

I kicked a shoe against the cement.

"'For I was hungry,'" he said softly, "'and you fed me. I was thirsty, and you gave me drink. I was a stranger, and you invited me into your home. I was naked and you clothed me, I was sick and you cared for me. I was in prison, and you came to me.' Matthew twenty-five." He looked out at the yard, the stone furnace. "It's a beautiful chapter."

"I don't need that bullshit right now," I said. "No offense."

He went silent.

"I mean, yeah, those are some nice words. But . . ." I rolled my head back. "Well, anyway, I didn't."

"You didn't what?"

"I didn't do what I was supposed to do. Or rather, I did something I shouldn't have done." I picked at the edge of the bench. "I think. I don't know."

"You mean helping him?"

"No. The opposite of that." I felt myself grow heavy. "I was angry with him. He told me . . . something. Not what they told us today, but something. And I . . ."

I found I couldn't finish.

"Listen," he said, and surprised me by touching my hand. "That anonymous tip."

My stomach turned. "Yeah?"

"It wasn't me."

"Of course it wasn't."

"And it wasn't you."

Flinching, I pulled my hand away and gazed at the roof of the porch, frowning.

"They said it was some guy who called this morning," he said gently. "It wasn't you. It wasn't either of us."

"Don't be so sure," I said.

"It was a man," he said again. "They told me."

My vision began to blur. I wiped my eyes tiredly, looking away.

"Then it was Jerry."

"Who?"

"Jerry Calaman."

"Jerry *Calaman*? What's any of this got to do with him?"

"He was angry with me. And he knew something was going on."

Martin ran a hand over his face, pulling the skin down. "Listen to me. When they arrested Danya, he was in his room. He wasn't in the basement. He was sitting there on his bed with his suitcase packed."

"So?"

"I think—well, I think it's pretty clear what happened."

"Yeah, he was waiting for me to pick him up."

"No." He sighed. "Well. Maybe. But I don't think so."

"What are you trying to say?" I asked.

He looked at me.

"I think he turned himself in," he said quietly.

I fixed him with a long stare. A kind of jerk, or shudder, ran through my body. He looked away.

"Why would he do that?" I said.

"Because there were risks he decided he couldn't bear to see you take on his behalf."

I stood up rapidly and walked to the edge of the porch, crossing my arms.

"Or because on some level he always meant for this to happen," Martin went on behind me. "Or both."

"What do you mean, always meant for this to happen?"

I heard the creak of the bench, could picture Martin hunching forward, staring down at his feet. "Regardless of what he is or isn't," he said slowly, "I think that man was carrying around some heavy burdens. And even though he was hiding here, he wasn't really hiding. He was running, but he also wasn't really running. I think—" He stopped before going on. "I think we may have been watching someone do slowly what many people do a lot more quickly. People who feel guilt. People who feel sadness. People who don't know how to ease either of those things. You didn't see it, and I didn't see it." His words grew softer. "Or maybe I did see it, but I didn't do enough. I wish I had."

I left the porch and walked onto the grass, to the edge of the hill, looking down over the trail and the park. Wrapping my arms around myself, feeling my own body under my clothes, I stared down at the blank stretch of the picnic grounds.

In my mind's eye, I saw the stranger as he had stood before me the previous night, turning his head away shyly, covering his nakedness with his hand. The image was more than I could bear.

Martin came and stood beside me.

The spring breeze passed over us, over the trees, stirring everything around us invisibly before fading and disappearing.

We were quiet for a time, side by side, the descending sun shining into our faces.

"I'm going," I said then.

He studied me for a moment before answering. "Okay."

"No, I mean I'm really going. I'm leaving."

Closing his eyes, he straightened as if bracing himself.

"All right," he said finally. "Where?"

"I don't know yet."

He took a deep breath. Then he motioned toward the hostel. "Come with me."

"No." I suddenly felt too exhausted to stand. "That's okay. Some other time."

"Oh, just come on. It won't take long."

He turned and walked up the hill, and I followed him.

I was afraid we would go down to the basement, but we didn't. Instead, he led me to the top floor, the one with the dormitory-style rooms that gave a view of the trail as it disappeared into the woods. The bunk beds inside had been pushed back against the walls, leaving a large space in the middle, and a strange contraption stood there, something with multiple wheels and bars and a set of protruding gears. There was some sort of seat in the middle of it, set at an angle, long and black. I thought I saw a handle jutting up somewhere, but I couldn't be sure. The linoleum around the thing was smeared with grease.

I stood in the doorway.

"I don't understand," I said after a pause.

"It was for you," he said. "If you wanted it. I had to guess your height, but I did my best." He stepped forward, placing a hand on what seemed to be a pair of pedals.

"But—" It was difficult not to feel as if I were moving through a dream. "What is it?"

"It's a recumbent bike." Slowly, he spun the pedals, looking thoughtful. "Although I've realized lately that you wouldn't want it. I originally thought—with your hip and everything—it would be easier on you than a regular bike. That you might enjoy it." He stole a glance at me. "But, you know, I think . . . well, I think I probably should've know you wouldn't want to use anything different from what everyone else uses."

I was still confounded. "You made this for me?"

"Yeah. But it's all right. It doesn't have to be for you. Somebody else will take it. I guess I just—" He laughed to himself. "I'm not sure what I was thinking, really."

I looked from him to the thing.

Penance, I thought.

"Martin," I said then, looking at him and, for the first time in all the years I'd known him, truly seeing him, this man with his quiet intelligence and unwavering compassion, his strident and almost foolish faith in human goodness. "I'm so sorry."

"What do you have to be sorry about?"

"I don't know. All of it. You're never anything but kind, and we all—"

"Oh," he interrupted, "nonsense. Now." He took his hand off the machine. "What do you need me to do?"

For a moment, I couldn't speak.

"Well," I said when I'd gathered myself, "if you could call Herman— you know, the store's owner—and maybe find somebody else who can watch the place—"

"Done. I have cousins. That's what they're for. Next?"

"And . . . and tell Herman I'll pay him back."

"Pay him back?"

"Yeah."

He seemed to consider this, but put his questions aside. "Okay. Anything else?"

I closed my eyes. "Nothing. That's all."

"Listen," he said. "Go ahead. Go." There was an effort in his voice, as if he were forcing himself to say the words. "This place will still be here when you get back."

"I don't think I'm coming back."

"I see." He looked down at the streaks of black on the floor, then back up. "Well, if that's how it's meant to be, then that's how it's meant to be."

We walked back down the stairs together, and for the second time in twenty-four hours, I found myself facing someone and not knowing what to say.

"Goodbye, then," he told me, reaching out to shake my hand, pressing mine in both of his. "You—you take care out there. And you know, the minute you need—"

"Yes," I said. "I know."

We held each other's gaze, our hands clasped.

"Go on, then," he said, his voice strained.

I went, not turning around, realizing that if I looked back at him, I would never go.

Outside, I noticed that one of the store's windows was open, yawning darkly like a toothless mouth. For a moment, I looked at it, feeling the cool air on my skin. Then I strode out of the parking lot and up the hill, leaving the car behind. In the shade that lined the sides of the road, I walked toward the sun, shielding my eyes. A pickup swept by me, its driver raising a hand in greeting. I turned my head, pretending I hadn't seen.

Fifteen minutes later, I turned onto the dirt path that led to the prison camp, not caring about the mud that soaked my shoes. I stood there at the entrance, gazing into the forest, taking from it the last peace it would ever give me, picturing the grasses and streams that would come with the summer, slowly covering the ruins as if to shield them, to keep them hidden from those who would seek to map them, to find meaning in what they once were. The fire hadn't touched this place. The only thing that could undo it, it seemed, was time, the time that would either continue to pull it open to the view of others like a wound or, someday, let it close and disappear and be forgotten.

By the time I returned to the parking lot, the sun was beginning to descend. A bird sang somewhere in the woods, and for the first time in months, I saw a column of smoke rising from the campground. I drove away, slowing only when I passed St. Eleanor Regina, the chapel named after a dead queen whose heart had been removed and buried miles away from her body. I knew how she felt, I thought, picturing the silent woman stretched out, her hands folded over the void in her chest, her eyes closed. I knew how she felt.

In town, I was careful, as I always was. I stopped at all the red lights, accelerated slowly on green, kept an eye out for pedestrians. Passing the two strip malls and the Joyride bar—its parking lot so full that two cars were waiting for spaces, their headlights glowing—I got onto the interstate.

At Harrisburg, I merged onto another highway, taking it north, past Hershey. The medical center where I had been treated after the accident was visible from the road, and as I watched, a helicopter landed on the flat roof of one of the buildings, illuminated by floodlights.

Moments later, it was gone, hidden by the trees on the side of the road.

Keeping my eyes fixed ahead, I passed it and left it behind.

The truth about the accident, of course, was that it hadn't been an accident; furthermore, as far as I knew, I hadn't been hurt at all in the wreck. I was the only one who knew that, and I had never told anyone, even though it would have been easy enough for someone to figure out. I had always expected to be asked about it, but I never was. Everyone was too frightened, I guessed; there was probably plenty that was frightening about me in those early days, bolted and sewn back together and drugged the way that I was. Even so, I always wondered why it was that everyone seemed happy to take the story I told them at face value, and that no one—not a single person—ever asked how it was possible that someone who had been sitting in the passenger's seat of a car had wound up with so very many injuries on her left side.

Memory is a funny thing. People, as I learned from the handful of psychology books I later found at the library, can be tortured and not remember, kidnapped and not remember, attacked on the street and not remember. Some do remember, but only peripheral things, like the shirt they were wearing or the face on the billboard across the street, the song that was playing on the radio, the color of the sky, the stains on the walls, the sound of some other terrible thing that was happening to someone else nearby. I remembered everything about that afternoon, though, maybe because it wasn't really such a surprise.

It was a Monday in March. Amos had been laid off a few days earlier after spending the long, cheerless winter working on a building site in Carlisle. Ever since the garage incident, I'd been locked in the house, unable to open the windows or doors. That day, however, he had decided to take me with him while he went fishing up at Possum Lake, on North Mountain, across the valley from the park where I would later work.

I would never know why he brought me along; it was a drizzly day, and maybe he thought he would be lonely, out at the end of the long wooden pier. I sat next to him on a plastic lawn chair, shivering. He had stopped bringing food to the house, eating on his way to and from work instead, with the result that he was increasingly puffy while I was becoming slighter with each passing week. I was determined to leave again, stowing my few possessions away in a corner of the attic, waiting for another chance, a better one, telling myself I would get it right this time, I would run to a place where he'd never find me. I knew it

was little more than a fantasy, but I fought hard to hang onto it, clinging to it on bad days, struggling to remember it on what seemed to be
good days, willing myself not to let go, not to forget.

I wasn't as brave as my grandmother had been; or rather, if I was, it
was in a different way. When he did the things he did, I didn't shout or
fight back, and after the day when I had fled so uselessly to the priest,
I didn't run. Instead, the war I fought was based on a single tactic:
patience. I waited. I waited for him to make a mistake.

For a long time, I was hopeful, but I discovered that hope is hard
to maintain when you're hungry. Hunger trumps everything; there
are no other thoughts, no other real desires or fears. Increasingly, I
spent my days wandering around the house in the quiet, searching
for something that would keep me from thinking about food, wishing
for the radios Amos had taken away, wondering if I would actually go
crazy from the silence. Often, I simply slept, since sleep was a place
where I couldn't feel the clamoring emptiness in my gut. But all the
time, I was waiting. Ready.

That day, on the edge of the dock, with no one else around to see
us, I stood up tentatively to stretch, then sat back down when Amos
yanked on my arm. He was tense; I could see that. He kept recasting
his line for no reason, his face an almost eerie blank as he stared out
at the gray water.

It was the loss of his job, I thought. It would pass.

For a while, I, too, stared out at the water. The pier stretched out
behind us, so long that it felt as if we were on an island by ourselves.
Amos clapped a hand to his neck, swatting a mosquito, then was still
again. There was no wind, and the long grasses and cattails seemed to
stand sentry, guarding the hostile and impenetrable marshes.

I dozed off for a time, perhaps a few minutes, perhaps an hour.
When I woke, everything around me was unchanged except the sky,
which had cleared slightly. Somehow, that quality of light, dusky and
variable even in the middle of the day, made me feel more than ever as
if we were alone in the world, trapped under a glass dome.

Finally, Amos's pole jerked down, bobbing and dancing in his
hands. With a noise of satisfaction, he pushed his chair back and
turned the reel with his large, rough fingers. The line, weighted with
the struggling fish, cut a path through the water. I watched it creep
toward us until he leaned back and pulled the fish out of the lake,
bringing it swinging into the air.

It was a rainbow trout, long and silverish, with a red streak on its side. Outraged, it bent its body convulsively at the end of the line, the dim light catching on its sides. It was young, but large enough to be worth keeping.

Amos was pleased.

"Hand me the knife," he said.

Rousing myself, I stood, holding onto the back of the lawn chair for a moment to steady myself. The green duffel bag with his fishing gear was behind us, and I loosened the ties that held it closed. Reaching into it, I felt my way past the tackle boxes and ponchos and coils of line. My fingers found the solid, heavy pocketknife at the bottom, and I grasped it, looking up.

The fish hung in the air, its tail still twitching, its soft, greenish belly glinting in the light. Its eyes were wide and shocked, its jaws stretched open. The tip of the hook pointed toward the sky, sharp and silver.

I turned my head, and the pier stretched out before me, almost surreally long, like a mirage. At the other end of it, the truck was parked at the edge of the lot, near the sand. As I looked at it, I imagined that I saw it slide backward, down the sloping asphalt. Straightening, I blinked hard at it, and the image dissipated. The truck wasn't moving.

But, I thought with a sudden jolt of adrenaline, it could.

I bent down over the duffel bag again and dropped the knife in, shoving it deep into the bottom.

"It's not here," I said.

Amos looked over his shoulder. "What?"

"The knife. It's not here."

He scowled. The fish twitched and gasped noiselessly. "What are you talking about? Where else would it be?"

I shrugged. "I don't know. Maybe in the truck." Retying the bag with trembling fingers, I summoned the courage to add, "I think I saw it on the dash."

"Then why didn't you say something? What's wrong with you?"

I looked out over the lake and didn't answer. It took all of my self-possession not to move, not to give myself away. I was sure he would see it, the fact that I was steeling myself, my heart racing. But he didn't.

"Go get it," he said disgustedly, and I closed my eyes, preparing the words that came next.

I turned to face him and waited.

"Go on!" he barked. "What's the holdup?"

"It's locked," I said, fighting to keep my tone indifferent, my voice steady. "I need the keys."

"What do you mean, it's locked?"

"It's locked. I locked it. I'm sorry."

He gave me a look of disbelief and contempt. "Up here? What are you, crazy?"

I bowed my head. He couldn't see my face, couldn't hear the pounding in my veins as it reached a crescendo, its sound filling my ears.

Reaching into his pocket, he handed me the keys. Then he turned back to the fish, sitting down and bending over, working the hook out of its mouth.

The keys shone in my palm. For the briefest of moments, I stared at the back of his head, hesitating, just like the thirteen deer I would one day count in the darkness, frozen by their fear just as they should have fled.

Then I saw it: his neck tensed, and he lifted his head. Realizing what he had done.

I ran.

My feet pounded on the boards of the pier, each step ringing through the air like a shot, one two one two one two. I heard a crash behind me as he leaped up, stumbling over his chair and shouting as it fell into the water. I was running forward, faster than I ever thought possible, my weak legs spurred on by sheer willpower, complete and utter fright. The lakes and trees around me blurred, a smear of gray and brown, unreal. All I could see were the boards in front of me, the reeds at the shoreline, the truck. Behind me, I heard Amos's strides slamming against the wood. I could picture his arm outstretched, grasping for me as he yelled. The shoreline approached, bobbing up and down in time with my panicked steps, and I flew, soaring off the end of the pier, landing in the sand, screaming, reaching out for the truck, my body lunging forward, my entire being stretching toward the door handle, my mind a white-hot blank, everything in me concentrated on the key, the key, the key.

My fingertips found the handle. I could see the ignition through the window.

I pulled, and the door opened. Gasping, I threw myself into the seat, holding the key to the ignition, hands shaking violently.

I dropped it.

Amos grabbed me and lifted me bodily, throwing me so hard I landed ten feet away, in the gravel, sending up a shower of dirt.

In a bound, he was at my side, standing over me. I panted, looking up at him, raising a hand to shield myself.

"You think you're so smart?" he shouted.

It was one of the last things I would ever hear him say.

Pulling his leg back, he kicked me sharply, driving the steel toe of his boot into me as I curled on my side. Then he did it again, and again. I sank my fingers into the gravel, trying to crawl away, but he simply followed me, his boot thudding into my flesh. Insanely, I was still reaching for the truck, trying to slide toward it, but that ended soon enough. I didn't feel the bones break, didn't feel my ribs fracture or my hip give way. What I felt was the points of the gravel pressing into my cheek as I lay with my arm resting limply, uselessly, in front of me. I thought I would never move again.

Our ordinary monsters. What are we supposed to see when we look at them, their monstrosity or their ordinariness?

He didn't kick me in the head, which was lucky; otherwise, I probably would have needed new eyes, a new face. When he was finished, he bent down and grabbed me under my arms, dragging me to the truck, not seeming to notice the twin ruts my heels left in the gravel. He fastened the seatbelt around me, which would seem odd in hindsight; maybe, at first, he intended to take me to the hospital, as he had done after the garage episode. I could only imagine, later, what kind of story he might have come up with this time in order to explain what had happened, but as it turned out, he managed to tell a tale that was completely convincing without even saying a word.

I must have been making some kind of noise, moaning maybe, but he sat down in the driver's seat and shut the door without looking over. The engine started, and he drove us out of the parking lot, pulling onto the curving road.

After a few minutes of calm, he began to gather speed, taking the turns hard, whipping us first right, then left. At first, I thought we might be rushing to the doctor, but as the tires began to skid with each curve, spraying gravel over the edges of the steep drops that lined the road, I realized that that wasn't it.

I said his name, and he glanced at me.

"There's blood on your mouth," he said. "You're drooling on yourself. Wipe it off."

Slowly, I did as I was told, lifting my hand to my face and then slid-ing it along the inside of the door, grasping the armrest, slumping for-ward in the seat, breathing through my mouth. He kept his eyes fixed on the road, his jaw set. The needle on the speedometer edged upward; the rocks and trees flew by. He wasn't blinking, and, looking at him through the strange film that was clouding my vision, I suddenly knew what was coming. He said nothing, just stared through the windshield, a harshly determined look coming into his eyes, bouncing in his seat whenever we hit something in the road. I didn't say anything, either, because I didn't know the words; because it hurt to breathe; because if I couldn't escape, I was content to die. Then, as the car went faster and faster and the engine screamed louder and louder, I thought I might say something, take the risk, even if he would be angry, even if he would strike me, and had just turned toward him when he spun the wheel and, with a flick of the wrist, steered us straight into a telephone pole at the edge of some stranger's yard.

There was a burst of dust, a sound so loud I thought a grenade had been dropped in my lap. Then it was over.

He hadn't been wearing his seatbelt, even though he'd put mine on. He went over the steering wheel, into the glass.

And that was that.

Later, I would hate him for having done it, for having done all of it on purpose, but by then it was too late. Whatever words I had for him were just empty sounds. What can you say to a dead man, especially one who's already been buried by the time you can sit up, by the time you can once again say your own name?

I went to the chapel once, the one in the hospital, while I was still in the wheelchair. It was nearly Easter. Most of the stitches were out by then, although the bones would take much longer to heal. It was a Protestant service, and the minister was giving a sermon on Matthew, the part that describes the Last Supper. "And Jesus said," he intoned, like someone who was trying to make himself sound important, "'This is my blood of the covenant, which is poured out for many for the for-giveness of sins.'" I began to titter, then laughed so loudly they had to wheel me out of the place. The pouring out of blood, as I could have told him, had nothing at all to do with forgiveness. Blood was blood, and suffering was suffering. It didn't redeem anyone. It couldn't. The world went on exactly as it had before, regardless of whose blood had been poured out for what reason. Jesus, I thought, had known what was in store for him and had only been trying to give it a meaning, to make it something other than the useless and routine act of cruelty it was.

The hospital psychologist told me I was very articulate.

I drove on in the Jeep, the miles passing. Very early in the morning, I reached New York, passing through a tunnel and emerging into a confusing thicket of streets, narrow and dark save for the few bars that still seemed to be open. Somewhere near a park, I pulled over, locked the doors, and climbed into the back of the car, pulling a blanket over me so I would be hidden from view, like a rabbit in a nest. When I woke up, my head aching, the sun had just begun to rise and I found that I had a parking ticket. I brushed my teeth with a bottle of water from the trunk, spitting into the gutter, and slipped the angry-looking sheet of paper into my pocket. At least the car hadn't gotten towed with me in it.

People began to appear in the street, most of them looking as if they had been out all night, the men rumpled, the women in sparkling disarray. One of them pointed me toward a convenience store, where I bought a city map, but I was already so impossibly lost that the grid of streets might as well have been a foreign alphabet. As I drove, the streets became canyons, surrounded by buildings that seemed soulless, the dull stone and glass interrupted only by a thumbprint-sized park here and there.

Finally I saw a bridge, a strangely ornate-looking one, and crossed it, half hoping it would take me out of the city but also thinking it might show me why I'd come here in the first place, why I'd thought that getting lost here, disappearing, might be the first step to a new life, might erase the previous twenty-four hours. For the moment, life seemed the same, except that I was now trailing a taxi—the first one I'd ever seen—and had no idea where I was.

On the other side of the bridge, the buildings seemed shorter, more open. I looked up and saw birds turning in wide circles: seagulls. In Centerville, we only saw them rarely, when they were driven inland by storms. But I was certain that was what they were.

Of course, I thought.

The sea.

I stopped to buy a doughnut and began to feel, if not better, then at least slightly more myself. I looked at the map again and followed what seemed to be the main road, even though it was taking me the opposite of the way I'd originally planned to go. I liked it better out here than in the place where the highways and tunnels had first deposited me. The buildings were still crowded together, but in a kind of matter-of-fact, shrugging way that somehow reminded me of home, even though there was no real resemblance.

At last, the road ended, and there I was, staring out at the sand, the boardwalk. Beyond that, I was sure, must be the ocean.

I stopped and climbed stiffly out, rubbing my face. The air had a smell, a feel, that was new to me. I stood still for a moment, then started to walk.

The shoreline, when I reached it, was narrow and dirty, the brown sand strewn with rocks and glass and bottle caps. No one was there; it was still almost too cold to be walking in such a place, let alone swimming. But there it was, the water, dark and rippling and stretching to my right and left as far as I could see. The wind blew my hair into my face as I knelt and touched a wave that had approached me. It seemed softer than the lake water somehow, warmer, darker, gentler. When it receded, it left behind a white foam, which was soon overtaken by the next wave.

Squatting there, I turned my face up to the sun. I imagined the stranger sitting beside me.

There was a dry throb in my chest, and I gripped my hands together, holding them against me, clenching my eyes shut.

Sand stung me, rough against my face.

I wanted you to be different. Oh, I wanted you to be different.

The waves crept forward, touched my shoes, crawled back. My fingers slid up my arms until I was clutching my elbows, holding myself in a tight knot, rocking back and forth, feeling something break open. Like lava released from the center of the earth, it rushed to the tips of my fingers, the roots of my hair.

Heartbroken, I thought. It was a word I'd never thought much of. But it was the right one, and I felt it in the depths of me in a way I never had before. In a way I'd never let myself.

It was like breaking; it was. It was like splitting in half. As if I would pour out of myself and dissolve into the water, spread out in a film of pain.

I opened my lips, making a voiceless sound.

The waves approached me and receded, slowly carving hollows around my feet. I stayed there for a long while, thinking about what I knew, what I didn't. What, if anything, I could choose not to know.

After a time, I raised my head again. My eyes were dry even though I felt as if I'd been weeping for days.

Slowly, I stood.

I didn't know what he was, who he was; I never would.

And I chose that, I thought. I chose not to know. Not to carry it with me, let it bind me, chain me up and drag me down and leave me trapped as the years went by, all those moments I would never get back once they were gone. I chose not to forgive him, and I chose not to refuse to. I chose not to look back on the decisions I'd made. They were over. He was gone. Nothing I could do would change that, would let me see him again, ask the questions that would fill this void, this terrible abyss in my center. The truth wasn't what mattered. An hour from now, I would still be here. I would wake up tomorrow, and the day after that. That was what I had to think about.

There was an empty plastic bottle floating on the water, and I waited until another wave brought it in. I stooped to catch it, then turned and walked away.

By the boardwalk, where the sand was drier, I filled the bottle with the loose grains, tucking it into my sweatshirt. Briefly, I faced the water again.

I missed him, this Daniil. I missed the person I had known. I could admit that. And I did; I did admit it. I could feel his absence.

And if he had been an illusion, then I missed the illusion.

There were voices behind me, and a gull cried, sweeping overhead.

I turned to go.

On the streets past the boardwalk, people were emerging, striding briskly off to work, opening shops with clangs and clatters, lugging grocery bags. In a souvenir store, I bought a postcard to send to Beth and, after a moment of thought, one for John. Then I climbed back into the Jeep—removing another parking ticket, which I stuffed into my pocket—and drove back the way I had come. Looking at the world through my own eyes, moving in my own body. Solid and real.

In my mind, I saw a woman who had been curled up on the forest floor stand up, brush the leaves from her dress, rub the decades of sleep from her eyes, button her cracked leather shoes, look around. See the road. Walk toward it.

Eventually, I found a highway that ran north and turned onto it, making my way out of the city and sailing on through the suburbs, like a leaf blown on a harsh breeze. I didn't belong in this place; I might not belong any place. But I would keep looking. I held the wheel steadily, listening to the radio, following the road as it unwound through the trees.

As the sun climbed overhead, slowly warming the car, I remembered a day in mid-summer, many years earlier, when my brother and I had been children. We'd been playing in the woods on the state game lands, a place where people liked to dump their garbage—not the ordinary kitchen bags, but big things, sofas and metal barrels and washers and dryers. We would jump on the things, push them together to make castles and cabins, hide under them. On this day, we were chasing each other when my brother suddenly stopped, shocked, and looked down at his shoe. A nail, long and sharp and rusting, had pierced right through the sole, biting deep into his skin. Frightened, I had picked him up, my older brother, struggling to carry him on my back until we reached the small, scorched-looking yard of a neighbor we had never met. The mailbox had an American flag painted on it, and there was a fake deer on the porch that had been used for target practice. An angry-looking dog watched me through the window as I knocked on the door.

After a minute, the neighbor appeared, a large man with thick glasses and a beard. His two front teeth were missing, and I would later learn that I didn't know him because he had spent ten years in prison, something to do with a fight that had ended badly. Too young to have any idea that I should be frightened, I stood there, looking up at him. Before I could explain, he saw the blood on my brother's shoe and closed the door behind him. In one smooth motion, he lifted my brother from my back and arranged him in his own arms, speaking in gruff murmurs, carrying him down the driveway. By the road, I took his hand—large, rough, with black grease written into the skin—and pulled him west, toward home. Together, we set off down the quiet road, walking the long mile, our three figures casting joined shadows. I touched a scar that crossed his fingers. The sun came through the trees, as it always does, light interrupted by darkness, darkness interrupted by light.

PINE GROVE FURNACE
POW INTERROGATION CAMP

*During WWII, the US War Dept. operated this secret facility
a mile north along Michaux Rd., one of three such sites in the
US. Military intelligence relating to topics such as weaponry
development and Axis operations was gained from thousands
of German and Japanese prisoners. Originally a farm serving
the iron industry, 1785–1919, the site was converted to Civilian
Conservation Corps Camp S-51-PA, 1933–42. After the war it
became church Camp Michaux, 1946–72.*

—Historical marker
Gardners, Pennsylvania

*ON THIS SPOT WERE FOUND THREE BABES IN THE
WOODS*
Nov.-24-1934

—Roadside sign
Gardners, Pennsylvania

ACKNOWLEDGMENTS

This book is rooted in many moments, but perhaps none so much as the evening in 2004 when I sat at a table at the Philadelphia organization Women in Transition, attending one of the training sessions required to become a volunteer for the local domestic violence hotline. The trainer handed out a sheet of paper that listed many forms of intimate-partner violence—not only physical mistreatment (punching, kicking, shoving), but also psychological, sexual, and financial. When I looked at it, a number of things came into focus for me in a way they never had before. Like many and perhaps most of us, I had previously understood "domestic violence" to refer only to the things I saw on TV and the shorthand images in the newspaper: the clenched fist, the cowering woman. But that isn't all family violence is, and my own life, at least, has benefited from that understanding.

Seven years later, I sat down one day and suddenly started writing the story of a young woman—one who had somehow been badly injured—who stood in a threadbare gray coat at the edge of a frozen lake. Eventually, I decided this would be a novel about domestic violence that contained neither clenched fists nor women who were only depicted as cowering. Whatever else it may be, I hope it's that.

The fact that the book ever reached publication is due to the patience, insight, and wonderful championing of the manuscript by Taylor Sperry, my editor at Melville House (who also helped come up with the title), and Stacia Decker, my incredible agent, who was offering feedback years before the draft was anywhere near ready for prime time. It also owes its existence to early encouragement and feedback from freelance editor Lauren Jolie LeBlanc, Amelia Keene, Rikin Shah, Jessica Howley, Tori Roth, Emily Marr, Elinathan Ohiomoba, Merryl Lawry-White, Brooke Dunbar, Gautam Hans, and Stephen St.Vincent, although any flaws in the story are my own doing. Many of my colleagues at the AIRE Centre, the Center for Democracy & Technology, and Human Rights Watch also offered warm words during the travails of the drafting and revision process, as did Eli James. My grandparents, parents, and extended family cheered me on during this project as during so many others.

The details about the prison camp are largely drawn from the work of local historians I've never met but for whose years of research I am extremely grateful. Some of the information they have gathered is available online at http://www.schaeffersite.com/michaux/.

Writing a novel in my spare hours while working full-time was in many ways an isolating experience, but friends such as Rachael Barza, Lauren Rogal, and Katie Ishibashi got me through it. Alison Stigora, fellow artist, nature-lover, and asker of deep questions, has also offered love and support at many critical junctures—and, many years ago, explored the woods of Pine Grove Furnace State Park with me when I briefly worked at the general store there.

Lastly, this story owes a vast amount to my women friends who are profoundly thoughtful about their faith and its meaning for their personal lives. They are forever teaching me what goodness is.